Behind You!

Linda Regan

CREME DE LA CRIME

First published in 2006
by Crème de la Crime
PO Box 523, Chesterfield, S40 9AT

Typesetting by Yvette Warren
Cover design by Yvette Warren
Front cover illustration by Peter Roman
Printed and bound in England by Biddles Ltd
King's Lynn, Norfolk

ISBN 09551589-2-3

A CIP catalogue reference for this book is available from
the British Library

www.cremedelacrime.com

Linda Regan is a successful actress. She is married to the actor Brian Murphy, and they live in Kent with their dog Mildred.

Acknowledgements

First I would like to lift my hat in a sweeping salute to Crème de la Crime and the risks it takes with first time authors.

And to thank Lynne Patrick, most sincerely, not only for making it happen but for making it fun.

Thank you too, to Steve Wade for his encouragement and expertise, and Meriel Patrick for her wisdom.

And I can never thank DC Paul Steed enough for his patience, answering endless questions on police procedure which I probably asked over and over again, and will probably ask again in the future.

A contract of eternal thanks, with no acting required, go to my very dear friends Roy and Debbie Hudd.

A big thank you to my special friend, the enormously talented crime writer Lesley Horton, for dusting me down and putting me back together.

And my husband deserves my love and eternal gratitude for the endless cups of tea, and the amount of time he spent retrieving my discarded manuals from rubbish bins and persuading me not to take it out on trees.

Thank you too to my family and close friends for getting me through.

And finally THANK YOU, Dr Ross Ellice, Dr John Hunt, Mr Frank Smedley, Dr Martin Leslie, Dr Terry Wong and everyone at the Sloane Hospital and London Bridge, who this book definitely wouldn't have happened without.

For Brian (my hero)
and for my mother
(for being Behind Me always)

What the "goodie" should really say -

I am the fairy godmother.
Love and joy I send.
I am immortal, don't you know.
I'm Cinderella's friend.

No demon king can do me in,
My eternal life revoke -
But by comedians I'll be murdered
If I kill one single joke!

Roy Hudd.

"Are you enjoying yourselves?"

"YES!" the audience shouted.

"Oh no you're not," the Ugly Sisters shouted back, goading the studio audience to join in.

"OH YES WE ARE!" came the animated response.

The smaller of the two over-dressed pantomime dames jumped up and down on the spot, squealing like a spoiled child. "OH NO YOU'RE NOT!"

The response was even louder. "OH YES WE ARE!"

"Blimey." Lottie Banham pointed to the television screen. "I'm sure that's Roy Hudd, but who's the thin one? I know his voice." She looked over to her brother, suddenly aware he wasn't watching. "Paul? Sorry, are you hating this? There's a rerun of three old comedies after."

Paul shook his head. "Not at all, I'm enjoying watching the kids enjoying it."

The children giggled and shouted at the screen, as if they were in the live audience. Lottie and eight-year-old Bobby still wore paper hats from their Boxing Day lunch; little Madeleine modelled a glittering tiara which matched the pink fairy outfit, complete with fluorescent wings and pink sparkling ballet pumps, that Paul had bought her for Christmas.

"I can't believe how big they're getting," he added.

Bobby screwed his face and Madeleine giggled. A smile spread across Paul Banham's face.

"Actually," he said to his sister, "I was just about to go anyway. I've got some things to do, and I'm on call so I should check in with the station."

Lottie gave her brother a knowing look. "Are you meeting Alison?" she asked.

"No, as I said, I'm on call."

"Shame," Lottie replied. "I approve of Alison, she's good

for you. And she really likes you."

"Alison is my sergeant, and that's as far as it goes, OK?"

"You fancy her," Madeleine chipped in, her uncle's love life suddenly more interesting than the pantomime. "Bobby told me you did."

"I'd just like to see you happy again," Lottie said.

Banham stood up, lifted his niece from the sofa and held her high in the air. "I think I'll put you on top of the Christmas tree. You look more like a fairy than the fairy that's up there."

Madeleine squealed and giggled, spitting chocolate over the front of Banham's denim shirt. He pulled a handkerchief from his trouser pocket and wiped the chocolate from her chin. "You're much prettier than Cinderella," he said, "even with chocolate all over your face. And one day I'll bet you'll marry a handsome prince and live happily ever after."

She giggled again and he put her back on the sofa as gently and carefully as he would a precious vase. "Watch the pantomime," he told her. "You can tell me about Prince Charming later."

"Oh, stay and watch it with us," Lottie pleaded, "and then I'll make us all turkey sarnies and fill you a doggy bag to take home, 'cos if you haven't got a date, I'll bet you've no food in the house."

Banham picked up the sparkling shoe and carefully put it back on Madeleine's foot. He caught Bobby looking dolefully at him. "What?" he asked him.

"I like Alison," Bobby said. "She's good at football."

"Ah, but she's not better than me," Banham told him. He nodded at the television. "It's Brian Murphy," he said to his sister.

"Who?"

"The other Ugly Sister. It's Brian Murphy, from *George and Mildred.*"

Alison Grainger had just put the word TREE on the Scrabble board. She scribbled down her score and looked up to see her father putting his letters either side of the R.

She frowned and shook her head. "No, you can't have MURDER, Dad. It's not Christmassy."

He looked indignantly at her from the other side of the onyx coffee table, but she didn't give him time to argue.

"We agreed only words with a Christmas theme," she said quietly. "MURDER has nothing to do with Christmas."

"Yes it has," he said gruffly. "You're a detective sergeant in the Murder Division, and you're on call, and it's Christmas."

Alison looked at her mother, but there was no support to be had there.

"If there's a murder it'll ruin our Christmas," her father argued. "Because you'll have to go and solve it, and your mother and I will be left here alone." He nodded his head. "So it has everything to do with our Christmas."

Alison shook her head. "No, that wouldn't wash in court."

"We're not in court, Alison," he said, raising his voice. "Tell her, Beryl. This is my house, and it's Christmas, and we're having a friendly game of Scrabble."

"Let him have it," her mother said anxiously. "It's only a game, Alison."

"That's double points too," her father said, stabbing his large finger at the scoresheet.

"No, it's cheating," Alison said firmly. "What's the point of playing Christmas Scrabble if we can cheat?"

There was a silence.

"OK, fine by me," Alison said at last, throwing her hands

in the air and standing up. "Absolutely fine. It's your go, Mum. I'm going to make some coffee. Do you want some?"

"I'll make it," her mother said, starting to get up.

"No," Alison told her. "It's your go; put a Christmas word down."

"I can't, I've got mainly vowels," Beryl Grainger said apologetically. "I'll miss this turn and make the coffee. You go again, Alison."

"I can't go either," Alison said. "I haven't got any vowels." She threw the pen down. "Oh, let's call it a day. You win, Dad."

There was another silence.

"What is it? What's getting to you?" Gerald asked his daughter.

Alison took a deep breath and put her hands to her eyes. "Nothing. Sorry, Dad. I've been busy lately. I'm tired, that's all, and it's making me a bit snappy. Sorry. Carry on, I'll change my letters and miss my go."

Gerald carefully studied his new letters for a few moments, then put six of them all down on the board under the last R in MURDER. They spelled ROMANCE.

"Romance happens at Christmas," he said innocently.

Banham closed his front door behind him and threw his keys on to the table by the door. He walked into the kitchen and put Lottie's doggy bags on an empty shelf, then opened the fridge and took out a can of lager. As he straightened up the photo on the wall made him catch his breath: a young blonde woman, proudly holding a new baby. He stared at it, then turned away and walked into the lounge.

But the memory was back. He looked around the bare room, imagining the Christmas they would have had if

Diane and Elizabeth were still here. Elizabeth would have been eleven – just a few years older than his beautiful niece Madeleine. Diane would have cooked the family dinner, and together they would have watched Elizabeth tearing her presents open. The memory invaded him: his adored eleven-month-old daughter, her tiny head bloody and unrecognisable on her bunny blanket. Diane, only inches away, covered in congealing blood from multiple stab wounds as she reached out to save her baby. Ten years, one week, and probably now one hour ago – but their killer had never been brought to justice. And he hadn't been there for his wife and child when they needed him most.

He knew Lottie was right; his life had to move on, and Alison was right for him. But when he had tried to get close to her, the memories and guilt came back and he couldn't go through with it.

He popped the lager and took a long gulp. He should have rung her, but he hadn't known what to say after shying off at the last minute with the feeble excuse that business and pleasure didn't mix. She was furious, but he just couldn't admit the truth.

He would keep his appointment with the counsellor this time; it was his new year's resolution. If the counselling worked, maybe they could try again. The Phil Collins CD that Alison had bought him for Christmas lay on the coffee table. He slipped it into his stereo and pressed Play. *Groovy Kind of Love* filled the air. He flopped into an armchair and closed his eyes.

Then the phone rang.

1

The alleyway to the back of the theatre building was cordoned off with the usual blue and white tape. Two police cars, silent flashing lights signalling the emergency, were parked either side of the road. The female officer standing guard gave Banham a shy smile and lifted the tape to allow him through.

He walked up the alleyway and opened the stage door. Half a dozen girls, none older than twelve, stood in the passageway. All were dressed identically: black leotards, black tights, black shoes. Some were crying, others looked dazed and bewildered. Banham's eyes were drawn to a very pretty blonde girl who looked about eleven years old.

Another blonde, this one attractive and middle-aged, appeared behind the group. "Can I help you?"

He flashed his warrant card and asked the woman where the stage area was.

"I'll take you."

She led him down the short corridor and turned left. A sign in the shape of a large hand with a pointing finger read STAGE LEFT. NO UNAUTHORISED ADMISSION DURING PERFORMANCE.

"It's through the swing doors," she said. "We've been told to wait in the Green Room, but I'll take you through if you like."

"I'll find my way, thanks."

"You don't think it was anything other than an accident, do you?"

"That's what we're here to find out," he said abruptly.

"How long will we have to wait? Only, there are children

in the show, and their parents…"

"I'll get someone to let you know as soon as I can," he told her. "I'm sorry, you are?"

"I'm Maggie, Maggie McCormak. My daughter's in the show, she's one of the principals."

Banham nodded. "Did you…?"

"She plays the cat," Maggie carried on. "My husband's the stage manager and I do the wardrobe…"

Her voice died away as he fixed his eyes firmly on her. "Did you see what happened?"

"No, I was watching the show from the audience," she said lowering her gaze and brushing her eye with a finger. "I knew something was very wrong when they brought the curtain in. So I rushed back. Everyone was crowded around at the edge of the stage. Barbara Denis told me she wasn't breathing and Vincent had gone to ring for an ambulance."

Banham nodded. "Thank you. Could you look after the children?"

He pushed open the swing door and found himself at the left-hand side of the stage, as the sign had indicated.

The house lights were turned on full and light flooded the stage area and auditorium. But where he was standing large and cumbersome pieces of scenery blocked both the light and his access to the stage. He found himself face to face with a tall, oddly-shaped and brightly painted piece of plywood, which he couldn't manoeuvre around.

Alison – Sergeant Alison Grainger – was on the other side of the stage with her back to him, talking to one of the forensic team. She was wearing an ankle-length grey military-style coat, with a maroon woollen scarf. A matching maroon cap with a hanging bobble covered her head, allowing her long mouse-coloured hair, frizzy from the December night air, to tumble freely down her back. He thought she looked beautiful. He recognised the officer she was talking to: Penny Starr, his young detective constable's current date; Afro-Caribbean hair peeped out from under the hood of her blue, head-to-toe plastic overall. She held a magnifying glass in one latex-gloved hand and a pair of tweezers in the other.

Max Pettifer, the senior SOCO officer, was there too, deep in conversation with Heather Draper, the police pathologist. They blocked Banham's view of the dead woman; he could see long, dark hair fanned out on the floor, but no face. Banham was glad; he hated looking at young female victims.

Banham put a foot on the piece of scenery to climb over it, but his foot slipped on the painted surface and he caught his leg on something sharp. "Fuck," he cursed loudly, feeling about for the offending object. It was a loose, sharp nail.

Alison looked up. "Don't try to climb over that ship, Guv, it's not safe," she shouted. "Best to walk round the back." She pointed to the area at the rear of the stage where a black cloth hung from ceiling to floor. "There's a thin passageway behind that black curtain, it'll bring you round this side. But be careful, there's scenery everywhere and very little light back there."

"Right," he said, looking around for the ship and realising that she meant the large piece of scenery. He picked his way around it and manoeuvred carefully around several smaller pieces before he found the passageway. Easy to have a fatal accident here, he thought. Perhaps the killer knew that – if there was a killer, of course. The health and safety officers would have a field day, especially with children working here.

He noticed a spiral staircase to his right, leading downward. So there was a basement too.

The passageway at the back of the stage was extremely narrow, and a solitary low-wattage lamp lay on the ground to help steer his way. If the actors had to squeeze down here every time they needed to cross the stage, he was glad he wasn't one. At the far end he bumped against a wobbling wooden trestle table, edged carefully around it and found himself next to another spiral staircase. So, two staircases leading to a basement area under the stage. The actors probably used that to get across.

The trestle table was another accident waiting to happen. Two identical long swords lay side by side on it, both blades blunt and rusting with age. Beside them was a large, furry black cat's head, with erect ears and large, green plastic eyes. The poster at the stage door read *The Wonderful Colourful, Star-Studded Pantomime – DICK WHITTINGTON and his VERSATILE CAT*. This cat didn't look versatile; it didn't even look appealing.

Someone poked him in the arm and he nearly jumped out of his skin.

"Thought you'd got lost," Alison Grainger said.

He turned to face her, and into the light. A few feet away at the side of the stage the dead girl lay, her head against a piece of scenery, next to a block of concrete about five inches square. Banham stared at the corpse.

"Guv, you may not want…"

Sometimes he thought Alison could read his mind. "May not want what?" he snapped before he could stop himself.

She took a breath before answering. "I was just going to say, there isn't a lot to be gained from looking at the body. Either she either banged her head against the concrete block as she fell, or someone lifted it and hit her with it. We can't do much until the forensics report comes back. It may not even be a murder case."

He looked over her shoulder again and studied the angle of the corpse. Alison spoke again.

"That new forensic officer, Penny Starr, was with DC Crowther when he got the call. She's offered to take the concrete block and do a light-source test…"

"Who's running this investigation?" he asked her. "You or me?"

"Sorry?"

"You heard me."

"You are, Guv. I was just… here, that's all."

There was a few seconds silence. He knew she had his best interests at heart, but he was the senior officer.

"As long as we've got that straight." He nodded his head in the direction of the corpse. "Is that the exact spot where she landed when she supposedly fell and hit her head?"

"No, one of the actors, Vincent Mann, has touched her. She was wearing a black balaclava and he pulled it off in the hope that it might help her breathe, so she's been moved. But only slightly, according to him."

Banham walked towards the body and crouched beside it.

"Evening, Guvnor," said Penny Starr, holding a magnifying glass over the concrete block. "It's tricky, this one; the girl apparently hit her head on this, but I can't get anything from the concrete here; I'll have to take it away and do a light-source treatment."

"Yes, Sergeant Grainger mentioned that. How long?"

"Three days. Sorry, can't go any faster – the reagents need to develop."

Banham looked up at Alison. "We'll need DNA from all the actors, to eliminate them."

As he straightened up he heard a woman's laugh. Heather Draper, the pathologist, was standing a few feet away with

Max Pettifer, head of the SOCO team. The smile left his face when he noticed Banham staring at him. "She died from a blow to the temple artery," he said. "It was very quick and she was dead before the paramedics got here."

"She died instantly, I suspect," Heather Draper agreed. "But that's off the record – as usual I've said nothing until the post mortem's done and you've had my report." She lifted the girl's head so Banham could get a good look at the blow.

"She must have hit the stage weight with a lot of force if she fell," he said.

Heather pointed to the girl's cheek. "Someone has been knocking her about too. Those bruises aren't fresh, a few days old at least."

Banham rubbed his hand across his face. "When can I have your report?"

"Hopefully tomorrow. I know the mortuary's free. I'll get it to you as soon as I can."

He knew she would do her best; they always worked well together.

Not so Max Pettifer, overweight and too fond of the sound of his own public school voice.

"I know it's urgent, old son," he said. "I'll do my best, but I didn't invent Christmas, nothing I can do if the laboratories are shut."

Penny Starr looked up from where she was examining the area around the corpse. "I'm happy to give up my Christmas leave," she said. "Colin is on the case anyway, so it's not as if we'd see much of each other. I'll give a couple of the technicians a ring - they'll be glad of the overtime."

"Thank you, Penny."

They might make some progress after all.

Alison Grainger was still beside him. "How far have we

got?" he asked her.

"Her name is Lucinda Benson," Alison said. "She was the principal girl in the pantomime. Uniform called us; they were told she fell against that stage weight, in the middle of a routine that took place in pitch black and included most of the cast."

"In pitch black? No wonder she fell! This place is a death-trap. And what was that stage weight thing doing there?"

"It's supposed to hold the scenery up."

"But it's not; the scenery is falling down. How easy would it be to lift that concrete block in the middle of a routine that took place in the dark?"

"You'd have to be quick, and strong, and know where to aim," Alison told him. "In the dark, that might be difficult. But all the people on stage with her know the backstage area extremely well, and they're used to the lighting."

"Have we got a list of the actors who were on stage yet?" he asked.

She pulled a sheet of paper from her pocket. "I got this from the producer. They're all waiting in the Green Room upstairs. DC Crowther got here first; they told him every-one was on stage when it happened, except the pantomime dame who was changing his costume. Crowther said he couldn't understand their technical jargon." A sheepish expression flicked briefly across her face. "I've… been in a few pantomimes myself… when I was a child, of course, not recently. So I told him to ask me if there was anything he didn't understand."

Banham suppressed a smile. "Good thinking, sergeant." A sudden thought struck him. "You haven't told anyone else, have you? That you've worked in pantomime?"

"No, Guv."

"Good. Keep it to yourself. We may need that card up

our sleeve. Where's Crowther, by the way?"

"I sent him out front with DC Walsh to take statements from the pianist, sound engineer and usherettes - not that any of them saw much. I said we'd all meet up in the Green Room when you arrived. I hope that's OK?" She looked at him apprehensively

"Do we know who was standing where on stage, at the time of the death?"

She shook her head. "All the children, and the actors except the dame, were walking on and off the stage carrying different coloured ultra-violet fish."

Banham blinked in bewilderment as Alison continued, "The routine is very precisely staged, so I'm sure the choreographer will know who was where in the scene."

"Good."

Alison began to walk off stage; he caught her up as she reached the wings. "Um, why were the fish ultra-violet?" he asked.

"It's called the underwater ballet scene. There's a storm at sea, and all the cast fall overboard and land in the ocean. They're all dressed from head to toe in black, and the stage is in darkness too, so the audience can't see them. When the actors walk across the stage holding the ultra-violet fish in the air, it looks as if the fish are swimming about on their own."

"Right," he said, completely bemused now. "So how do we know who was next to her when she fell?"

"According to the producer, she fell at the end of the routine. He said the actress who plays Dick Whittington, the star of the show, Barbara Denis, should have been standing next to her."

"Should have been?"

"He said we'd have to double check that with the

choreographer. He told me all the cast have said the same – they heard a bump at the end of the routine, just before the lights came up, and they thought someone had fainted or fallen over. Then when the lights did come up Lucinda was lying in a heap on the floor. They all knew something was seriously wrong, so they dropped the curtain."

"How many actors were there on the stage?"

"According to this list, there are five actors, four adult dancers and six children in the cast. Plus the choreographer, and the stage manager who's mostly in the wings."

"So DNA swabs from all the adults if they'll give them, and bag all the costumes for forensics."

"Crowther was already doing that when I arrived. He's been here a while."

"And there I was thinking you were the one trying to take over the investigation," Banham said dryly. "How did he get here so quickly? He lives the other side of town."

Alison grinned. "Penny Starr doesn't – she lives around the corner from here, and he spent Christmas with her."

Crowther always managed to pull the women, Banham thought. The DC was no oil painting; what was his secret? He stole a glance at Alison; he'd managed to mess that up before it started.

He dragged his hand across his face wearily and walked over to the high desk at the corner of the stage. A copy of the script lay on the stool beside it, open at a page headed Underwater Ballet. He flicked through it, but made no sense at all of the different coloured underlinings and other marks.

"They call that the prompt corner, Guv," Alison said.

"Does someone sit there during the show?" Banham asked.

"The stage manager should," Alison told him. "Apparently

tonight he was in the pub. And yes, uniform are checking on that."

"So who brought the curtain down? Isn't that his job?"

"He didn't say. I'll make sure I ask him."

"What's up there?" he asked her, pointing to the rows of lights and twisted ropes hanging from the ceiling over the stage.

"They call it the flies. Sometimes the sound engineer and the electrician operate from up there, but in this show the sound engineer is at the back of the auditorium. So there wouldn't have been anyone up there today."

"Shouldn't," Banham corrected. "Something else to check."

"Everyone involved in the show backstage is in the Green Room." Alison handed him the notebook she was holding. "This is a list of the whole cast and crew, made up by the producer."

She was still wearing her gloves, maroon wool to match her cap and scarf, with pom-poms dangling from the wrists. He reached out and grabbed her hand.

"What's with the pom-poms?" he asked.

She pulled away. "A Christmas present from my mother."

Her embarrassment was almost tangible. "We do need to talk," she said lowering her voice.

"About what?"

"About last week?"

He looked down. "There's no point, Alison. It was my fault, I shouldn't have tried to mix business with pleasure. It won't happen again."

His heart was in his boots. Why couldn't he be honest with her, and tell her how he felt? What he really needed was to move more slowly.

But he'd said it now, and blown any chance he had of trying again.

"It wasn't anyone's fault," she said after an agonising couple of seconds. "It wasn't a crime scene. But never mind; if you think business and pleasure don't mix, I won't say any more. End of chapter. OK?"

The black flecks her eyes turned blacker when she was angry. He had once told her that her eyes were a shade of sludge. That had made her furious; the flecks had turned jet black and she had told him to go to night-school and take a course in romance. Everything he said came out wrong.

She was waiting for him to speak. OK, business, not pleasure. "Right, sergeant, let's get on with this enquiry. Start with the children; take their statements and let them go. I'm going to see what Crowther has found out, and then I'll talk to the producer."

"Yes, Guv."

He looked up and found himself staring into shiny black flecks in her sludge-coloured eyes. She turned away and headed for the swing door that led to the corridor. He followed. She pushed the door wide open, walked through it, and left it to fly back and hit Banham in the face.

2

No matter what Detective Constable Colin Crowther was wearing he always looked as if his clothes belonged to somebody else. Today his jeans were a little too baggy and his grey jacket a touch too long in the arms. The front of his short, over-gelled brown hair stood erect from his head, and the rest with its natural curl lay flat against his skull. He had a boyish face with big brown eyes, a wide smile and a cockney accent.

Crowther was ambitious. Banham knew he was desperate to make sergeant, so it came as no surprise when the young officer hailed him loudly and launched into an account of everything he had done in the hour that he'd been at the crime scene.

The DC had arranged a liaison officer to go round and break the news to the dead girl's parents, then organised the available uniform officers, supervised by DC Isabelle Walsh, to secure the area. He had personally labelled each of the black outfits that were worn by the actors and bagged them in evidence bags, all ready for Penny to take away to test for fragments of concrete. Then he had spoken to the staff in the pub next door, who had confirmed that Alan McCormak, the stage manager, had been in there at the exact time that the accident happened.

Crowther reminded Banham of a spaniel waiting for a rewarding bone.

"You take a lot on yourself, don't you, lad? The post mortem won't be done till tomorrow. Until then we don't even know if we're looking at a murder enquiry."

The young constable's face fell. "I kept Sergeant Grainger

in the loop, Guv. I just thought…"

The truth was he'd done extremely well. Banham relented. "OK – just wait for instructions from now on."

Crowther tapped the side of his nose and lowered his voice. "I've found out a little something of interest, Guvnor."

Banham lifted his eyebrows.

"I had a quick word with the girl who set the dance routines," Crowther said. "Sophie Flint. She explained what happened at the time of the death."

"Go on."

"Apparently, the geezer who plays the pantomime dame, Stephen Coombs is his name, isn't on stage in that part of the show because he has to change his costume during that routine. But tonight, when the routine was over and…" Crowther screwed the side of face up as he often did when in thinking mode… "Vincent Mann, that's the feller, rang for the ambulance, Sophie Flint said Stephen Coombs was standing in the corridor – and he hadn't changed his costume."

"She told you this?"

"Yes, Guv."

"We'll need an official statement."

They started to climb the stairs to the first floor. "Have you spoken to anyone else?" Banham asked.

"I had a quick word with the chorus dancers, Guvnor."

"All young and pretty were they?"

"The three girls are a bit gorgeous, I'll admit, Guvnor," Crowther said with a grin. "I daresay the black bloke is somebody's type; not mine though."

Banham couldn't help liking Crowther. He had too much confidence and not enough experience, and his enthusiasm was inclined to run away with him unless he was kept on a leash; but he worked hard, and had a good future.

"Keep your eye on the ball," Banham told him, stopping as they reached the top of the stairs. "Don't for goodness' sake start flirting with any of the women. At the moment they're all suspects."

"I wouldn't dream of it, Guv."

"Besides," Banham added, "I'm relying on you not to upset Penny. She's offered to work through her leave and keep us ahead on the forensics side, but only because you're here."

Crowther lifted his lapels and pulled his shoulders back. "I train 'em well, Guv."

Banham fought the urge to smile. How did Crowther do it? He couldn't get it right with one woman, but this lad managed to juggle two or three at once.

"Sergeant Grainger is taking statements from the children," he said, "so you and I will make a start up here. How many...?" He looked down the list he had torn from Alison's notebook and started to count the names.

"Just four actors, Guv," Crowther prompted. "There's also four adult dancers, and the dame who wasn't on stage at the time. Sophie Flint said she also plays the fairy."

Banham looked at the list again. "Vincent Mann, the comic. He's the one who rang for the ambulance. He pulled the girl's balaclava off, leaving his sweaty handprints all over her."

"DNA. Don't help matters," said Crowther.

"Barbara Denis plays Dick Whittington," Banham read, "And Alan McCormak, the stage manager, also plays Alderman Fitzwarren - and was in the pub this evening."

Crowther shook his head. "How can you be on stage playing a part, if you're in the pub?"

"And also be at the side of the stage keeping an eye on

things," Banham said. He looked back at his list. "Fay McCormak, she's Alan's daughter. She plays the cat."

They were now standing outside a door bearing the sign:

OFFICIAL COMPANY OFFICE
SOPHIE FLINT (Choreographer)
MICHAEL HOGAN (Producer)

"What happens in the official company office?" Banham asked.

"Don't know, Guv."

"Is it unlocked?" Banham asked.

"Let's find out." Crowther turned the handle and the door opened.

The man at the far end of the office nearly jumped out of his skin. He was tall and middle-aged with longish dark hair streaked with silver. He reminded Banham of a seventies pop-star, with his lived-in face and long grey-green cardigan over dated green corduroy trousers finished with scuffed black cowboy boots. The bags under his eyes were very prominent, and he clicked an electric kettle off and on nervously.

"This is Michael Hogan, the producer of the show," Crowther told Banham. "Mr Hogan, you were asked you to wait in the Green Room with everyone else."

"I just spoke to your sergeant," Hogan said. "She's taken the children down to the basement to interview them in their dressing room. It's getting cold down there now the heating's off, so I'm making a pot of hot coffee for her. Would you gentlemen like some?"

"White, two sugars," Banham said with a thin smile.

"One sugar for me," Crowther added.

"How is your enquiry progressing?" Hogan asked, taking a packet of fresh coffee out of a cupboard and spooning some into a pot which stood beside the kettle.

"It's hardly started yet."

"But it was an accident, wasn't it?"

"We can't say anything yet, we need to make some enquiries."

Michael poured boiling water into the coffee pot. The rich smell filled the air, and Banham suddenly felt in desperate need of a large cup to keep him going.

"I'm going to sound callous," Michael said concentrating his attention on the coffee. "But as all the seats for tomorrow's matinee are sold, I have to ask." He looked sheepishly at Banham. "This won't have any repercussions on the rest of the pantomime run, will it, Inspector?"

Banham eyed the man for a second before replying. "I can't answer that yet. We'll have to wait to see how long forensics need the area. I'll try and let you know how things are progressing in an hour or so." He folded his arms and leaned against the doorframe. "Were you in the building during the performance this evening?"

Hogan's attention was back on the coffee. "I've been in the building all night." He looked back to Banham again. "The cast didn't know that, though. I arrived after the show had started."

Crowther took out his notebook and started scribbling.

"I wouldn't have come in at all, except that the show needs to be cut. Sophie, my assistant, is the choreographer. She said there were too many ad-libs creeping in, and the show was getting longer. I have to keep the running time down to two and a half hours, to give the front of house staff time to get the afternoon audience out and clear the sweet papers and ice cream cartons before the evening performance."

"So you came in this evening?"

"Yes. To watch the show, and look for cuts."

"You were in the audience?"

Hogan nodded.

"So someone could vouch for that?"

He nodded again, then shrugged. "Actually, only the first half of the show. I had a drink in the bar at the interval, to give me a bit a bit of Dutch courage." He smiled and gave a nervous laugh.

Banham noticed how straight and white his teeth were. Probably all capped: expensive job! So he hadn't always been so desperate for box-office profits.

Michael continued, "I had to go and see my ex-wife, Barbara Denis, the star of the show." Another nervous laugh. "She can be a force to be reckoned with if she doesn't get her own way – and I had decided to cut her love duet with Lucinda. It wasn't very good." He paused again and then stretched his mouth down like a scolded schoolboy. "I needed a drink first."

He slowly pressed the filter downwards on the steaming coffee. It smelt delicious.

"So did you tell Barbara and Lucinda you were cutting their song before the second act started?" he asked.

"No. I intended to, but I got sidetracked."

"Who by?"

"First I bumped into Maggie McCormak as I came through to the backstage area. She's my wardrobe mistress, and my stage manager's wife. And general all-round helper."

"Was your stage manager there at that time, or had he gone to the pub?"

"He was on the stage. He's in the show too. He plays the part of Alderman Fitzwarren." Hogan looked slightly embarrassed. "It's a bit of a tight budget this year, I'm afraid. Everyone is doubling up."

Banham nodded dismissively. "How soon was this before the scene in the dark?"

"The ultra-violet scene, you mean? About ten minutes. It starts approximately twenty minutes after the curtain goes up on act two, and the second act was about ten minutes in when I left the bar."

"So when, exactly, did he go to the pub?" Crowther asked.

"Then, actually. He walked off stage during the scene. He's always doing that. There's a clash of personalities between the dame and the comic, and they argue on stage. That happened tonight, and Alan hates it. He walked off and went to the pub."

"You saw him?"

"Yes."

"And you let him go?"

Michael shrugged. "It's complicated. I've employed him for years, and I'm used to it."

"What did you do then?" Banham asked.

"I put the head-cans on and spoke to the lighting and sound director. He works from the box at the back of the auditorium. I told him that Alan had buggered off and asked him to take his own cues from the stage. He's used to it. He's used to Alan too, he just gets on with it. So are the other actors, they just say his lines and no one notices."

Crowther and Banham exchanged glances.

"And when was the last time you saw Lucinda?" Banham asked.

"Actually at that moment," Michael answered. "As I finished speaking to Robert. Lucinda came off stage and saw me in the wings. She came straight over to me. She'd been crying."

"You must have good eyesight," Banham said. "Isn't it

dark backstage?"

"I could tell by her voice," he said quickly.

"What did she say?"

"She said she wanted to talk to me, before Barbara did. She said Barbara had been picking on her for days, accusing her of singing flat. They'd had a terrible row over it."

"Was Barbara jealous of Lucinda?" Crowther asked.

Hogan gave a little laugh. He reached up to the top of the metal filing cabinet in the corner of the office and took down three mugs and a tray. "Barbara is over fifty. She's in the menopause and riddled with insecurities." He set the mugs on the tray and sighed loudly. "Lucinda is..." He shook his head and corrected himself quietly. "Lucinda was a beginner. Sometimes she did sing flat, and Barbara shouted at her. It's not personal, Barbara's very professional, she needs the show to be good, she needs to get other work, she wants to relaunch her career! So she gave Lucinda a hard time, but she wouldn't have murdered her for singing off key."

"Did Lucinda argue with anyone else?"

"Not that I know of."

"What did you say to Lucinda?"

"I told her I'd try and sort it out. Then she went back on stage." Hogan put his hand to his face. "Then Vincent Mann, the comic, came off the stage and made a beeline for me. He was furious. He told me to do something about Barbara. He said I was to tell her to stop picking on Lucinda, or he would do something about it himself."

"What do you think he meant?"

Hogan shook his head. "I've no idea. He made things worse by telling Lucinda to stand up for herself. The rest of us have worked with Barbara before, we know her well, and we know it's best not to argue with her. Her bark is much worse than her bite."

The producer was visibly upset. "Take your time," Banham said.

"That wasn't the time to tell Barbara I was cutting the duet," Hogan continued after a brief pause. "It would have made things worse. So I decided to wait until the end of the show, then call the whole company together for a pep talk. I just wanted them all to do their jobs. I need to make as much money as I can this season." He closed his eyes. "My debts are closing in on me. I'm fighting not to go bankrupt."

Banham gave him a moment to compose himself before asking, "What happened then?"

Michael Hogan shook his head. "I walked away from Vincent Mann."

"And went where?"

"Oh, up here. Sophie wasn't on stage, I knew she'd be here, changing into her black costume for the ultra-violet scene. I wanted to ask her what she knew about the arguments."

"While she was changing?" Banham asked.

Hogan turned back to the tray and busied himself with the cups. "Or doing her hair."

"And what did she say?"

"She said she thought Vincent Mann was behind it all."

Banham watched him, but said nothing.

Michael turned to face him. "Sophie told me Barbara was behaving even worse than usual this year, picking on everyone. She thought it was because Barbara wasn't getting enough attention; the audiences liked Vincent more than her, and she was terribly insecure. She told Sophie she wanted all her solo numbers re-choreographed." He smiled. "Sophie refused of course, and Barbara threw a terrible tantrum. It all went in one ear and out the other with

Sophie." He smiled again, like a proud father. "She's very good at handling people. She's also very shrewd. She knew we had a serious problem."

Crowther scribbled in his notebook. Hogan looked from Banham to Crowther and back again. Banham said nothing.

"Sophie suggested I sack Vincent," Hogan continued after a few seconds. "She thought that would sort out all our problems." He lifted the top off a tin and picked up a spoon. "I told her that wasn't an option. Vincent is a well-known television presenter and the audiences were buying tickets to see him." He pulled a sideways expression. "Sophie had already thought about that. I might have known she'd have worked it out." He spooned sugar into a mug of coffee which he handed to Banham. "She said I should play the role." He turned his back and Banham watched him adding sugar to another cup as he explained. "She said we didn't need him to pull in audiences any more, as the tickets were already sold for most of the run. Barbara would be less insecure if I was playing the comic, and I could sort out Lucinda and Barbara's differences."

"Could anyone have overheard this discussion?" Banham asked him.

"Everyone else was on stage at the time." Hogan handed Crowther the coffee. "And by then it was getting near the ultra-violet scene and Sophie had to go down herself. But I agreed to give it some thought."

"And did you?"

"Yes. I walked Sophie to the stage, then I went down to the basement, into the juveniles' room; the kids were all on stage so I knew I would have ten minutes of peace and quiet."

Crowther looked up from his notebook. "So you were on your own in the juveniles' room when the UV scene took place?" he asked.

"Actually no." He paused. "Maggie McCormak came in."

"I thought you said you saw her earlier going out through to the auditorium to watch the show," Banham said quickly.

"Yes, yes I did. But she came back… for her binoculars."

Crowther was having trouble writing; his pen seemed to be running out of ink.

"And I stayed there, thinking, right through that scene," Hogan said.

"Did you come to any decision?" Banham asked.

Hogan lowered his eyes again. "Yes, I decided that I would go with Sophie's suggestion and get rid of Vincent Mann."

The only sound was from Crowther's biro scribbling on the corner of the note-pad. Banham pulled a pen from his pocket and handed it to him.

"Is there anything else?" Hogan asked. "Only I want to take this coffee down to your sergeant."

"What alerted you to the incident on the stage?" Banham asked.

"The tannoy was on in the children's room and I heard the curtain being brought in. So I ran upstairs and… well, Sophie said there'd been an accident, and the ambulance was on its way. I made the announcement to the audience, I told them they could all have tickets for another show. Not that there are many left."

Michael indicated the coffee. "Yes, go ahead," Banham said.

"And you'll let me know if I can run the show tomorrow?"

Banham tried not to let his irritation show. A nineteen-year-old girl had just lost her life, yet the man only seemed interested in keeping the ticket sales going. "I can't make a decision on that just yet," he said. "The forensics team have a lot to do."

"Will I know tonight? Only I'll have a lot to sort out."

"You won't get the costumes back by tomorrow," Banham said abruptly. "Forensics will need them for quite some time."

Hogan gripped the tray more tightly. He looked at Crowther and then back to Banham. "I see," he said hesitantly.

Banham opened the door for him. "I'll keep you informed," he said.

Hogan still didn't leave the room.

"The cast are planning to stay here tonight," he said apprehensively. "The roads are pretty bad, and the last buses and trains have gone now. They've all slept on the floor many times when the weather's been too bad to travel. I hope that's all right with you."

Banham nodded. "As long as they stay away from the stage."

Banham had been looking forward to the coffee, but screwed his face up after the first mouthful. "Not enough sugar," he said as soon as Michael Hogan was out of earshot.

"I'll drink it, Guv," Crowther said. "There's a machine in the Green Room. As it's the season of goodwill, I'll treat you to a plastic cup of instant."

"I'd sooner you treated yourself to a biro that works," Banham told him.

The door to the Green Room was next to an enormous mirror that took up three-quarters of the wall at the end of the corridor. The door was ajar, and the mirror reflected the inside of the room. Banham stopped a few feet from the open door and took the opportunity to study the cast members who were gathered there.

In one corner of the Green Room stood the vending machine, and beside it a lopsided plastic Christmas tree had been carelessly planted in a black bucket with torn Christmas paper round it. The tree was bare, apart from a grubby white fairy who had slipped and now hung sideways from the dusty top branch. On the floor beside the tree sat three young blonde women and a large black man.

"The chorus?" Banham asked Crowther in a low voice.

Crowther nodded, and pointed to another blonde girl, wearing a pink velour track suit and pink trainers with flashing lights on the sides. Her hair was pulled off her face and secured with a raspberry pink velour scrunchy, into a long ponytail that trailed down her back. She was sitting on her own, sipping from a plastic cup.

"Sophie Flint, the choreographer, Guv. And that –" Crowther pointed to an enormous man sitting a few yards away, his large bulk overhanging both sides of his canvas-backed chair. "That's the man that plays the dame, and hadn't changed his costume when he should have."

Banham studied the fat man, then turned his attention to a tall, handsome woman who sat in the next chair. "Presumably the older woman is the formidable Barbara Denis," he asked.

Crowther nodded.

"Now why did I know you'd have spoken to all the young women, but not the older one?"

"Not on purpose, Guv."

"Good! You can interview Barbara Denis now. I'll talk to the fat man. That just leaves Vincent Mann, the one who dialled 999."

"And took the balaclava off the dead girl," Crowther reminded his boss.

Vincent Mann was easy to spot in the mirror, even though his head was buried in his hands. He wore a bright yellow, blue and red jacket and bright buttercup yellow shoes. Another man sat in the chair next to him, holding a half-full glass. He was older, with flyaway grey hair, and a red, blotchy complexion. Alan McCormak, Banham thought, the stage manager who had been in the pub.

"Make sure uniform takes a statement from the stage manager," he told Crowther.

"So are we releasing the actors after we talk to them?"

Banham rubbed his fingers across his mouth. "They're staying in the building tonight. If possible, I'd like to let the show go on. It'll keep the suspects together while we gather information."

Crowther took his notebook from his pocket. "All right if I hang on to your biro till the morning, Guv?"

"Do I have a choice?"

"You know, I reckon that pathologist woman fancies you." Crowther gave Banham a cheeky wink.

"Whatever gives you that idea?"

"She's going to get the post mortem done in the morning. It's holiday time – that's a favour she's doing you."

"She'll get paid," Banham said crisply, to cover his embarrassment. "And you said yourself, it's the season of goodwill."

"True."

"I'm glad you agree." Banham smiled. "In that case, you can stay here for the night with the actors." He lowered his voice. "This wasn't a freak accident. You know it, and I know it. Someone in this building has committed murder."

Alison tried to push her hurt feelings to the back of her mind and get on with her job. She and Paul Banham had been friends as well as close colleagues for years, and he always asked for her to be assigned to his murder enquiries. He had spent months dropping hints, and when she finally agreed to an evening out they'd had a great time – then he came out with the business and pleasure don't mix number.

Despite her confusion and anger she wanted to be here working with him. He was a great detective, and her work was her life. She had six shivering children to interview in the freezing basement under the stage. So she had to put the personal issues out of her mind.

As she entered the children's dressing room a sudden flood of childhood memories hit her. Nothing seemed to have changed since her own days as a pantomime juvenile. White ballerina costumes, silver lurex finale dresses, sailor costumes, coloured peasant skirts, chiffon harem outfits were all bunched on a sagging clothes rail on the far side of the long room. In a tidy row at the base of the rail were rows of tiny ballet slippers, black tap-dancing shoes and small black flippers.

Chairs spread with brightly coloured towels marked each child's territory. On the towels stood bright lipsticks and black eye pencils, and photographs of Robbie Williams or Will Young, and one of a beautiful chestnut pony mounted in heart-shaped, pink fluffy photo frame.

Suddenly the face of Simon le Bon jumped into Alison's mind. He was the one who smiled down from the mirror beside Alison's place in the dressing room and got the plump teenager through the endless costume changes and teasing.

She had been a chubby tomboy who liked nothing more

than playing football with her army sergeant father. But her mother had sent her to a local dance academy, telling her it would help with her weight and posture.

All the children in the class were expected to be babes in the pantomime at the local theatre every Christmas, and they all loved it. All except Alison. She had been a fish out of water. But she said nothing; her mother so enjoyed being backstage, sewing sequins and making costumes that made Alison look slimmer. It was then, at the age of nine, that she began to watch what she ate, and her weight started to drop.

The dance classes continued till she was fourteen. Then one of her classmates ran away from home, and she was allowed to help with the search; once involved with the local police she was hooked, and told her parents she wanted to be a detective. Her mother offered self-defence classes in place of dancing school, and she happily swapped pink leotards and tap shoes for judo kit. She was a natural; even now she would happily barge into a fight, and could always hold her own with the boys.

But she continued to count calories, and feel guilty every time she ate a large meal. Even now, aged thirty-four and five feet seven, she weighed less than nine stone. She still sometimes swallowed too many laxatives, and often fasted for a couple of days. The rest of the team often joked about how skinny she was, and secretly she enjoyed it.

She stared at herself in the huge mirrors, despising the two extra pounds that clung to her body after Christmas, and wondering if Banham might find her desirable when she shed them.

She rubbed her gloved hands together to keep her circulation moving. It was far too cold in here to keep children hanging around. She left the dressing room and made her way along the under-stage passageway, where the little girls were sitting with their parents, huddled into their coats and scarves.

"I won't be a minute – I'm going to look for some heaters," she told them.

"They're not allowed," said one of the mothers. "Fire regulations."

"If they're so keen they should put in a fire escape," Alison retorted. "Those spiral staircases aren't much good in an emergency."

"It's there." The mother indicated a large double door with a fat double lock on the inside, only just visible behind three heavy wicker skips, overflowing and piled high with dusty costumes.

Alison tried to pull one of the skips back and the mother jumped up to help. "Sorry," she said as one of the dads joined her and dragged it away from the exit. "It's my fault, I'm in charge of the costumes. We're so short of space down here."

"One accident is enough," Alison snapped. She released the bolt on the fire doors, and icy air and snow blew down the steep ramp. She shut the doors quickly and tapped the snow from her gloves.

"Where does that lead to?" she asked the woman.

"The street up the side. We're not allowed to use it, no matter how bad the weather is – we have to walk all the way round to the stage door."

Alison nodded a thank you to the woman. "I'd sort those skips out if I were you," she told her. "The health and safety officers will have a field day if you block a fire exit, especially with children in the show."

She headed back to the dressing room before the children froze to death.

The smallest girl was still crying and frightened. All she could tell Alison was that she heard a bump at the end of the routine. The next told a similar story: she heard a thump at the end of the scene and thought someone had fallen over.

The rest of the interviews were a formality; all the children gave exactly the same account of the incident, much as Alison had expected. She sent the last one home and looked around the dressing room for the shoulder bag that accompanied her everywhere.

Suddenly she was aware of a noise. It sounded like footsteps, and seemed to be coming from the opposite wall, behind the rail of costumes. She stood as close as she could and listened: yes, someone was definitely walking about on the other side of the rough, unpainted brickwork. She ran a hand along the bricks and found a small silver handle. She turned it, and part of the wall opened like a door, releasing a damp smell like a secret cellar.

The footsteps seemed to be getting nearer, and in the darkness she could just make out the shape of another spiral staircase directly in front of her. But leading where? She moved her fingers along the wall in search of a light switch. "Is someone there?" she called.

3

"What do people call you?" Crowther asked, following Barbara Denis through a door adorned with a large, white plastic star and the words NUMBER 1 DRESSING ROOM.

"Quite a lot of things, and some of them not very nice," she said with a laugh.

He noticed her back teeth were slightly discoloured. Always a sign of age in a woman, he thought smugly; she must be over fifty.

So what was a woman her age doing playing Dick Whittington?

She settled herself in an old, comfortable armchair in front of a mirror that covered the whole of one wall, and smiled at her reflection. "You can call me Barbara."

The actress's skin was still shiny from the cream she'd used to remove her heavy stage make-up. Her long, thin legs were covered in well-worn black leggings; she curled them under her in the chair, pulling her floor-length grey cardigan more closely around her shoulders.

Crowther was a streetwise boy, and her large, brown eyes held no secrets for him. He'd seen that lonely haunted look all his life – on the hookers that walked the beat in his home town of Chingford.

"Please make yourself at home," she said, waving at the large brown sofa that took up the whole of the opposite wall. He obeyed, and coffee from Banham's unwanted cup splashed on to his hand as he sank into the cushions. Aware of her eyes on him, he quickly sat upright, put the coffee down and took out his notebook and Banham's pen.

She swung her armchair around to face him. Over the black wool leggings she wore a black Bardot-style boatneck jumper, which bared part of a shoulder. She pulled the jumper up and tugged her cardigan even closer. "What do you want me to call you?" she asked, widening her eyes.

"Detective," he answered, meeting her gaze.

"Would you like something a bit stronger than that coffee, Detective? Do help yourself to a gin and tonic. Gin on top of the fridge, tonic inside it. There's a lemon too – I like to do things properly."

She had taken a shine to him. He knew he had a way with women, especially the older ones. Even from several feet away he could see that the crow's feet around her eyes came from the biggest bird in the flock. And she wasn't a real blonde either; tell-tale grey roots peeped through her fine, shoulder-length, honey-coloured hair. He gave her an insincere smile and told her that the coffee was fine.

"How did you and Lucinda get on?" he asked.

The smile left her face. "Not well, to be honest. We had to work very closely together. Principal boy, that's me, and principal girl… We had to sing love duets together, that sort of thing. And I can't deny I found working with her difficult."

"Because she was young and beautiful?"

"No, Detective, because she sang flat and that reflected on my work." She pulled her face back into a smile and he noticed the fine lines above her top lip; she was, or used to be, a heavy smoker.

"I often have to work with young hopefuls, and often ones without talent." She sighed and closed her eyes. "I work a lot for Michael, the producer of the show. He's my ex-husband. He uses a lot of beginners in his productions.

I call them his baby birds."

"Come again?" Crowther said.

"Cheap cheap."

Crowther still looked blank.

"They don't cost him a lot," she explained patiently. "They want to get into show business, and he wants to save money. It suits them both."

Crowther slurped his coffee. Barbara stood up and walked over to the tall rusting fridge that stood by the window. She poured herself a small gin and opened the fridge to take out the tonic. "Are you sure you won't change your mind?" she asked him, shaving a slice off a half-used lemon with a small kitchen knife.

He shook his head.

"Actually I felt sorry for her." She took a sip of the drink. "She wouldn't have got anywhere. She was dim, naïve and untalented."

Crowther looked at her. After a second he asked, "And what about you? Where have you got?"

"Oh, I had a hit record, Detective. *Oh Ho, You Know.*"

He fought the urge to laugh. "When was that?"

"1984. It made the top one hundred."

"Maybe my dad remembers it," he said tactlessly. "How old were you then?"

She looked unamused. "Work it out for yourself. A woman should never have to give her age away."

"So you're self-conscious about your age?"

"All female singers are, Detective. It is a hazard of our job."

"Then you must have hated working with Lucinda. You said yourself that she was young and beautiful."

"Actually you said that." Her voice grew louder. "I said she was naïve and dim."

"Was she?"

Barbara sat back in her chair and faced the mirror. "Beautiful?" She wiped a spot of black from under her eye, then swivelled the chair to face him again. "Yes, I suppose she was." She shrugged and gave a little smile. "She looked... foreign, but if you like that then yes, she was beautiful." She uncurled her long legs, stretched them in front of her then crossed one over the other, pulling her cardigan over her shoulders again. "Detective, I don't know what you're trying to imply, but I wasn't jealous of her. I need to get more work, and that means sounding my best on stage. So a principal girl who sings off key is irritating."

Crowther slurped his coffee again. "OK," he said. "Talk me through..." He glanced at his notebook. "The ultraviolet scene, is that right?"

"Yes, that's right."

"Could you see the other people on the stage?"

"I was aware of them. We know exactly where the other actors are because we've rehearsed it. For instance, if I stopped in the middle of the stage Sophie would bump into me. I know she's always behind me, although I can't actually see her."

"So if someone was there who isn't normally, you would know?

Barbara squeezed her lips together and seemed to weigh this up before shaking her head. "Well, no, I couldn't swear to that. But I'd say it's highly unlikely. It's so tightly rehearsed. If someone was there that shouldn't be, someone would bump into them, and someone else into them. And that didn't happen. Everything seemed normal until I heard that thump." Barbara put her hand to her cheek. "It came from my right side, where Lucinda stands at the end of the line." She moved her hand away from her face. "It's very hot and stuffy under those black balaclavas, and my first thought was that she was pregnant and she'd fainted."

Crowther frowned.

She continued. "I would have heard something out of the ordinary if anyone else was there. But I didn't – all I heard was the thump as she fell."

He scribbled *pregnant?* in his notebook, then looked at her again. "Does your stage manager often disappear when he should be working?"

She rolled her eyes. "Yes. Don't ask, it's a long story."

"I am asking," he said firmly.

She rubbed her neck and edged her cardigan up again. "He's married to Maggie McCormak," she explained. "Maggie does the wardrobe. They have a daughter, Fay, who plays my cat. I play Dick Whittington."

"Yes, I know," he responded sharply. "The question was about your stage manager."

She obviously wasn't used to being told to get to the point. But it was past midnight and they had a lot to do. He just wanted the facts.

"It's all relevant," she said crisply. "Michael, my ex-husband, had an affair with Maggie, many years ago, after our marriage had split up. Alan started drinking. Then, predictably, Michael got tired of Maggie. But Alan carried on drinking, and Michael feels responsible, so he carries on employing him, even though the man is incapable of doing the job." Barbara's tone hardened. "Alan and Maggie take advantage of that kindness. So in answer to your question, yes, Alan is frequently in the pub when he should be working, and Maggie covers for him. Like tonight, at the beginning of the UV scene, he had gone to the pub, so she was in the wings helping give out the fish."

"The fish?"

"Plastic sea creatures. They have ultra-violet lights inside them. That helps us see our way across the stage. "There are workers in the wings too, by the prop table, to help us pick up the right ones."

Now Crowther really was confused. "Workers?"

"Small blue lights, by each prop table."

"Ah. Not people, then."

"No, but there are stagehands around. Two of them, young boys." She rolled her eyes. "Cheap cheap! Work experience boys. Michael cutting corners again. They move the scenery at that point, so they aren't involved in the UV routine."

Crowther had already spoken to the stagehands. He decided it was time to change the subject. "Why isn't Stephen Coombs in the routine?"

She raised her eyebrows. "He's twenty stone, detective. Isn't that enough of a reason?"

"Come again?"

"He used to be in it, until a few years ago. But he's a very large man, and he can't dance. He gets it all wrong and gets in everyone's way."

"Was it the same routine? When he was in it?"

"Yes."

"So he knows the steps?"

She paused and then frowned. "Well, yes, I suppose he would. If he remembers them."

"So what does he do when the routine is on?"

"He was given a costume change. A tactful way of keeping him out of it."

"Whose idea was that?"

"Michael's."

"Kind of him."

"He's a very kind man."

"Surprised you let him go then."

The smile dropped from her face, and for a moment Crowther glimpsed the real Barbara Denis, nervous, insecure and vulnerable. He was pleased with himself. He was getting somewhere.

Alison's fumbling hands found the light switch. She found herself facing Michael Hogan, a tray of coffee in his hands.

"Sorry if I gave you a fright," he said. "I had my hands full, but I know my way down in the dark."

She followed him into the dressing room.

"You poor girl, it's freezing down here," he said. "This coffee will soon warm you up."

"Thank you. So where does that passageway lead to?"

"It comes out near the ground floor dressing rooms, then another staircase to the first floor comes out next to the mirror by the Green Room. Hardly anyone uses it though." He grinned. "The theatre ghost is rumoured to be walled up in there, and supposedly gets violent if you disturb her. That's if you believe that sort of rubbish."

Alison didn't return his smile. As he put the tray down on the laundry basket she noticed the elbow of his cardigan was worn through.

"I've been putting shows on here for thirteen years now," he told her, "and I've never met the ghost."

Alison cupped her hands around the coffee pot. "Whose dressing rooms are on the ground floor?"

"Everyone is on the first floor. Oh, except Sophie. She plays the fairy, and she's my assistant and my choreographer so she shares the company office with me."

He lifted the milk jug to pour. "No milk," she said brusquely. "I take it black."

"I'll leave you to help yourself."

The coffee wasn't too hot and she downed a full cup quickly, glad of its warmth. Michael had disappeared into the corridor, but she heard voices and went to investigate. He was talking to Maggie McCormak; they both fell silent when they saw Alison.

"I was telling Michael we must move the skips and keep the fire exit free," Maggie said quickly. "We don't want the fire officer after us."

"Yes, and I'd check the obstructions the scenery is causing in the wings upstairs while you're at it," Alison said. "I'm sure health and safety will be paying you a visit very soon."

There was an awkward silence, then Michael Hogan said, "Would you like some more hot coffee?"

"No thanks."

She turned back into the dressing room, and he followed her.

"Look, I know this sounds bad under the circumstances," he said, "but I'm kind of desperate. I have to keep this show running. I rely on the pantomime for most of my income. Nearly all the tickets are sold for the matinee tomorrow, and I'll lose a lot of money if they all have to be refunded."

"I'm sorry," she told him. "It's not down to me. Detective Inspector Banham is in charge of the case."

Banham was upstairs in the company office, sitting in front of the mirror where there was enough space to lean and write on the dresser. Beside him, Stephen Coombs the pantomime dame was trying to get comfortable in an upright chair too small for his bulk. Stephen was late middle-aged and balding badly. Smudges of black make-up mixed with perspiration sat in the bags under his eyes, and the blotchy remains of a dark foundation streaked his neck. He either wasn't aware or didn't care that he hadn't fully removed his stage make-up.

Banham found the aroma of the man's stale sweat and cheap deodorant offensive. His fingers rubbed his mouth as he studied the cast list Michael Hogan had supplied.

"You play the part of Sarah the Cook," he said.

Stephen Coombs blew his nose on a greying and over-used handkerchief. "I do, yes. I'm the dame. So I wasn't on stage in the fatal scene," he answered defensively. "I don't have to do that scene, because I'm the dame, see." The words spilled nervously and hurriedly from the man's large, thick mouth. "I have to change my frock, see. I change every time I come and go on stage. It's what dames do. I have to wear wigs an' all, so I couldn't be in those chorus scenes. I need the time to get changed and ready for my next entrance, and to do my wig. The others, they have to wear balaclavas over their heads, so they can come and go unseen. So the audience think the fishes are flying across the stage on their own, instead of the actors waving them about like mad things, see."

It was the second time that someone had explained the scene to him, but Banham still didn't see. He made no reply, but leaned his elbow on the table and stared at the large man.

Stephen bit a nail then pulled his fat thumb from his mouth and shifted uncomfortably in his seat. "The choreographer works out the staging for that scene, that's the steps that the cast have to do when they are going from one side of the stage to the other in the dark with the fishes," he said. "That's to stop the actors bumping into each other, see. Mind you, we have so little rehearsal time, no one really knows where they're supposed to be, so they do bump into each other and get in the wrong place. It happens all the time."

Banham raised his eyebrows.

Stephen carried on talking at top speed.

"Nobody knows who is beside them, or who bumps into them, because the stage is in darkness. Someone knew that, somebody bloody knew they could creep on stage and not be noticed."

Banham thought the man's brown eyes were like a frightened animal's. He let a few seconds go by before saying, "So you don't think it was an accident?

"No, I don't."

Banham looked at him expectantly, but Coombs looked away. He pulled the grubby handkerchief from his pocket and blew his nose again. "Excuse me," he said. "I've got a cold coming."

There was a small patch of greasy blackheads at the side of the man's nose. Banham wondered if that was the result of plastering layers of make-up on his face every day. He was suddenly glad that he was a policeman.

"Anyone in the cast could easily have hit her with that stage weight, you know. Except me," Coombs added quickly. He moved his head nearer to Banham's and lowered his voice. "I wasn't on stage in that routine, see. It's chorus work really. But work is so scarce nowadays, no one would dare refuse to do it. The producer's a cheapskate; he makes the principals do chorus work and muck in far more than usual to earn their pay packet."

Banham didn't reply.

"Something else that might interest you," Stephen Coombs said after another short silence. "Michael Hogan is going bankrupt."

Banham's shrewd blue eyes remained fixed on the man. "Does it make you angry that all the principals have to muck in?" he asked after a moment.

"Well, not me it don't," he said. "No skin off my nose. Pantomime dame is all-consuming, see. If I'm not on stage, I'm changing. I have ten full changes, tights, knickers, eyelashes, all that sort of thing. So I don't have a minute's peace from curtain up till curtain down."

"And you were in your dressing room, changing, during the ultra-violet scene tonight?"

Stephen nodded.

Banham scribbled in his notebook. "Could anyone vouch for that? Was anyone with you?"

"Well, no, as I explained, he's a penny-pinching bastard. He won't even pay for me to have a dresser, and I really need it. I mean I have to change tights, and…"

"Yes, understood," Banham broke in quickly. The last thing he needed at midnight was this petty whinging.

"So no one to confirm your alibi then?"

"Such as who?" He seemed to be getting worked up. "There was no one. They were all in the scene."

"Apart from the stage-hands?"

"The stage crew was very thin tonight. It was just two work experience boys, and they were busy changing the set."

"How long does it take you to change?"

"I didn't do it," Stephen blurted.

Banham looked up from his notes. "I didn't say you did," he said mildly. "I asked how long it takes you to change."

"About three minutes for that change into the Island costume. I'm supposed to be shipwrecked, so it's a minimal change, you see."

Banham didn't. "And no one else was around."

Stephen shuffled uncomfortably in his chair. He brought his fat hand to his mouth and bit on a nail like a hungry squirrel who had found a nut. Banham noticed how dirty his hands and nails were.

"How well did you know the dead girl, Lucinda Benson?"

"Not well. I only met her this year. She was new to the business, like. She was very young."

"Did you get on with her?"

"Actually, I thought she was a bit naïve and too inexperienced for the job. She had a nice voice, but you couldn't hear it past the footlights. What bloody good's that? She bored the arses off of the kids 'cos they couldn't bloody hear her. Then the likes of me then has to go on and work bloody hard to get them back, see. That's why he books me every year, like, 'cos I know how to get the audience going." He moved in closer to Banham. "She only got the job because she was the producer's bit on the side, if you really want to know. So no one dared to say much to her. But she got right on everyone's nerves, I can tell you."

Banham studied his notes again. "You've worked for Michael Hogan for the last thirteen pantomimes?"

"That's right. I do dame for him every year."

"So you know him very well?"

Stephen nodded. "I do, yes."

"Is he married?"

"Not now. He was, though – twice. The last one's the mother of the girl what plays the fairy and choreographs the show. The marriage only lasted for a few years." He curled his mouth. "She wouldn't put up with his infidelities, so she threw him out."

"What about his first wife?"

Stephen removed a bit of fingernail from his mouth. "His first wife was Barbara Denis. She's our star – plays the title role, Dick Whittington, the principal boy. It was years ago, mind, and the marriage hardly lasted. She made a record called *Oh Ho, You Know.* You might remember it?"

Banham had been a follower of pop music in the eighties. He searched his memory. He couldn't remember ever having heard the song. He shook his head.

"Does she work for him every year? Or is it just this one?

"He usually gives her a pantomime at Christmas. He must feel sorry for her. It's hard to get work when you're a woman in your fifties, and let's face it, over the hill."

"How did she get on with Lucinda Benson?"

Stephen pulled a pained face and scratched the inside of his ear. "She bloody hated her. They argued all through rehearsals. They had to work closely together too, sing love duets an' all. Barbara kept saying Lucinda was singing flat, which she was. Michael wouldn't get involved. He's afraid of Barbara, she's a monster, see, and Lucinda had him well wrapped around her finger too. He never could resist a pretty girl. Barbara tried to get me involved, but I said it didn't matter how bloody flat the girl sang, seeing that she couldn't project neither; even with a microphone you couldn't hear her past the footlights."

"And the rest of the cast? How did they get on with Lucinda?"

He shrugged. "No one said much. The producer was giving her one, and they all wanted to work next year. But no one really liked her. Except for Vincent…"

"Vincent Mann," Banham said studying his piece of paper. "He plays Idle Jack, the comic."

"That's right. Well, I know for a fact they were having a bit of a fling on the side too. I'm sure Michael didn't know. He wouldn't have been pleased. Vincent works very closely with her in the show. He has to pretend to be in love with her. And you know, in this business, one thing leads to another."

"So she was having a fling with Vincent, and with Michael?"

Stephen nodded solemnly.

"Do the rest of the cast know?"

Stephen opened his fat arms and shrugged. "I couldn't say for sure. I'm not one for gossiping you see…"

Banham chose to ignore that remark. "How do you get on with Vincent Mann?" he asked.

Stephen scratched his ear again. "Well, I'll tell you straight, the man's an idiot. He doesn't know comedy. He presents a children's series on morning television so he thinks he's a star. Pantomime is an art, it takes experience. I've been working with live audiences all my life…"

Banham was getting tired of this. "How do you get on with him?" he snapped.

Stephen blinked. "Like I say, he has a lot to learn, he thinks he knows comedy, but he don't and I do. So, not well at all."

Banham said nothing. Stephen carried on, "He is a married man, with two daughters. And he's giving a nineteen-year-old girl a length. The man is an arsehole of the first degree, ain't that a bloody fact."

Banham look back at his notes. "Right, thank you, that'll be all for now," he said.

"Can I go?" Coombs said uncertainly.

"You can." Banham looked up at the man. "But I believe you'll be staying here tonight. There's no public transport at this time and the roads are terrible. I might need to ask you some more questions, but that's all for now."

"The show's on tomorrow then?"

"We'll see about that."

Stephen stood up, and Banham noticed he was shaking.

He paused as if about to say something else, but appeared to change his mind.

"You don't have to worry about anything you say to me," Banham said. "Everything is in confidence."

Stephen nodded, seeming reassured, but said no more. Then he left the room.

Banham dragged his hands over his face. It was going to be a long night. The packet of fresh coffee stood on top of the fridge by the kettle, but the coffee-pot was downstairs. He picked up his vending machine cup and drained the remains of the cold, muddy liquid. It tasted disgusting. He wondered if there might be another coffee-pot.

A grey metal filing cabinet stood in the corner of the room. He opened each of the three drawers in turn. Nothing in the first; some papers in second. When he pulled open the bottom one he found himself gazing at a black leotard, black gloves, and a pair of black tights.

4

Crowther said he had personally name-tagged, counted and bagged up all the black costumes the actors were wearing at the time of the suspected murder, and given them to Penny to take away for forensic testing. The young DC sometimes got above himself, but Banham was confident he was thorough. This was the company office; they probably kept a spare costume here for emergencies.

He quickly took an evidence container from his briefcase and pulled on the latex gloves he kept in his pocket. He bagged the costume and dropped it back into the case, which he locked again right away.

When he left the office a man was standing at the top of the stairs. Banham recognised the thick-rimmed black glasses, red, blue and yellow jacket and bright yellow shoes. It was Vincent Mann, the television presenter.

"I have to talk to you, alone," Mann whispered desperately.

"No problem," Banham said. "One of us would have got round to you before the evening was out." He turned back towards the company office.

"Not up there, it's not safe." Vincent raised his hand and shook it nervously. "I wouldn't be surprised if he's had that office bugged. That's probably why he offered it to you."

The man seemed unable to keep still; his whole body was shivering. Banham wondered if he took drugs. "OK, where is safe?" he asked him.

"Nowhere backstage." Vincent turned and hurried down the stairs. "Follow me."

Banham followed him – down the stairs, along the corridor, through the swing doors to the stage, where Penny

Starr and the police exhibits officer were still working. Camera bulbs flashed and a video camera was trained on the area around the body. Banham lifted a hand to get Penny's attention and pointed at his briefcase, mouthing, "Another evidence bag."

Vincent Mann was disappearing through the pass door into the auditorium. Banham followed him into the stalls, scanning the area to check where the exits were.

The auditorium wasn't large; Banham's sharp eyes estimated there were about five hundred seats. Apart from the pass door, there were two exits at the back, both leading to the foyer, but no emergency access to the street.

Vincent Mann was hurrying up the aisle towards the back of the stalls. In those bright clothes the man looked like a clown, but Banham had the impression he was the exact opposite.

Mann pulled down the scarlet velvet seat next to the end of the back row and covered his face with his hands. "Lucinda's death wasn't an accident," he said, his voice only just audible.

"OK. Tell me everything you know," Banham said non-committally.

Two tears fell from Vincent's eyes and he lifted the back of his hand to catch them as they rolled down one side of his nose.

Banham sat very still.

Vincent sniffed loudly and said, "She's been murdered. I know that for sure."

"How do you know for sure?" Banham asked.

"Lucinda was new to all this, and Stephen and Barbara were jealous of her." He felt around in his pocket, for a handkerchief, Banham assumed. He didn't find one. "They bullied her," he said. "And she couldn't stand up for herself, so I decided I would." He paused, sniffed again, and more tears fell. He wiped them away with the back of his hand. Banham waited in silence.

"I went to Michael and threatened to walk out if he didn't deal with it," Vincent said. "Michael needs me because the children know me – I'm on television every Saturday, so I pull the audiences in." He brushed his hands down both cheeks in an attempt to control his tears. "When Michael offered me the job, he told me he had very little money, that he was going bankrupt, so I said I'd work for free if he employed Lucinda as principal girl." He felt in his top pocket and found a tissue, which he used to wipe first his glasses then his eyes before putting it, practically disintegrated, back in his pocket. "If I hadn't done that, she would still be here today."

"Were you having a relationship with her?" Banham asked him.

"Yes, I'm in love with her. We've been together for two years."

Banham rubbed his mouth with the back of his hand. "Go on."

"If I walked out Michael would have to pay someone to take my place, and I knew he wouldn't want to do that. So I believed he'd sort it out."

"What did Michael say when you told him to sort it out?"

"He said he'd tell my wife about Lucinda. Then he dismissed me as if I was an old sock." His voice rose, and Banham had to concentrate to understand what he was saying. He retrieved the crumpled tissue and rubbed one eye with what was left of it.

"Take your time," Banham said, watching him roll the tissue into a ball.

"I was furious. I followed Michael upstairs to his office. He slammed the door in my face. So I stood outside and listened." He paused and clenched his teeth. "I heard him tell Sophie that Lucinda had to go. I assumed he meant that he would sack her. I was going to have it out with him after the show." He put his hand to his mouth. "But then… they murdered her." He shook his head and stared at the floor.

"What exactly did he say?"

"His exact words were, Lucinda has to go, at any cost!" He looked up and almost shouted at Banham. "At any cost, she had to go. That's what they said."

He wiped his face in circular movements with one of the cuffs of his coloured jacket, reminding Banham of a cat washing itself.

"They didn't mention murder?"

Vincent shook his head. "Of course not." His face crumpled like an unhappy child's. More tears rolled down his face, and he lifted his sleeve to wipe them again. "I know they've murdered her," he whispered.

Banham gave him a couple of seconds to compose himself. "Tell me about the ultra-violet scene," he said. "The scene where she was killed."

Vincent ignored the question. "I got her the job. If I hadn't got her the job she'd still be alive. They murdered her."

"How?"

"They hit her with that concrete block. She was standing next to it at the end of the routine."

"Michael isn't in the ultra-violet scene," Banham said. "He isn't in the show at all. How are you suggesting he murdered her?

The man was becoming hysterical. "Everyone is covered

from head to foot in black; anyone could have been there."

"Could they?" Banham asked.

Vincent didn't answer.

"Do you know who is behind and in front of you in the scene?" Banham asked him.

"I don't know anything. I'm useless at all that movement stuff. I don't dance, I'm a television presenter. Sophie blames me, she says it's my fault that people bump into each other all the time. I pick up the wrong fish too, but that's because there isn't anyone to help, and you can't see much in those black balaclavas."

"When you bump into people, do you know who they are?"

He seemed to be calming down. "No, I don't."

"Do any of the others?"

"Sophie does, she choreographed it, she always knows exactly who went wrong."

Banham became thoughtful. "Is everyone about the same height in the routine?" he asked.

"I think so, apart from Sophie and Fay and the children, but the children are in a different line, in front of us."

"Is it just the children in that line?"

"The professional dancers are with them, supposedly to help them. The children don't need help though – they don't go wrong. It's us lot that picks up the wrong fish and bumps into each other."

Banham had heard enough. "Thank you," he said. "I'll let you if I need to speak to you again."

Vincent turned to face him. "That's it?"

"For now, yes."

"You're not arresting anyone?"

Banham looked him in the eye. "We are making further enquiries. Meanwhile, I believe Michael has arranged for

54

you to stay here tonight. The weather is bad and you have a show tomorrow."

"Will there be a post mortem?"

"Yes."

"I want to know the results!"

Banham said nothing.

"What about her parents? Has someone informed them?"

"A liaison officer has gone to see them."

Mann stood up and clambered past Banham. "I'm not staying here," he said defiantly. "I'm driving home to my family."

Banham returned to the stage and gave Penny the forensic bag containing the black costume, imploring her to get a result as soon as possible. Then he decided to check on Alison. He wondered if she would have turned out as neurotic and theatrical as the people in this show if she had pursued a career in the theatre. He was glad that she hadn't and even gladder she was on this case with him; other things aside, her knowledge of theatre and pantomime would be a great help.

At the bottom of the spiral staircase he had to manoeuvre around about a dozen battered wooden skips overflowing with dusty costumes. He could hear Alison's voice, and followed it toward a room at the side of the basement, with JUVENILES written on the door. He hesitated outside the door; there were no children waiting to be interviewed, so she must be taking the last statement. His reflection glared at him from a full-length mirror on the wall next to the door; normally he avoided them, but this building was infested with them. At least now he understood why performers were so image-conscious; they were forced to spend most of their lives looking at themselves. He turned his head to get a view of his crown; the patch of thinning hair was more prominent than he had hoped. As a child he'd hated his baby-fine hair; the way the ends curled in the rain had earned him no end of teasing from his schoolmates and the nickname 'Girly-whirly.' Suddenly that curly fine hair didn't seem so bad, compared with none at all. The big four-oh was fast approaching, and he smiled to himself as he realised that it wasn't the age that life began, especially not for hair!

He undid the button of his heavy sheepskin coat and turned sideways, quickly pulling his stomach in. His denim shirt was crumpled – and he'd only bought it because the label had stated clearly Non Iron.

That was when he saw the toy bunny rabbit, stuck to the top of the mirror with Blu-tak. It wore a white sash bearing the words Good Luck in large red letters. He turned sharply away, but the memory was back: his tiny daughter Elizabeth, her head unrecognisable, on her yellow bunny blanket. Her little body was covered in blood, and one hand reached out for help from her already dead mother.

He took three deep breaths and the image receded. A few minutes went by before he felt able to open the door behind which Alison was working.

She was sitting behind a large laundry basket, opposite the attractive middle-aged blonde woman he had met when he arrived. Beside the woman on a child-sized bench sat a slightly built girl with long dark hair.

Alison looked up as he walked in. He leaned against the wall and folded his arms; she held his eyes for a moment, and when he didn't speak she lowered her head and carried on writing her statement. "Was anyone with you, Maggie, when you were watching the show from the audience?" she asked the woman.

"No, I was alone."

"Where did you sit exactly?"

The woman took a couple of seconds to think. "In the front stalls, row D, at the end. It's an usherette's seat."

"Which side?"

"Stage left, the same side as the pass door, but from the auditorium it would be on the right. Does that make sense?"

"Perfectly," Alison nodded curtly. "It says here that you do the wardrobe and look after the children and generally help backstage."

"Yes, that's right." The woman's smile was as artificial as her nails, Alison thought. "I'm married to the stage manager who also plays Alderman Fitzwarren. So I help out if he's on stage, or…" She paused. "Or not around." A frown spread across her forehead. "I thought they could manage in the UV scene, they normally do, so I popped out to watch the routine from the front."

"Could the usherettes vouch for you being there?"

Maggie lifted a beautifully manicured hand and raked her fingers though her highlighted hair. A thick gold watch was evident, and her nails were painted to match the maroon sheepskin jacket she wore over brown leather trousers.

Alison waited, pen poised.

"Yes," Maggie said. "If they were down the front they would have seen me."

"And you saw the entire ultra-violet routine?"

"Yes. I knew something was wrong at the end, because they don't usually bring in the curtain. That's when I ran back." She swallowed and paused to compose herself. "That's when I saw poor Lucinda."

"How did the routine appear to you, up until then?" Alison asked her.

"No different from usual."

"Go on."

Maggie turned to her daughter. "Fay would be the best person to ask. She's in the show – she plays Dick Whittington's cat."

Fay should have been in the Green Room with the rest of the cast, Banham thought. But he let Alison continue.

Alison's eyes remained on Maggie. She put her hand up to hush Fay before she could speak. "I was asking you how the scene looked from the audience."

"You don't notice the bad choreography from the front," Maggie said after a beat. "I only know because I was a dancer, and Fay knows because she is in it. But the audience ooh and aah in all the right places, so they obviously enjoy it."

"OK, what do you think?" Alison asked Fay.

"I'm in the row in front of the other principals," the girl said. "We can't see the row behind, but ours never goes wrong. We don't make mistakes."

Banham interrupted. "Do you ever hear them bump into each other?" he asked her.

She threw him a look of pure disdain. "We can't hear very much, we're wearing balaclavas over our heads and ears."

"But you heard the bump at the end of the routine when Lucinda fell?" Alison asked.

"Yes. You can hear a bit. Sometimes I hear Barbara telling people to fuck off. She goes wrong all the time and blames everyone else."

"Fay! Language!"

Maggie gave her daughter's shoulder a little shake and

Fay tossed her head. "Well, she does."

The girl lapsed into sullen silence and Alison looked from mother to daughter and back again. "The show's only been open for what, a week?" she asked.

They both nodded, Fay with a show of reluctance.

"So what do you mean, she goes wrong all the time?"

"Oh, we do this routine every year," the girl said.

"Which of the principals have done it before?" Banham cut in.

"I have," Fay said quickly. "I'm a principal now."

Alison smiled, remembering how desperately her young dancer friends wanted to be principals. The thought had filled her with horror.

"Anyone else?" she asked.

"Sophie." Fay's mouth twisted into a scowl. "She's in it every year, and she's choreographed since she was eighteen."

"Don't you like her?" Alison asked.

"They were juves together, it's just childish competition," Maggie said with a shrug. "They get on fine really. Barbara's the unpopular one, everyone hates her."

"Is Barbara unpopular with all the cast?" Alison asked Fay.

Fay looked at her mother; Maggie nodded.

"Yes, we all hate her. She picks on everyone. She's always telling us that she is the star. I play her cat, so I have to trail around by her heels right through the show. She's always telling me I go wrong in the dances, but it's her that goes wrong, not me."

"Fay has been dancing all her life," Maggie said.

"Is she the star, or is Vincent Mann?" Banham interrupted.

"Oh, the audiences love Vincent," Fay said. "He's really famous, he's on television. But Barbara has her name on top of the poster and is in the star dressing room, so she thinks she can pick on everyone."

"Did she pick on Lucinda today?" Banham asked.

Fay nodded. "She made her cry."

"Why?"

"Because she said Lucinda was messing up the love duet and singing flat."

"What did you think of Lucinda?" Banham asked Fay.

The girl looked sad. "I felt sorry for her. She was always crying."

Banham spoke gently. "Did she talk to you a lot?"

Maggie frowned at her daughter and Fay shook her head.

"Who picked on her the most?"

Maggie and Fay spoke together. "Sophie Flint."

Alison's eyes widened.

"Sophie is Michael's adopted daughter, and she thinks she's the bee's knees," Maggie said. "She isn't even very good, which is why the dances are a mess, but she'd never admit that. She walks around wearing a t-shirt with *I'm a Choreographer, Call Me God* written across it. That just about sums her up."

Banham picked up a plastic chair and placed it beside Alison. "Sorry," he said, "I didn't introduce myself. I'm Paul Banham, I work with Alison. He looked at Fay. "So Sophie blamed Lucinda if things went wrong?"

"Well, she couldn't pick on Barbara," Maggie cut in quickly. "Barbara's even tougher than she is. So she took it out on Lucinda. There wasn't anyone else." She faced the two detectives. "She knows my Fay doesn't make mistakes."

Alison lowered her eyes. Nothing changes, she thought. In her day all the mothers including her own believed their little girls were stars in the making. They were so seldom right.

"Tell me about the male members of the cast." Banham

said to Fay.

Again Maggie answered. "Stephen Coombs has got a terrible temper, so Sophie stays out of his way. And Vincent Mann is terribly neurotic so Sophie wouldn't want to upset him. He's the one pulling in the audiences."

"Did any of the men pick on Lucinda?" Alison said.

Again Maggie looked at Fay.

"She irritated Uncle Stephen," the girl said. "He was always telling her off, and they had a terrible row on the first night."

"What over?" Banham asked.

"He said she killed one of his laughs."

Banham looked puzzled and Alison explained. "She spoke her line without waiting for the audience to react to his, so he missed getting the laugh on one of his jokes."

"You are well informed," Maggie said.

"I read a lot. And it's fairly obvious!"

"How were the other men with Lucinda?" Banham asked Fay.

"Vincent liked her a lot. He stuck up for her when Barbara and Stephen picked on her."

"Is that all the men?" Banham asked.

"Apart from Alan, my husband," Maggie said.

"And there's Trevor, the black dancer," Fay said. "But he's only chorus, and dancers always keep themselves to themselves."

Alison scribbled in her notebook as Banham asked Fay, "What about tonight? Did you see Lucinda fall at the end of the routine?"

Fay's voice rose a notch, and she started to get distressed. "No, I heard scrambling behind me. That was the principals trying to get into their places. I'm in the line in front with the children, not because I'm a juvenile, but because I'm small. Then I heard a crash on my right."

"Where exactly were you standing?"

Her eyes widened in surprise. "I'm centre stage at the end of the routine of course."

Alison fought the urge to smile. The girl was so proud of being centre stage, in the dark, in a black costume that no one would see.

Fay continued, "I looked over in the direction of the noise but I couldn't see anything. I assumed someone had fallen getting into position. Then we got up, and the children walked off…" She paused. "Lucinda didn't move," she said, fighting back tears. "Someone shouted, 'Bring the curtain in.' Lindsay, one of the dancers, ran off and started to bring the curtain in. Vincent was kneeling beside Lucinda; he was pulling her balaclava from her head and trying to wake her."

Banham and Alison made eye contact.

"Then Trevor, the black dancer, ran to help Lindsay. The curtain is so heavy, it's impossible to do on your own. It always gets stuck."

"And was Stephen around?" Banham asked.

"I didn't notice," Maggie answered quickly.

"Did you notice?" he asked Fay.

"No, we had balaclavas on, it's hard to see anything."

"But you saw Lindsay and Trevor pull in the curtain and Vincent run to Lucinda?"

She nodded. "Yes."

"Thank you," Alison said. She lifted the untidy bundle of statements and tapped the edges together on the laundry basket.

"Can we go?" Maggie asked. "It's freezing down here."

Banham huddled into his sheepskin coat. He couldn't argue with that.

"I've spoken to all the juveniles," Alison said when Maggie and Fay had gone.

"I thought that young madam was a principal. Why wasn't she in the Green Room?"

"Her mother was down here sorting out the children's costumes. I suppose she was helping."

Banham sighed. "Not very good as doing as they're told, are they?"

"Anyway," Alison went on, "she reckons the principals often go wrong in that UV routine." She looked at Banham. "If that's the case, it could mean not everyone was where they should have been when Lucinda fell."

Banham picked up her train of thought. "And no one is sure who is who, with everyone from head to toe in black, and no lighting."

Alison nodded, and they said almost in unison, "So someone could have been trying to kill someone else."

In the pause that followed Alison pulled off her woolly cap and shook her long, crinkly, mousy hair free. It fell over her face, and she lifted it with the cup of her hand and pushed it back over her head, then squashed the cap into her coat pocket.

Banham loved her hair. It reminded him of an Airedale dog.

She saw him looking at her. "Something on your mind?" she said.

He cast about for something to say. "I hope you enjoyed the coffee," was the best he could come up with. "The vending machine stuff was disgusting."

"I think Michael Hogan was trying to get round me. He kept asking if the show would be able to carry on. His year's income depends on what he makes at Christmas apparently." She looked him in the eyes. "I told him I was only a sergeant, and you make all the decisions."

Banham opened the coffee pot and smelled the dregs of the coffee. "I'm letting the show continue," he said. "We can't do anything until we get the results of the post mortem. And if we keep it running, we'll know where all the suspects are." He rubbed his hands to warm them. "Eight o'clock tomorrow morning for a briefing. Hopefully we'll have the post mortem result around lunchtime. You can come back here before tomorrow's matinee, and take DNA swabs from everyone."

She nodded, and he gazed at her for a moment.

"What?" she said with a small smile.

"I like your hair loose," he said quietly. "And I am sorry for last week," he added after a pause.

He turned and left the room. She followed, and found him by the fire exit. "That's it, is it?" she said. "You lead me on, let me down at the last minute then say sorry and it's all forgotten?"

"I don't know what else to…"

"Oh, leave it," she said sharply. "We've got a job to do."

She wasn't sure, but she thought he gave a small sigh of relief.

Her throat thickened and she coughed to clear it. "There's something else you should know about." She turned back into the juveniles' room. "There's a door, behind that clothes rail." She pointed to the corner of the room. "Michael Hogan brought the coffee through it. There's another of those spiral staircases – according to Michael, it comes out next to the dressing rooms on the ground floor. Then if you go up another staircase, there's another door next to the mirror by the Green Room. He said no one ever uses it. It's rumoured to be haunted."

Banham stepped behind the clothes rail and examined the wall. "The weather's getting worse," he said. "Do you want a lift home?" He took a deep breath. "You could leave your car here; we're coming back after the morning meeting." He rattled the door handle as an excuse to keep his back to Alison.

"No, thank you. I'd sooner take my own car."

He turned the handle and felt for the light switch. The passageway was filthy, but the centre was noticeably less dusty. "Either ghosts walk up and down this passageway or else it is used quite a lot," he said. "I'll get forensics to have a look in here after they finish on stage." He paused. "It's snowing hard out there. It makes sense to take one car."

"Why?"

"Because I'll know you got home safely. And I need you on this case. And… you're tired."

"Yes, I am," she agreed. "I'm tired of being patronised. You're a bad driver."

He smiled. "I thought for a minute you were going to say I was a bad lover."

"How would I know?"

5

The full investigation team was gathered around the video machine watching footage taken the previous night by the police photographer. The camera shot showed Lucinda's body lying at the side of the stage with the concrete weight beside her head, then widened out to take in the area that surrounded the fatality.

The fact that the very pretty DC Isabelle Walsh had seated herself next to Banham hadn't gone unnoticed by Alison Grainger.

DC Crowther entered the incident room and the aroma of fried bacon, freshly baked bread and tomato sauce followed. He handed a bap overflowing with bacon and a greasy fried egg to Banham.

"Good man," Banham said unwrapping the serviette. "How was your night in the theatre?"

"Very interesting," Crowther said with a mischievous wink. "I slept on a chair in the chorus room, with three blondes huddled together in sleeping bags on the floor and a six foot black poof next to them. Sarge?" He offered the leaking paper carrier bag to Alison. She would have loved a bacon and egg roll but she shook her head. She intended to shed those two pounds that she had put on over Christmas as quickly as possible. She buried her nose in the cardboard cup of black coffee she was nursing, to stop herself inhaling the scent and giving in to the temptation.

"Only Know-all Col could find a café open on Sunday morning two days after Christmas," DC Isabelle Walsh said, taking a sandwich from him without so much as a thank-you.

Crowther had earned his nickname Know-all Col in the murder squad because he always seemed to know where to go for what was needed, and at the exactly the right moment. His dad was a scrap metal dealer, and his consequent connections with some of the most notorious gangsters in the area accessed some useful contacts. He was still in his twenties, and, like DC Walsh, desperate for promotion.

He had tried his luck with Isabelle many times, but always got turned down. Alison knew Isabelle was too ambitious to settle for a DC; she had her sights set much higher. She had been in CID for two years; Alison still remembered sourly how stunning she used to look in uniform. She was like a young Vivien Leigh: perfect features, delicate ears and a cute button nose, and no matter how she wore her shoulder length dark hair, the hat always flattered her. Most of the men in the station fancied her, and she made full use of it to get what she wanted in the force; it hadn't taken her long to make the jump to Murder Division.

Alison's own morale was low after the time she had been forced to spend staring at her reflection in the theatre's wall-to-wall and floor-to-ceiling mirrors. She was only too aware that her own nose was anything but cute, and her wide face far from perfect. She watched Isabelle bite into the sandwich and hoover the bacon into her mouth. The amount of carbohydrate the girl could eat seriously irritated her. She'd have to starve herself for a waist as tiny as Isabelle's.

Suddenly she was aware Banham was looking at her. She immediately took a large swig of the black coffee. It tasted less than exciting.

"Not hungry?" he asked her.

She shook her head. "I've eaten," she lied.

He stood up to start the briefing. She noticed he hadn't shaved, and found that a turn-on. She gave herself a shake; business only, she reminded herself firmly.

"At this moment, we have nothing but gut instinct to tell us this is a murder enquiry," Banham said. "We should have the results of the post mortem by midday today; that will tell us whether there was brain movement after the blow and before the fall. If there was, we have a case."

DC Crowther, keen to let everyone know he was pulling strings, interrupted through a mouthful of BLT. "Penny is at the lab, working her holiday to try to get us something."

Banham nodded. "She's light-source testing the concrete block for fingerprints, skin cells and maybe some hair. But we're looking at least forty-eight hours for some results, so..."

"What was the concrete block doing there?" one of the older detectives asked.

"It's supposed to weigh down the scenery," Alison told him.

Crowther interrupted again. "Penny's also got all the black costumes the actors were wearing at the time of the fatality."

"Plus another one I found in a drawer in the producer's office," Banham added. "We're hoping fibre from the concrete will show up on one of the costumes, and Alison will take buccal swabs from every member of the cast today." He looked across at her. "You can do that during the lunchtime show."

"Guv." She nodded.

"If we're lucky we'll get skin cells from the light-source treatment and match them to the perpetrator's. Meanwhile I've decided to let the show continue, because I can't hold any suspects..."

"Until we have concrete evidence of murder." Crowther burst out laughing at his own joke, and everyone else groaned.

Banham glared at him and carried on. "And also because it keeps them in the theatre, and we know where they all are."

"There were two young work experience boys moving the scenery at the back during that scene," Alison said. "So whoever killed Lucinda couldn't have walked in at the stage door and round to the other side without passing them. The only other way was across the stage during the routine. So that narrows it right down. It has to be someone who was either on the stage and in the routine, or knew it well enough to join in, unnoticed by everyone on the stage."

"That wouldn't be difficult if everyone on stage could barely see or hear," Isabelle argued.

Alison shook her head. "They'd still have to know the steps. It has to be one of the actors."

"Sergeant Grainger understands the theatre," Banham announced to the room. "She used to be in pantomime."

"Blimey!" Crowther put the end of his sandwich into his mouth and wiped his lips on the cuff of his yellow shirt. "Did you wear those arse-length skirts and thigh-boots?" He fanned himself with the remains of the greasy brown paper bag. "I'd have paid to see that."

Alison was lost for words. An older DC came to her rescue. "How many actors is that in the routine?"

Alison walked to the large white-board at the front of the room and started to draw the stage, and the placing of the suspects during the routine.

Some of the men were still sniggering; Alison felt herself flush.

"Just ignore them," Isabelle Walsh piped up. "They're

jealous 'cos they can't wear arse-length skirts. If they did we'd see how small their cocks are."

Silence descended, and Alison decided it was time to take control again. She pointed to the board. "Here's the stage, with two lines of actors in the routine where the fatality happened. Lucinda was here, at the end of the back line, with just three others. It isn't possible that anyone in the row in front row could have hit her; that would have thrown the routine out of sync, and according to everyone we spoke to, that row didn't go wrong and never has. It was mainly children anyway."

"Plus the four chorus dancers," Banham added. "So that eliminates all of them, plus Fay McCormak, who plays the cat. She was in the front row too."

"Barbara Denis, Vincent Mann and Sophie Flint were in the back row with Lucinda," Alison said. "They have to be our main suspects. And the dame, Stephen Coombs, who was supposed to be changing his costume at the time, but – according to Sophie Flint – didn't."

Banham jumped in. "There's also the black costume I found in the producer's office. With the stage manager in the pub and the stage unguarded, someone could have slipped into that costume and gone on stage…"

"But only if they knew the routine," Alison added. "Or they would have been noticed."

"So add Michael Hogan, the producer, to the list of suspects," Banham said. "He could know the steps in the routine, just like Stephen Coombs."

Alison thought for a moment. "The wardrobe mistress, Maggie McCormak, claims she was in the audience during the show and came backstage after it happened."

"But Michael Hogan said he saw her backstage, just before the UV routine started and again during it," Banham said. "So one of them is lying."

"Could she know the routine?" Crowther asked.

Alison nodded. "Definitely. She told me she used to be a dancer."

"She had very little time to get up to the office and get into the costume unnoticed," Crowther said.

"No one was around," Banham pointed out. "The stage manager was in the pub next door, leaving the coast conveniently clear."

"But it wasn't clear," Crowther argued. "Michael Hogan was in the company office just before the routine started."

"The routine is about ten minutes long," Alison said. "That's ten minutes to slip into a black leotard and pull a balaclava over her head, come down and join in the end of the routine, pick up the scenery block and hit Lucinda, walk back across the stage behind the actors – and it was pitch black, remember, so the stage hands wouldn't have noticed an extra person – then go upstairs and change while everyone is fussing around the dead girl. It's pushing it, I grant you, but it could be done."

The list of potential suspects was growing.

Banham gave the squad a chance to absorb Alison's points, then added, "A few other things came out of the interviews too. Vincent Mann claims that just before the routine started he was listening outside the company office door and heard Michael Hogan and Sophie Flint saying they were going to sack Lucinda. But Michael Hogan's version is that he wanted to get rid of Vincent Mann."

"What do we think about Michael Hogan sharing a dressing room with his adopted daughter?" Crowther asked. "Seems a bit of an old perv to me."

"I thought that," Isabelle Walsh said, rolling her paper napkin into a ball and throwing it at the waste-paper bin.

It missed. Alison picked it up and dropped it in the bin before she could stop herself. "They're not short of dressing rooms," Isabelle went on. "Barbara Denis has a room all to herself. Why doesn't Sophie share that?"

"The star always has a room to herself," Alison pointed out. "Barbara wouldn't take kindly to sharing."

"Besides, it's an office, not a dressing room," Banham shrugged. "Sophie Flint is the assistant director as well as the choreographer. Where's the problem?"

"Colin does have a point, though," Alison said. "He was discussing business matters with her while she was changing."

Banham shrugged again. "Maybe, but it doesn't seem of any consequence at the moment."

Did he really believe that, or was he being naïve, Alison wondered, a little irritated.

"Listen up, everyone," he continued. "Time we made a move. Forensics have finished with the area, so the theatre is open for business. They have a show at lunchtime, and Crowther, Isabelle, Alison and I will be there. Mickey Hutchens is on liaison duty with Lucinda's parents; I've asked him to get her phone records, and let me know if anything else turns up. And I'm hoping we'll have results of the post mortem by about one o'clock. The rest of you can take a break till then." He turned to Crowther. "Did all the actors stay the night at the theatre?"

"All except Vincent Mann, Guv. He drove home. Didn't please Michael Hogan, they had words over it. But Vincent said he wanted to get home to his wife and children, and no way would he sleep in the same room as Stephen Coombs."

"Perhaps Stephen Coombs wore the other black costume," the older detective piped up, "and meant to murder Vincent but got the wrong person."

"Good point." Banham said. "It would be hard to tell who was who in those outfits in the pitch black, especially if they aren't standing in the right place."

"And Vincent is only five foot seven," Alison added.

"As soon as the afternoon show is over," Banham said, "I want Sophie Flint brought to the station to make an official statement about Coombs not changing his costume during the UV scene. Meanwhile we'll be at the theatre, keeping our eyes and ears open. Alison, can you drive me?"

"So what's all this with you and the boss?" Isabelle asked Alison as they were washing their hands in the locker room.

Alison was tired and hungry and not in the mood. "Because he asks me for a lift to the theatre?" She noticed again how small Isabelle's waist was, as the other woman fastened the buckle on her brown leather trousers.

"No – because the whole department knows you bought him a CD of greatest all-time love songs for Christmas," she said, lifting her perfectly shaped eyebrows.

Alison opened her mouth to argue, but Isabelle got in first. "It's all right, he hasn't been telling tales. Crowther saw the card."

"And Crowther decided something was going on between us, and told the whole department? Well, it's not true." She was tired and upset, and this was the last thing she needed. "I don't mix business with pleasure," she snapped. "And I'm not looking for a leg up the promotion ladder; I can get there on merit. I bought him a CD, yes, but not Greatest Love Songs. It was Phil Collins, who happens to be his favourite singer. He's a friend, and I felt sorry for him – Christmas is the anniversary of the murder of his wife and baby and…"

The shrill of the phone in her handbag left her floundering. She pulled the phone out and flipped it open, aware Isabelle was staring at her.

"Mickey, yes." She turned away and groped in her bag for a pen. Isabelle handed her one silently, still staring.

"Her parents… Vincent Mann's mobile…" She scribbled on a scrap of paper. "And outgoing calls? Michael Hogan's mobile… few to Vincent Mann… one to Sophie Flint. Good work, Mickey; thanks."

"So why did she keep ringing her boss?" she said, more to herself than to Isabelle.

"To complain she was being bullied by Barbara Denis?" the other woman suggested.

"But why keep ringing him? We know she went to talk to him in the wings, but he implied that was the first he'd heard of it."

"Perhaps she wanted a leg up the promotional ladder?"

The quip broke the tension; Alison smiled. "And Sophie Flint found out? It's possible. That's a lot of secrets in that company."

Isabelle laughed. "Affairs are always secret ones," she said. "No one ever admits they are happening – more exciting that way." She raised her dark eyebrows. "You don't need a CID badge to know that."

6

The headline on the board outside the newsagent made Banham's heart sink.

OH NO IT ISN'T! OH YES IT IS! MURDER!

Alison had just come out of the building. He waved to her and pointed towards the shop.

As he took his wallet out to pay, the appointment card from the sex therapist slipped to the floor. He bent down to retrieve it, just as Alison walked in.

"So how did that leak out, Guv?"

He swiftly pushed the card back into his pocket, hoping she hadn't noticed it. His stomach tightened; the thought of Alison knowing he really cared about her but couldn't do anything about it was too awful to bear.

Suddenly the image of baby Elizabeth flooded his mind again, her body covered in blood.

"Are you all right, Guv?" Alison asked with great concern. "You've gone a funny colour. I wouldn't trust Crowther's bacon and egg butties."

The image receded and he managed a smile. "No one would sell Crowther duff butties," he told her. "They wouldn't dare mess with him."

She picked up a paper and flicked the pages. "Good publicity for the show," she said. "Big picture of Vincent Mann on page two. Small ones of Stephen Coombs, Barbara Denis, and Sophie Flint." She blew out a breath. "Now, that could make for bad feeling."

He relaxed; she hadn't seen the card. "I'd like to know how the press got the story," he said.

"Someone in the cast rang them?"

He nodded. "It certainly wasn't us!" He picked up a couple of reduced price chocolate Christmas puddings from the counter in front of him and paid for them.

"Do you want one?" he asked as they made their way back to the car.

"No, I don't," she snapped.

He was still in her bad books, then. He unwrapped a chocolate pudding from its coloured paper.

"So who stands to gain from the publicity?" he asked. "Surely not Michael Hogan? It could have the reverse effect on the ticket sales."

Alison shook her head. "There's a very old saying: all publicity is good publicity."

"I'll bow to your knowledge." He crunched into the chocolate. "Who would the publicity help?"

"All of them! Barbara Denis wants to make a comeback, she needs all the publicity she can get." She tutted irritably. "You've already eaten an enormous fried breakfast bun, wasn't that enough?"

"What about Sophie Flint? And it wouldn't look too good for Vincent Mann – a top children's presenter, involved in a murder case?"

Alison tried not to look at the chocolate pudding. "Sophie is assistant director and choreographer," she said. "She's probably on a percentage of the takings. Vincent Mann... well, if he's convinced she was murdered, he might care more for her than the bad publicity, and it's going to get out eventually." She flicked the automatic unlock on her dark green Golf a few paces away. "The same goes for Stephen Coombs," she mused. "Actually the only person it could reflect badly on is the stage manager Alan McCormak. Don't get chocolate on my car seats."

Banham put the rest of the chocolate pudding in his

mouth. "He's the only one with a cast iron alibi," he said, opening the passenger door. "Three of the pub staff saw him drinking in the Feathers."

Alison grimaced. "Didn't your mother tell you it's rude to speak with your mouth full?" The ignition fired; she indicated and pulled out, blowing her horn at another driver. Banham took a deep breath. Her driving was bad enough under normal circumstances, but when she was in a foul mood he feared for everyone she came into contact with. He didn't understand; she was all right at the briefing, and since then all he'd done was bought her some chocolate, which he'd ended up eating himself.

"I want you to talk to the terribly young and terribly bossy choreographer when we get to the theatre," he told her. "You may not charm her the way Crowther would, but you'll have more idea of what she's talking about."

She said nothing for a few seconds, then returned his smile. "OK, boss."

He wiped the front window to make sure she could see clearly, then clicked on the rear window heater. "Crowther is driving her to the station after the show to take an official statement," he reminded Alison. "So see if you can get any more relevant info out of her first."

"I'll tell her we're doing her a favour waiting until this show finishes," Alison said. "Then I'll grill her."

The rest of the journey passed in silence. Banham gazed through the window at the Christmas decorations still hanging across the streets. He opened his mouth to tell her how much he enjoyed her company, and that he'd like to see her again, but lost his nerve and closed it again. Women were very complicated.

They entered the theatre from the front and walked into the auditorium. Michael Hogan and Sophie were both leaning against the orchestra pit talking to the cast, who were spread out around the auditorium, apart from the four chorus dancers who sat huddled together.

Alison and Banham slipped quietly into the back row and listened.

"Both teams of juveniles have left," Michael was telling the cast. "Red Team's parents all pulled them out of the show last night, and I've had calls from the mothers of five of the Blue Team kids this morning. I couldn't say anything under the circumstances. So you'll need to spread out and use the stage. Fay is taking over as principal girl, and Maggie has kindly offered to play the cat."

The end chorus girl sat up. "I'm Lucinda's understudy," she said indignantly. "I've learned the part and I know the songs."

"Sonia, darling, I can't spare you from the chorus," Michael pleaded. "I've lost my juvenile dancers and you four have to make up for ten. Maggie's too old for the chorus, but she'll be fine in the cat's skin."

Sophie stifled a little laugh, and Maggie tossed her head. "Charming!"

Michael smiled placatingly at Maggie and turned back to Sonia. "This is the best way," he said. "Please bear with me."

Sonia's disappointment was clear. The black boy put his arm around her.

Sophie noticed Alison and Banham for the first time. "Anything we can help with?" she called. "Or are you just watching?"

"I'd like a few words with you, Sophie," Alison said politely. "But no hurry – after you've sorted your rehearsal is fine."

"We can do it now. Come through the pass door; we'll go up to my office. You can take the rehearsal, Michael."

As if she was the producer and he the employee, Alison thought.

Sophie was wearing the sugar-pink track suit she'd had on the night before, her waist-length, silky blonde hair pulled off her face into a ponytail twisted and secured with a large zebra-print clip. Half the hair had slid from the clip and hung down her back. Alison often dealt with under-age prostitutes, and knew untidy ponytails were all the rage. Sophie's hard front was reminiscent of those girls, but she felt sure it wouldn't take too much to knock her off her perch and find a way into her insecurities and fears.

Alison sat on the flip-up chair in front of the Formica shelving. Sophie leaned against the shelves and folded her arms. Her eyes were an unusual colour, a clear, bright indigo, like Elizabeth Taylor's; but unlike the star's, they were small, hard, and calculating.

"Sorry to pull you away," she said. "I need to ask you a couple of questions."

"Fire away."

Alison managed a small smile. "You told DC Crowther that Stephen Coombs hadn't changed his costume after the ultra-violet scene last night."

"Correct."

Alison hadn't been in the best of moods to start with, but this girl's clipped and patronising tone was irritating her.

"OK. We need you to come to the station and make an official statement about that." The girl opened her mouth to object. "But it can wait until after the afternoon show. DC Crowther will drive you there and get you back in good time for the evening performance."

Sophie swallowed hard and her mouth began to tremble. Good, Alison thought; the hard edge is crumbling.

"Oh, and we're a bit confused," she added casually. "Does everyone pick up the same fish in that routine every night?"

Sophie hesitated.

"You should know; you choreographed that scene," Alison pressed her.

"Yeah, yeah." Sophie pushed a tendril of hair behind her ear with her forefinger. Diamante studs were stuck to the edge of each nail.

"The truth is, sometimes it goes a bit awry. I know I told the other detective it works fine, but, well, I turn a blind eye, because it don't really matter what fish go on when, as long as the audience enjoys the scene." The nervous finger wound around another tendril and slid it behind her ear. She gave a tiny false laugh. "The actors aren't good with steps. I may as well be talking to a brick wall." She paused. "But I'm there, hands on, so we get through, even when Alan doesn't turn up."

"So the order of the line varies from show to show?"

She shrugged and curled her mouth. "Yeah, it can. Not by much, though."

"It couldn't, with only four in the row."

Sophie fixed Alison with her unusual eyes. "It don't make no odds. As I say, as long as ultra-violet fish move across the stage and the audience get to see them all, it doesn't matter to me."

"It matters to our enquiry," Alison said briskly. "Did you know who was where in the line last night, and who was holding which fish?"

Sophie shook her head and dropped her gaze for a fraction of a second, then lifted it again. "No, I've said, it went a bit awry last night," She shook her head again. "I don't know who was holding what."

"Could anyone have been holding a stage weight?"

Sophie took her time before replying. "Only if they could lift it."

"I can lift it," Alison said. "And doesn't dance training build up your muscles?"

"I suppose."

Neither spoke for a few seconds. Sophie's hands gripped the shelf behind her. The girl's discomfort was almost tangible.

"Is that it? Only I'm needed downstairs."

"No, not quite," Alison said. She let another few seconds pass, then asked casually, "Are you and Michael Hogan lovers?"

Sophie straightened up and folded her arms in front of her. "I don't have to answer that question," she said. "It's got nothing to do with you."

"I'll take that as a yes, then." Alison kept her tone friendly.

Sophie didn't take the bait. "Up to you. I ain't answering the question. Look, I need to…"

Alison cut in, "Just before the UV scene last night, were you and Michael discussing sacking Vincent Mann?"

Sophie lowered her gaze again. Alison could practically see her razor-sharp mind working. She looked up. "Did Michael tell you that?"

"No, Sophie, you don't ask the questions." Time to get tough, Alison decided. "This is a suspected murder case. I ask, you answer. Now – were you and Michael discussing sacking Vincent Mann before the UV scene last night?"

Sophie's eyes once again pierced Alison. "Yeah, we were discussing it." She started to make for the door.

"I haven't finished yet," Alison rapped.

Sophie stood still, her back to Alison.

"First I need to take a DNA swab from you." She opened

her bag and took out a pack.

Sophie turned to face her, panic spreading across her face. "What for?"

"For elimination, that's all."

"But Lucinda wasn't murdered; it was an accident."

"We're waiting on the results of the post mortem. I just need to brush the inside of your cheek with this." She held up the little tooth-sized brush. "It doesn't hurt."

Sophie opened her mouth. Alison took the sample and sealed the swab in its pack. She started to feel sorry for the girl. It hadn't taken much. Now those hard eyes looked like a terrified little bird.

"I'll make a deal with you," she said to her. "I said I was happy to wait until after the show for you to come to the station and make an official statement. My boss is less happy. But if you tell me about your relationship with Michael Hogan, I'll talk to DI Banham and make sure we don't interfere with your lunchtime performance."

Before Sophie had time to protest, Alison continued. "I wouldn't ask if I didn't think it had anything to do with our enquiry."

Sophie stared at the floor. "He's my stepfather."

Banham was looking around the little sound booth at the back of the stalls. The electrics were turned on and Michael's voice was coming through the speakers.

"It was a tragic accident," Michael told the cast. "Tragic, and I still can't believe it's happened. He paused and gave a painful sigh. "The police will be around backstage today. There's no need to let them bother us; we'll do our jobs and they'll do theirs. There will be a plain clothes police-man in the wings…"

"We'd rather have the blond bloke from The Bill," one of

82

the dancers quipped.

"I'm glad you find it such a huge joke, Tanya," Vincent Mann shouted angrily across the auditorium. "I don't agree that it was an accident, nor that we should carry on. I'm very glad that the police are here, and if you had any sense you'd take it very seriously indeed."

There was a long silence, eventually broken by Stephen Coombs. "Don't fret, Tanya. You meant no harm, pet."

Banham watched through the glass as Stephen looked across the auditorium at Vincent Mann. "God knows we're short of jokes around here," he said bitterly.

Michael quickly raised his hands. "OK, let's keep it together. We are all edgy, and that's understandable. But let's not fight. One accident was enough." He looked directly at Vincent. "And of course it was an accident."

"Please!" Barbara Denis's voice boomed out. "Can we just do our jobs and keep personal feelings to ourselves?"

Everyone mumbled their agreement.

"Alan has faithfully promised that he'll be at the side of the stage every moment that he isn't actually on it today," Michael said.

Alan pulled up the collar of his overcoat and shuffled uncomfortably.

Michael's voice started to crack with emotion. "No one need feel threatened or frightened," he said. "It won't be easy, but we're professionals and we'll get through."

He walked off, through the pass door into the backstage area, towards the steps that led to his office.

He hadn't got further than the foot of the stairs when he heard the clacking of high heels behind him. He turned to face Sonia, the tallest of the three dancers. "I'm sorry if you're disappointed not to be playing principal girl," he said flatly. "But I've had to do what's best for the show.

I really need you to dance today."

"You said I was her understudy. I learned it all." She was angry. "You promised…"

"Keep your voice down," he urged her, looking around to make sure no one was close by. "Please, Sonia, don't do this. I've got a lot on my mind."

She made no reply.

"Sonia, I can't give you that part. Wait another year, get some voice lessons, learn to project. Then I'll keep my promise and cast you next year."

"Lucinda hadn't any experience," she spat. "She hadn't had voice lessons, and you couldn't even bloody hear her. What did she do for you that I haven't?"

Michael froze for a second then turned away towards the stairs. "I'm sorry you feel like that. I will keep my promise – next year."

Sophie Flint was on the landing. She had heard every word. When she heard Michael approach, she quickly slipped behind the door of the toilet along the corridor. Michael went straight into their shared office; Sophie watched Sonia follow, and stand hesitantly outside the door for a few seconds before retracing her steps.

Sophie checked the cubicles to make sure she was alone, and she settled herself in the one farthest from the door. She flipped her phone open and stabbed in some numbers.

The phone the other end rang only twice.

"I'm not going to play games with you," Sophie said when it was picked up. "I know what you did to Lucinda. And I know it was you."

There was no response.

"You must have known I'd work it out," Sophie said.

Still no response.

"Oh, you don't have to worry," she said sweetly. "I'm not the type to tell tales." She waited a beat. "But I need to be rewarded."

The voice at the other end raged for a few moments.

"No, it's not blackmail," Sophie replied, her voice still sweet as sugar. "Let's call it a late Christmas gift…"

Banham was feeding coins into the vending machine in the Green Room. Alison leaned against the side of the machine, reading the paper. She was dressed in heavy donkey brown corduroy trousers, a beige polo neck jumper, and a grey wool tunic which reached her thighs, if you included the twelve inches of tassles that hung from the hem. The arm-holes seemed to go half way down to her ribcage and did precious little to keep out the cold. A russet coloured ribbon and tortoiseshell slide held her long, crinkly, light brown hair in a ponytail.

"Coffee," he said, holding out the plastic cup.

She wore very little make-up, but he noticed she had put on fresh lipstick in a soft brownish shade. He thought she looked beautiful. He turned back to the machine and fed more coins in. Some man was going to very lucky, he thought with a smile, despite that terrible temper.

He was still smiling as he took his own sugared, white coffee from the machine.

"Is something funny?" she asked.

"Is smiling a crime, Sergeant?"

"You don't do it very often, that's all."

He wished he was brave enough to tell her what had made him smile.

"How can you drink that stuff without sugar?" he said. "It's disgusting enough with!"

"Can we talk about the case?"

She was definitely still angry with him.

"Sophie has confirmed that the fish don't run in the same order every night. So if a fish was missing last night, it wouldn't help – we wouldn't know who should have been holding it."

She had a rim of coffee froth around her mouth, making her look clownish. He fought to keep a straight face, glad when his phone rang to distract him.

"That was the mortuary," he told her after ending the call. He pulled a handkerchief from his pocket and handed it to her. "Take a look at your face in the mirror."

She glanced in the mirror and quickly wiped her mouth. "I didn't tell you that you had chocolate on your teeth this morning," she said defensively.

"You should have."

"What did the pathologist say?"

"Lucinda wasn't pregnant, but she'd had sex within a few hours. And they need forty-eight hours for the results of the brain trauma. So we'll have to play for more time."

"She must have had sex between the shows," Alison said. "I suppose that proves she and Vincent hadn't been rowing."

"There are marks on her face," Banham said. "She's been slapped around quite a bit, and there's heavy bruising to the tops of her arms, a few days old."

"Perhaps he likes rough sex," Alison said.

Banham looked shocked. "Or perhaps someone else hurt her," he offered. "You finish the buccal swabs, and get Isabelle to drive them over to the lab. I'll go and have a good look around the building, and check all the nooks and crannies in the so-called haunted passage. Crowther can stay on duty in the wings."

"That'll make him a very happy bunny," Alison said. "Watching the dancers doing their quick changes."

"He's a bloke," Banham shrugged.

"He certainly is."

"We'll all gather there for the second act," Banham said. "That's when the UV scene is."

"They're still doing it, then?"

"Oh yes. Hogan has managed to get more costumes."

She swallowed the last of her machine coffee and nodded. "I'm going to track down Stephen Coombs. He never seems to be in his dressing room – I don't know if he's avoiding me or Vincent Mann." She tossed her cup into the bin and headed for the door.

Just as she reached the door he called to her. She turned back. There was still some froth on the side of her mouth but he decided against mentioning it. "What's your instinct on this?"

"I haven't got one yet, Guv. You're the one with the reputation for instinct; what's yours?"

"We need to find a motive," he said. "That's what bothers me most. Lucinda had only known these people about a month. Who would be driven to kill someone they have only known for a few weeks?"

Alison didn't reply. He went on, "I've got a full team on this, because of my instinct. But it's not even confirmed as murder until the brain trauma report comes through."

"Go with your gut, Guv," Alison said. "I agree with you, this wasn't an accident. The light-source test should come back from Penny tomorrow – that might turn something up. And have you noticed, this company is unusually incestuous? They are all involved with each other or have been. Only Stephen Coombs seems to have no romantic link with any of them. Yet at the moment he is our main suspect. So why? is a good question?"

Banham rubbed his mouth thoughtfully. "And how?"

7

Stephen Coombs walked purposefully into the Feathers and looked around, craning his head to peer into each alcove. After a few moments he spotted the stage manager. As Alan McCormak lifted his first pint of the day with a shaking hand, Stephen slid quickly into the bench beside him.

"That sergeant who looks as if she's got a carrot stuck up her arse is after me for a DNA sample," Stephen said careful to keep his voice low.

Alan licked spilt beer from his dirty hands. "Damn you, you nearly gave me a heart attack, sneaking up on me like that,"

Stephen ignored him. "They're checking everyone out. They'll want yours too."

"I'll take what's coming." Alan held his palm up defensively. "I killed her."

"Don't give me the fucking theatricals," Stephen shouted. He looked around to check no one was in hearing distance before continuing, "You didn't kill her. There are witnesses who saw you in here."

"Oh, I killed her all right, and won't I feel the guilt of it now until they lay my bones in the brown earth," Alan said. His head bobbed up and down like a nodding dog, and Stephen grabbed his scrawny arm.

"Get a grip, man. And listen up. I've had to put my thinking cap on. A DNA test might bring a few things to light, right?"

Alan nodded nervously.

"And we can't afford any complications. Am I making myself quite clear?"

"Whatever you say, boy, whatever you say." Alan dipped his mouth over the rim of his glass and gulped greedily. The scattered broken veins over his reddened complexion made him look a lot older than his fifty-five years.

A few feet away Sophie Flint pressed her slim body tightly against the large beam that ran from ceiling to the floor behind the alcove.

"Come in."

Vincent Mann hesitated before walking in and pushing the door shut behind him. He watched Barbara gaze into the mirror to see who had entered her dressing room; confusion mingled with fear when she saw it was him. A flowery bandeau held her hair off her face, and dots of dark make-up spotted her face. She held a small triangular sponge in one hand and a stick of old fashioned pan-cake in the other.

"What do you want?"

"Just a chat." He leaned back against the door and folded his arms across his chest. She turned back to the mirror and dropped the sponge on the dresser, then quickly rubbed the spots of make-up into her face before tapping a small black cigar out of her tortoiseshell cigarette case. Their eyes met in the mirror as she took the holder between her teeth and flicked her lighter. Then she turned back to face him.

"I am devastated about Lucinda," he said quietly.

"We all are."

He nodded, and a beat passed. "You didn't exactly get on."

She inhaled on her cigar. "We had strong professional differences, but nothing personal. I'm sorry she's dead." She inhaled again and blew smoke out of the side of her mouth.

"Michael won't release me from this contract," he said quietly. "He said I have to finish the run."

"That's only right."

"Maybe." He paused. "It's tough having to work under these circumstances." Her face seemed to soften, and he continued. "So... I'd like to try to work together. Can we bury the hatchet?"

"Unfortunate choice of words," she said with a flicker of a smile. "But yes. Let's try." She lowered her eyes and blew out more smoke. "I understand how bad you must feel. I knew about the deal you made with Michael to get Lucinda a job."

"I'd prefer that wasn't made public," he said quickly.

She gazed at him squarely. "Vincent, I'm a perfectionist and a career woman, so I get short-tempered when the show isn't good. But I'm not a gossipmonger, and your affair with Lucinda is nobody's business but your own."

He pulled his mouth into a small smile. "Thanks."

"Nor will I say anything about the row you had with her after the first night. Unless it turns out not to have been an accident, of course."

The smile dropped from his face immediately. "That was just a tiff."

"You hit her across the face. I saw you."

"I..." Vincent took a deep breath.

"But I don't see any point in mentioning it to the police. Unless, as I say, it turns out to be a suspicious death. Then I wouldn't have any choice."

"Thank you." His heart dropped into his boots.

"Nothing to thank me for. I want the show to continue. So let's try to work together." She balanced the cigar on the glass ashtray in front of her and held out her hand. He took it and they shook. "But in return I'd like a little respect," she told him. "I know you're on television every week, but I am very much more experienced than you in pantomime. That's why it's my name on the poster."

He gave her a tight smile and adjusted his glasses. The posters had already been printed when he signed the contract, but Michael pointed out that everyone in the country knew who he was, and the local press would only be interested in him. So he was the real star. He hadn't thought it mattered, but he hadn't figured on a principal boy with an ego the size of a football.

"I know what's best for the show, you see," she said, pulling the cigar free of the holder and stubbing it into the ashtray.

"Fine by me," he answered, keeping the smile pinned on his face.

She laughed politely. "New beginnings."

"New beginnings," he repeated. Lost pride was a small price to pay.

Besides, he had other things on his mind.

For a woman in her middle forties, Maggie McCormak still looked great. Her years of professional dancing had given her the discipline and desire to keep her slim body toned and in shape. She also knew how to dress. Today she wore a red figure-hugging angora jumper with the very tightest of jeans that were torn and frayed at the back to show the firm flesh of her thigh. Michael Hogan gazed appreciatively as she perched next to his papers.

"It's understandable that the mothers won't let their children carry on," she said to him.

"I wish that was my only problem."

"As usual, this is all Alan's fault."

He used to find that demure expression irresistible. Now it was rather irritating. "Don't, Maggie," he snapped, flinging his pen on to the dresser. "You know he can't help himself."

Maggie crossed one leg over the other. "He's always been your downfall. Yet you employ him year after year."

A laugh burst from Michael's mouth. "No, Maggie, you've been my downfall." He reached for the pen and stared at the papers in front of him. "But that's history."

"You wouldn't be without Fay."

"I wouldn't be without any of my children," he answered. "And how would Fay feel if I sacked her father? Besides, I'm responsible for his drinking."

"I've been thinking, maybe we should tell her the truth," Maggie said.

"Oh no, oh no." Michael put a hand out in front of him. "The time for the truth is long in the past. Much better she goes on thinking he's her dad."

"Better for who?"

"For everyone." He threw the pen down again. "What's brought this on? Come on, Maggie, you know as long as I'm in business, Alan will be in work. I'd never forgive myself if anything happened to him."

"Fair enough." Maggie tugged at the hem of her angora jumper, revealing more cleavage. "But what's he ever done for her?"

"He only started drinking because of us."

"He started drinking because his religion doesn't allow divorce. And I have to live with it."

Michael sighed. "Whichever way you look at it, we're responsible. So as long as I have a show, he'll have a job."

She raised her eyebrows but said nothing.

He bit on his lower lip. "I know that look. What is it?"

She shrugged. "I don't want Fay to spend her life in this stinking business. I want her to have a future..."

"Christ, Maggie, I'm broke! My whole life is hanging on

the money that I make on this show."

She raised an eyebrow again. "You've enough to keep your little choreographer in a luxury flat."

"She's my daughter too."

"But not your own flesh and blood, like Fay. Yet you spend enough of your money on her." Her toned soured, "Anyway, we all know the truth…"

"I have given Fay everything you asked for. You have your home, holidays, and I pay the fees at the dancing school."

"I don't want her to be a dancer, unemployed most of the time and finished at forty. I want her to go to university and have a decent career."

Michael sighed. "I'm sorry. I have more pressing concerns at this moment." He picked up his pen and chewed the end.

"The police have just questioned me again, and I had to give a specimen of DNA from inside my mouth."

"And?"

"Did you tell them that I came backstage during the UV scene last night?"

He closed his eyes. "Yes, I think I did. I needed a witness to vouch for seeing me backstage. Otherwise it might get complicated."

"That detective woman asked me why I didn't mention it last night."

A muscle under his eye started to twitch. "What did you say?"

"I said when you're in a state of shock, as we all are at the moment, your brain doesn't work properly. I told her that after I went into the auditorium I popped back for my binoculars and saw you in the juveniles' dressing room, but I didn't think it was important enough to mention last night."

"Thanks."

"And obviously I didn't say anything about how close you and Sophie are."

They stared at each other, and she was first to look away.

"Anyway, I'd better go and get into that smelly cat skin." She didn't move.

"I'm just doing the wages," he said quietly. "I've made money this week, so I'll give you a bonus. You could have a late holiday with Fay before she goes back to school."

Hair curlers, hair straighteners, hair gel, hair lacquer, pots and palettes of different make-up colours, varying sized make-up brushes, magnifying mirrors, chocolate bars, discarded sweet wrappers and bottled water filled every inch of the available space on the dresser in front of the three girl dancers. The six clothes rails were all overladen with identical costumes and positioned at odd angles to allow easy access for the girls' quick changes.

Trevor Bruce was in the end seat. Less than twenty-four hours earlier Lucinda had sat there. He was dressed in a peasant outfit, ready for the start of the show.

Sonia was curling her hair, Tanya was straightening hers with another gadget and Lindsay was spraying deodorant over her feet and into her shoes. The air in the room reeked of perfume and muscle sprays.

"You're eager," Sonia said to Trevor. "We've got twenty minutes before curtain up."

"I wanted to spend some time cheering us all up before the show starts."

"You'll need more than twenty minutes," Lindsay said.

"Oh shit!" Tanya tugged violently at a lock of hair that was stuck in the hot tongs.

"Hey, hey," Trevor soothed. "Calm, Tans."

"Oh, shut up," she snapped. "There may be a murderer on the loose, and all Michael Hogan cares about is keeping the show running so he can make money. Calm, my arse!"

"No." Trevor shook his head. "It was a freak accident. The police would have closed the show down if they thought there was a murderer out there. They've even put a detective in the wings to make you feel better." He stood up and kneaded Tanya's back with his strong, light brown hands. "Ease up, babe, I'm gonna be looking out for you." He felt her relax under his touch, and moved to Sonia in the next seat. He pressed the heels of his hands into her back and slid them sensuously down her spine. She moaned with pleasure.

He did it a couple more times then went on to Lindsay. "Wow, you are one tense lady," he told her, massaging her shoulder muscles. "Don't worry; I'm here, and I'm even changing with you. No one'll get past me."

The girls looked at each other.

"Not that anyone is going to try," he quickly added.

"Who are you trying to kid, Trevor?" Tanya said. "You were in that routine. Lucinda didn't just fall over and bang her head. That stage weight had been moved. Someone had lifted it. "

Trevor shook his head. "Michael is such a cheapskate. Pieces of scenery blocking entrances and exits, stage weights left where people can trip over them. The stagehands are just work experience – they don't have a clue what they're doing. This place was an accident waiting to happen. They'll sort it now, but it's too late. And that's the truth of it." He kneaded Tanya's shoulder again. "Now, come on, get a grip. We have to get through this contract, and we can do it if we look out for each other."

"But we were all standing there," Tanya said. "I heard a

crunching sound, then I heard her hit the floor. You must have all heard the same?"

"We all heard a noise," Sonia said. "We all thought some-one had fainted."

"I didn't hear a crunching sound," Lindsay added. "And I wouldn't know if the stage weight was in the wrong place. This is my first theatre job, remember?"

"Can we change the subject?" Sonia's voice developed a tremble. Trevor started massaging the base of her spine. "Come on, babe, it's going to be OK," he said softly.

"Wouldn't the scenery collapse if someone moved the stage weight?" Lindsay asked cautiously.

Trevor shook his head. "No scenery was attached to it. The stage hands didn't secure it."

"Please," Sonia said. "I'm beginning to feel sick."

"Change the subject," Trevor said firmly.

No one spoke for a few moments.

"Could someone have sneaked in?" Lindsay asked Trevor.

"Unlikely, darling. Who would know the exact time of the UV scene? Or that Alan wasn't there? Sorry, babe, I don't buy that." He rolled his large brown eyes. "This isn't helping no one," he said. "We have to get out there and do a show. Fay and Maggie will be in here to change in a minute, and we don't want to scare them, do we?"

"I wonder if Vincent's wife knows he was having it off with Lucinda?" Sonia said.

"Do we know for sure that he was?" Trevor asked. "We all think they were, because they were always together, and he stuck up for her when Barbara and Stephen gave her a hard time, but we don't have no actual proof they were humping."

"I do," Lindsay told him. "I wouldn't have said anything before. But I caught them at it, after the first show three days ago, and yesterday, before the first show. They were doing it at the back of the stage, where it's really dark."

"No kidding?" Trevor said, his eyes bulging like a friendly frog.

"So perhaps the wife done her in," Sonia said.

Trevor screwed his face in disbelief "Oh, get a grip, ladies, please."

"Actually," Lindsay said, "there's a spare black costume, in the company office."

Trevor looked astounded. "Michael has spare costumes?" he joked. "That's harder to believe than a stranger creeping in and committing murder."

"No, there is one," Lindsay insisted. "Only one though. Anyway, Michael's had to pay out now; he's had to hire some more because the police won't release the others."

Trevor nodded. "And he's more upset about that than about Lucinda."

The tannoy in the dressing room suddenly came to life. "This is your fifteen minute call, ladies and gentlemen; fifteen minutes to curtain up."

"Blimey," Sonia said. "Alan sounds sober for once."

"Oh don't," Lindsay said. "Imagine how he must be feeling."

"Serves him right," Trevor said. "If he'd done his job the stage weight wouldn't have been loose, the accident wouldn't have happened, and you lot wouldn't all be letting your imagination run away with you."

"You're right," Lindsay said decisively.

They all nodded agreement, and silence fell for a few moments. Then Tanya put down her eyelash curlers and said, "I was wondering if the killer had made a mistake."

All the others stopped what they were doing.

"Lucinda should have been next to Barbara, but they'd

all got out of sync again. One of the juves, that tall girl, was next to me."

"No, I was next to you," Sonia said. "I was holding the pink sea dragon. When have I ever gone wrong?"

"Never," Lindsay and Trevor chorussed.

"Well, the back row were all over the place," Tanya said.

"They always are," Sonia pointed out. "Except Sophie."

"Actually I thought Sophie went wrong last night," Trevor said thoughtfully. "And Barbara…"

"So what are you saying?"

"Everyone hates Barbara, but no one hates Lucinda. So what if someone meant to hit Barbara?"

Sonia shuddered. "It's best not to think about it. I'm just glad that that detective is going to be around backstage."

8

Through the backstage tannoy came the sound of excited chatter and rustling sweet papers. With only five minutes to go, the audience were in their seats, eagerly waiting for the curtain to rise and the fun to begin.

Banham and Alison walked into the semi-darkness of the wings and stood next to DC Crowther, who was so engrossed in the rehearsal on stage that he didn't notice them.

Alison found his keen interest in the scantily dressed dancers chauvinistic and annoying. But she was aware that all that had passed her lips since yesterday was too much coffee, and low blood sugar was making her irritable. Tomorrow, she told herself, looking at the slim, shivering girls on the stage, tomorrow she would have shed a pound, then she would feel better; a few more, and perhaps men would find her attractive again.

Sophie Flint was trying to restage the whole show in the few minutes before the curtain went up. The nervous cast stood on the unlit stage, and she pushed them around like chess pieces.

"You've got to try and fill the stage," she reminded them for the umpteenth time, moving Vincent one way and Barbara in the opposite direction. Alison noticed the shove she gave Barbara; the older woman ignored it and stepped back to her original position, right in the centre of the stage.

Sophie turned her attention to Fay, who was dressed in Lucinda's principal girl costume. Her long dark hair was tied back in a plait and decorated with a pretty red ribbon.

Even in the dim lighting, Alison could see her young face was caked in make-up, her eyebrows pencilled heavily, and her lips shining with too much red lipstick.

Fay put her hands out to stop Sophie. "It's all right," she said with the authority of a forty-year-old. "I know exactly what to do, and so does Mummy."

Maggie McCormak's head peeped out from the oversized, ragged black cat costume. She carried the large, eerie feline head under her arm, and the tail draped across her wrist as she trailed behind Barbara.

Sophie looked from Fay to Maggie and back again. "I wish I was that confident," she said sarcastically.

Stephen Coombs was standing so far back that Alison hadn't realised he was there. He moved toward the centre of the stage, dressed in a vast orange tent, with a matching hat, yellow wig and full make-up.

"Why don't you just let us get on and do it?" he said to Sophie. "It's going to be hard enough. Everyone's nervous enough – we don't need all this fucking staging. Let's just get through it."

"Mind your own business, Stephen." Sophie didn't even glance in his direction. "It's very important to know where we're supposed to stand."

"But we do know," Fay argued.

Alan's voice suddenly boomed out from the prompt corner. "One minute to curtain up. Time's up, Sophie. Opening positions; stand by, please."

"No, you'll have to wait," Sophie shouted back. "We're just sorting something out."

"We're sorted," Stephen said defiantly, walking into the wings. Vincent, Maggie, Barbara, and Fay followed him, leaving Sophie on stage with the four chorus dancers. She shouted, "I'm the choreographer, and if I say hold the curtain, we hold the curtain!"

Michael walked on to the stage from the other side, his face thunderous. "Don't give Sophie grief," he said angrily. "She's in charge, and I'd like you to remember that."

"It's not possible to forget, boss," Stephen said sarcastically. He grabbed the supermarket trolley full of sweets and novelties which he threw out to the audience during his first scene, and knocked Barbara in the back with it.

Sophie walked into the wings on the opposite side of the stage and snatched up her fairy wand ready to start the show. Michael followed her and they started whispering.

The four dancers stayed on the stage and spread out as best they could. Sonia, the tallest, moved to the corner nearest Crowther, and waited till she was sure he was watching her before lifting a leg and stretching it straight up in the air and against her shoulder, her lacy white knickers in full view.

Crowther made the most of the opportunity. Aware she had his attention, Sonia told the other dancers how nervous she was about going home alone to her empty flat. Crowther moved in on the girl, assuring her she had no need to feel afraid when he was around, and he would see her home safely. Alison shook her head, half-amused, half-appalled.

"Get off the fucking stage, ye stupid get," Alan yelled at Crowther. "We're about to bring the curtain up."

Crowther stepped back like a chided schoolboy.

"Any word from Penny?" Banham asked him.

Crowther coughed in embarrassment. "She's working away like a good un, Guv," said. "Isabelle's just driven the cast's buccal swabs over, and she'll keep us posted."

"Good." Banham twitched his nose. "Any reason why you're wearing so much aftershave today?"

"It's to drown the whiff of him," Crowther said, jerking

his head in Alan McCormak's direction. "I've got to stand next to him for the next half hour and he don't 'alf bloody stink."

Banham was edgy. He knew there was nothing he could do until he got some results back from forensics, or the brain trauma test results from the pathologist. That might mean another day or two. The way he felt now he wanted to close the show and arrest the whole cast. There was a killer among them, and he had a hunch who it was – but he was only too aware hunches couldn't put people in prison. And if he was wrong, he'd have lost the opportunity to get evidence to trap the real killer. He wasn't a patient man, but he had to bide his time.

A chord crashed from the piano, and suddenly everything was in full swing: music was playing, Alan and Michael were hauling the curtain, the girls on stage had started to sing and dance.

Maggie McCormak put the cat's head over her own, rushed on stage, leapt in the air and turned a cartwheel. Alison stared open-mouthed. "I'm ten years younger than her, and I couldn't begin to do that," she said.

"You've got other talents," Banham whispered.

"Oh, right, like you'd know," she snapped.

She turned away and he immediately regretted speaking. He wished he understood women.

The opening number finished and the audience applauded, then Vincent Mann made his first entrance and they went wild, clapping and cheering and whooping. Banham glanced at Barbara Denis, standing in the wings with a face like thunder.

"She's not a happy bunny," he whispered to Alison.

"It's called professional jealousy," Alison replied.

The dancers ran off and started changing at the side of

the stage. The embarrassment of standing so close to half-dressed women was too much for Banham. "I'm sure Crowther can manage here," he said to Alison. "Let's go and check out the security backstage. We'll have a look around the dressing rooms. If anyone says anything, we're checking the windows."

The first door they came to was the chorus room. Banham knocked and put his head in. The room smelt strongly of muscle spray and deodorant. No one was around so they walked in. "None of these could possibly be suspects, could they?" he asked Alison. "Not if they were in the line in front of Lucinda?"

Alison shook her head. "What about Maggie and Fay? They're changing in here too."

"Fay was in the same line as the children, and Maggie was watching from out front. We'd be better off using the time to look round Stephen Coombs's room."

The dressing room Stephen shared with Vincent Mann and Alan McCormak was directly next to the chorus room. The room smelled of stale sweat. Banham swiftly searched Stephen's pockets and the cheap canvas bag on the back of his chair. He found his cheque book and flicked through it. "Looks like he gets five hundred pounds a week salary," he said.

"That's about right," Alison answered. "A little on the low side, but then he isn't very good."

Vincent's mobile phone was on the dresser next to a photo of his children. Banham scrolled through the numbers. "Texts from Lucinda on here, from yesterday. 'I love yous' mostly. So they were on good terms." He carried on scrolling. "He phoned his wife five times yesterday as well."

"Sweet," Alison said sarcastically.

"She's phoned him this morning twice already. Sophie's

called him once, and so has Michael Hogan."

"And he went home last night. He was the only one, remember, Guv."

"Yes, I do. He said he missed his wife." Banham stared at a pair of enormous black cardboard eyelashes in an old rusty tin next to Stephen Coombs's tissues. They reminded him of spider's legs. "I can't see a mobile for Stephen."

"Perhaps he hasn't got one. I can't imagine him having many friends."

"Pity. OK, let's have a quick look next door."

The next room smelled of expensive perfume. There was a fridge with a kettle and a bottle of gin on the top of it, and a vase of fresh winter flowers stood by the window. Banham read the attached card. "Good luck, darling, with love from Michael."

He picked up a mobile from the dresser and turned it on. "Just a couple of recent calls – Michael and Sophie," he said. "Barbara Denis strikes me as quite a lonely woman. Does she live alone, do we know?"

"Just because a woman lives alone, it doesn't make her lonely, Guv. Some of us prefer it that way."

"And some don't," he said frostily. "Alison, can you cut the snide remarks? We've got a killer to find. Let's just concentrate on the job."

She nodded, looking a little embarrassed. "Yes, Guv. I'm sorry."

They closed the door behind them and retraced their steps up the corridor to the stairs. On the first floor, Banham knocked on the company office door and pushed it open. Michael Hogan was perched on the side of the dresser, talking on the phone. He looked surprised to see them and cut the call short.

"We're checking the whole of the backstage area," Banham

said. "Sorry to interrupt your phone call. Business, was it?"

"Personal, actually."

"Mind if we sit down?" Banham asked, pulling out the only two chairs in the room. Alison sat on one, and took out her notebook; he settled in the other. "Something I wanted to clear up," he said

"That looks official." Michael indicated the notebook.

"Just routine. You said you and Sophie were in here last night discussing giving Vincent Mann the sack."

"Yes, that's right."

"Another member of your cast has told us it was Lucinda Benson you wanted rid of."

"Who told you that?" Michael replied indignantly.

"Just answer the question," Banham said crisply.

"It could only have been Sophie; no one else knew."

"So which of them did you want to sack?" Alison asked.

"Vincent Mann," Michael said, looking her in the eyes. "Sophie said he was the cause of all the trouble. But I said it wasn't financially viable." An uncomfortable few seconds passed, then he continued, "It isn't a crime to sack an actor who is making trouble. Although I still feel responsible."

Banham stared at him. "Meaning?"

Michael dragged his hand down his face. "I had a thing with Lucinda. Well, more a fling, really, but if someone found out…"

"When?"

"When did I have sex with her?"

"Was it just the once?" Alison asked.

He nodded. "She came on to me and I couldn't resist. Please don't write this down," he asked Alison. She put her pen down, and he looked at Banham. "I'm sure you'd agree know how hard it is to turn down sex when it's handed to you on a plate."

Banham took a deep breath but said nothing. Michael turned back to Alison. "I know at forty-eight years of age I'm old enough to know better, but I'm afraid I can't resist a pretty woman," he said.

Banham suddenly wanted to hit him. "When did you have sex with Lucinda Benson?" he demanded.

Hogan sighed heavily. "Yesterday. Between shows."

"Does Vincent Mann know?"

"No, and I hope there's no need for him to find out."

"What about Sophie?"

Panic filled Michael's eyes. "No, and she must never find out."

"Why?" Alison asked.

"Because she's my adopted daughter. I couldn't bear it."

"Could anyone else know?" Banham asked.

"I doubt it. Everyone was out having tea. She came up here and told me Barbara was picking on her and asked me to talk to her. I said I couldn't intervene." He scratched the back of his neck and looked pleadingly at Banham. "She took every stitch of clothing off, right here in front of me. I'm a man, for God's sake. I'm sure you would have done the same."

Alison turned away in disgust.

Michael's forehead furrowed. "God, I hope it had no bearing on what happened to her."

"Did you notice any bruising on her body?" Alison asked.

"Yes, as a matter of fact I did. But all dancers collect bruises."

"Surely not on their faces?"

"I didn't notice that. But then I wasn't looking at her face."

The show was being relayed at low volume through the tannoy system; it suddenly caught Michael's attention. "I'm

106

sorry, I have to go," he said. "Alan is about to go on as Alderman Fitzwarren and I have to run the corner until he comes off stage at the interval." He looked from Banham to Alison and back again. "I hope what we've said will remain confidential."

They followed him back down the stairs and into the wings, where Crowther was still standing. Michael helped the two young stagehands shift scenery, then sat on Alan's high stool in the corner, put on the head-cans over his head and spoke to the sound and lighting engineer at the back of the stalls.

"Do you believe they only did it once?" Alison said.

"I think so," Banham said. "Otherwise why tell us at all?"

"So we won't think he wanted to get rid of her. We already know from the post mortem that she had sex yesterday. The DNA samples will tell us who with."

The dancers came flying towards the stage for their next cue. "We're in the way," Alison said. "Shall I nip down and check the basement, and see if the fire escape is locked?"

"I'll do that," Banham said quickly. "I'm not used to all these half-dressed women. I don't want them to think I'm watching them."

"I'm sure they'd think you were quite normal if you did," Alison said. "I'll check the other side of the stage then, and meet you back here in five."

If Alison was honest with herself, she was glad of a break from Banham. She knew what a difficult time Christmas was for him, but he hadn't made it easy to show sympathy and understanding. She was angry with herself, for letting him know she was up for a relationship with him, but angrier with him for turning her down.

That was all history now. Embarrassing though it was, she'd get over it. He was far too complicated for a relationship anyway. But he was a great detective and a good boss, and she didn't want to jeopardise their working partnership. He had put his head on the block and called out the murder team on a hunch, so the least she could do was back him up. If they did have a murderer to catch, they had to get on with it.

She made her way along the narrow passageway at the back of the stage and checked that none of the stage weights were loose, or where someone could trip over them in the dark. When she was satisfied she returned to the left side of the stage, where the three girl dancers were in the process of another quick change, wriggling into skimpy white leotards. Crowther was watching as they discarded their flimsy peasant dresses, threw them on the floor and stood naked apart from the tiniest of white G-strings. His testosterone level must be at a record high, Alison thought, registering the eye contact between him and Sonia, the tallest dancer.

Banham came up the iron staircase. "It's pitch black down there," he said. "I had to use a torch."

Did you check the fire exit?" she asked.

"Locked from the inside," he said. Though the dancers who were now fully clothed in leotards and tights, he averted his gaze. Crowther was grinning; if Banham had come up those stairs one minute earlier, he would have passed out with embarrassment.

The lights on stage dimmed, and bells started ringing loudly. "What's happening now?" Banham asked.

"This is the ballet on Highgate Hill," Alison told him. "It means the interval is only a few minutes away."

"Good." He set off for the corridor and the first floor dressing rooms. "Come on. Barbara Denis will be free at the interval, and I want to talk to her about her ex-husband."

Barbara was clearly on edge, nervously smoking a small cigar and sipping a glass of gin. "I don't normally drink when I'm working," she said, "but the UV scene is twenty minutes away, and I can't remember ever feeling this afraid."

Banham indicated the sofa. "May we?" he asked her.

She shrugged. "Sure. Would you like a drink?"

They both declined. "I wanted a little chat, off the record," Banham said. "If nothing else it'll keep your mind occupied for a few minutes."

"What do you want to know?"

"You've worked for Michael for a long time, and you must know all the cast. Tell me about them."

She inhaled heavily on the thin cigar. "Michael and I were married many years ago," she said, a sad note creeping into her voice. "I know them all, except Vincent Mann and poor Lucinda. I only met them this year." She sipped on her gin, and her teeth chattered against the side of the glass.

"Do they always argue a lot?" Alison asked. "Or is it just today, because everyone's nerves are frayed?"

She placed the glass on the dresser in front of her and frowned thoughtfully. "They do argue a lot," she said. "Especially Stephen and Sophie. Stephen is Alan's brother, Fay is Alan's daughter, Sophie picks on Fay, so Stephen stands up to her. I just try and keep to myself, unless I think something isn't right for the show. I'm unpopular because I fight for high standards of work."

No one spoke for a few minutes. Barbara picked up a large sable make-up brush and dipped it in a tin of dark powder, carefully powdered the skin between her lips and nose and squeezed her lips together to check the result. Facing the two detectives again, she said softly, "I gave Lucinda a hard time. We had a terrible row yesterday. She

109

got the harmonies all wrong and I lost my temper with her."

"I heard," Banham said. "She went to Michael to complain about you, didn't she?"

Barbara lifted her eyebrows. "Did she? Well, that wouldn't have done her any good. Michael and I may have divorced eighteen years ago, but he still has enormous professional respect for me." She turned back to the mirror, untied and retied the bow holding her tiny ponytail in place, then checked the clips either side of it.

"Michael gives me the best dressing room, the best salary, and the best billing. That proves what he thinks of my work." She lifted her chin. "And he relies on me to keep the show together."

"How does that go down with Sophie Flint?" Alison asked her.

Barbara laughed nervously and reached for her glass. "Not well. Sophie is Michael's current favourite." She took a sip of gin. "Blondes. You must have noticed – every female in the show is blonde, except the McCormak girl. It's Michael's little weakness. He can't help himself, but he doesn't respect any of them."

"Them?"

"He's highly sexed. He can't help it." She turned back to the mirror and picked up a dark lipstick. "He had a fling with Alan's wife, Maggie, a long time ago." She painted her lips and rubbed them together. "It's always blondes. He can't stop himself." She picked up the sable brush and powdered again over the same spot, stretching her mouth downwards as she did so.

"So are you saying Sophie is his mistress, as well as his daughter?" Alison asked.

"Adopted daughter. Yes. But it won't last; none of them

ever do."

"Who is Fay's father?" Banham asked quickly.

"Alan of course. Oh, I see what you mean." She shook her head. "No, no, definitely not Michael."

There was another silence as she sipped her drink, and her teeth chattered against the glass again. "I'm glad you're here," she said to Banham.

"Did you see Stephen Coombs after the UV scene last night?" Alison asked her.

"Yes, he came on stage just after the accident to see what was happening. He isn't in the scene."

"Did you notice what he was wearing?"

"Has someone else told you that he wasn't wearing the right costume?"

"Was he?"

"I'm not sure." She put her hand to her mouth. "He has a criminal record for GBH. I didn't want to be the one to tell you, but I expect you'd have found out."

This was news to Banham, but he replied noncommittally, "Yes, I expect we would. What happened?"

"He attacked someone with a kitchen knife and I believe he got a suspended sentence. He's hotheaded and acts before he thinks. That's not to say I believe he hit Lucinda. I still think it was an accident. But for the record he threatened and bullied her all through rehearsals and he has threatened me many times."

"In what way?" Alison asked.

"Threatened to punch me, nothing more, but that in itself is scary. My face is my fortune, and I need to keep working."

"And you're not sure whether he changed his costume during the UV scene?" Banham asked.

"I can't be sure," she said. "I was on stage doing the scene.

111

Alan wasn't there and Maggie was giving out the wrong fish in the dark. It was total bedlam…"

"Maggie was in the wings?" Banham interrupted.

"Only briefly, at the beginning of the routine, just before Michael."

"Michael? You saw Michael in the wings as well?"

"Yes, but as I said, only at the beginning of the UV. It goes on for eleven minutes. I saw Stephen at the end of it, after the accident. Sophie said he hadn't changed, but I can't for the life of me remember what he was wearing. Something dark I think, but I'm really not sure."

Alan's voice sounded over the tannoy. "All artists to the stage, please, to rehearse the UV scene before the start of act two."

Barbara downed the last of her gin and started to undo her dressing gown. Banham jumped up. "We'll leave you to it," he said quickly.

She opened her mouth then closed it again.

"Is there something else," he asked her.

"Yes, actually, Inspector, there is." She let the dressing gown fall, revealing a lacy black teddy. "I wondered if you were married," she said, lowering her eyelashes, "because I find you very attractive."

A few minutes later all the cast were on the stage, working in tense silence. Alison, Banham and Crowther stood in the wings with a fidgety Stephen Coombs.

Sophie was first to speak. "It'll be all right. There are four detectives in the wings, so nothing can go wrong."

No one answered.

Sophie tried again. "Don't worry which fish you carry across the stage today…"

"No one ever does," Stephen heckled.

Sophie glared at him. "Just take whichever one Alan or Michael gives you." She was moving the cast around like chess pieces again.

Fay snapped, "Stop pushing me."

"I have to," Sophie said. "It's the quickest way."

"We should have rehearsed it last night, when we had more time," Fay flounced.

"Come on, Fay," Michael said sternly. "Sophie's trying to get it right."

"I never go wrong," Fay defended herself. "And she's always in the wrong place."

Alison and Banham exchanged glances.

"Just do as you're told, Fay." Sophie sounded like a school prefect. "In ten minutes we'll be doing this for real, and if anyone bumps into anyone else we'll all die of fright." She gave Fay another shove and turned to Vincent Mann, pulling and turning him into another place in the line, like a clockwork train. He moved obediently and said nothing.

Barbara bristled as Sophie approached her. "Tell me where to go," she said quietly, "But don't push me."

"We're short of time," Sophie said. "It's easier if I show you."

"Then show me," Barbara said firmly. "Don't shove me."

"Mummy knows where she has to be," Fay said. "I told her earlier." Maggie McCormak moved into a space in the front line.

"No, not there," Sophie shouted at her. "If Fay has been standing there, that's why it's been going wrong. Listen to me, not her."

"That's where I always stood," Fay argued. "Our line never went wrong – it's yours that's a mess."

"Fay, just shut up and let me get on with it," Sophie snapped.

Again Michael intervened. "You'll get done quicker if you just do what Sophie says," he said to Fay.

"I know all the cat's moves better than anyone," Fay protested.

"I taught you the moves, but you don't always get them right," Sophie said irritably. "Just shut up and do as you're told."

Banham's eyes never left the stage.

"Bossy little cow isn't she?" Stephen Coombs whispered. "Twenty-two years old and she thinks she's Gillian Lynne."

"Who's Gillian Lynne?" Banham asked Alison.

"The most prominent theatre choreographer of the last fifty years," she told him. "She choreographed *Cats.*"

Michael Hogan hadn't taken his eyes off Sophie, and Maggie McCormak's were firmly fixed on him. Banham made a mental note. The relationships between these people were a maze.

"Did Trevor Bruce, the black boy, give a DNA sample?" Stephen asked Alison.

"Yes. I told you. We asked everyone in the company."

"What a waste of taxpayer's money," Stephen said, adjusting his skirt. "Neither of us would know what to do with a woman if she gave us a compass."

"The women too," Alison told him. "It's so we can eliminate you all…"

"The audience are getting impatient," Alan McCormak shouted from the corner. "How much longer are you going to be, for Chrissake, Sophie?

Michael stormed off to the prompt corner. "She's had to restage the whole routine," he told him. "She'll take as long as it takes."

Alan putting his hand up defensively. "I'm only looking out for your interests, boss. If we take the curtain up late,

114

we'll be pushed getting this house out before the evening lot'll be coming in."

"Are we all clear where we're going?" Sophie asked the cast.

The tension spoke for itself, but no one demurred.

"OK, we're ready," Sophie shouted to Alan.

The cast all walked solemnly into the wings to stand by for the opening of act two. Only the dancers remained on stage. Maggie, Fay, Barbara, Vincent and Stephen stood in the wings near Banham.

"There'll be two police either side of the stage," Banham assured them. "You'll all be perfectly safe."

Maggie put her cat's head on and stood beside her husband in the prompt corner as she tied the clip at the back. Fay followed, muttering her lines for the opening scene, immersed in her own world.

Barbara, aware she had an audience in Banham, stretched her arms in the air and flexed her back to loosen up. Banham looked the other way.

Vincent Mann stood a foot away, watching Barbara.

The four dancers were on the sparse stage, limbering up. Sonia turned to make sure Crowther was watching her, and he winked.

Lindsay, the youngest dancer, called to Alan. "Do you need help getting the curtain up?"

"I'm right here," Michael called back. "I'll help him."

Suddenly a loud duff note blasted from the pianist out front, followed by the tinkling of piano keys, playing a happy song. The chatter from the audience immediately hushed.

"Stand by," Alan shouted.

Banham struggled to the back of the stage and felt his way along the dark passage to the other side of the stage.

Sophie was standing in the wings holding her sparkling wand, ready to make her entrance as the fairy after the opening routine.

As the dancing started Michael appeared beside her. Banham stood a few feet away watching them. Sophie nodded and Michael spoke; then he curled her long silky blonde hair round his finger and pulled her towards him. Banham looked across to the other side of the stage; Stephen, Barbara, Vincent, Maggie and Fay all watched Michael kiss Sophie gently on the cheek...

9

The backstage tension didn't seem to affect the audience's enjoyment. As soon as the curtain went up, the actors had them cheering and booing in all the right places, shouting, "Oh no he doesn't! Oh yes he does!" and "Behind You!" in true pantomime fashion.

The cast were standing on the enormous plywood ship; Stephen Coombs, in a red and white nautical dress with a matching sailor's hat, was on the bow goading the audience on. It reminded Banham, standing in the wings stage right, of his childhood in Brighton.

A storm was brewing and the ship was going to sink. The ship's captain, played by Trevor, told the actors to jump overboard, and Stephen Coombs teetered on the edge. Banham was surprised that the cheaply made scenery could take his weight .

The other actors were behind him, pushing and shoving to get to the front of the queue and jump over the side. Banham didn't know whether the pushing was part of the story until he saw Barbara Denis sidle up beside Stephen and elbow him in the ribs in an attempt to push herself to centre stage.

The floor of the stage was cleverly lit to resemble angry water. As the actors landed in the lights, they rolled from side to side and bumped each other as if they were at the bottom of the sea. Someone rolled a few feet from Banham, but in the dim lighting he couldn't make out who it was. Then a vivid beam flashed like lightning, and he recognised Barbara Denis. She hugged her leg, and whispered, "Fuck, fuck, fuckety fuck!" Banham hoped that the sound man had had enough sense to switch her radio mike off. She had obviously caught herself on the same loose nail he had walked into himself when he first arrived at the theatre.

Fay McCormak had also rolled over to that side, and ended up next to Barbara.

"Get out of my fucking way," Barbara hissed at her. "You pushed me and I've cut my leg."

Fay whispered back, "Tough shit, I hope it turns poisonous."

Until then Banham had felt sorry for Fay. She was only seventeen, and despite everything that had happened she had taken over a leading part in the show and was managing remarkably well. Even now he understood that everyone's nerves were stretched to the limit. Michael Hogan was insisting that they do the ultra-violet scene, and it was only moments away.

At the back of the set Michael was helping the two work experience boys to pull the ship into the wings. DC Isabelle Walsh was talking to Alison Grainger at the other side. Alison signalled to Banham. He squeezed past the ship and followed her and Isabelle to the corridor where they wouldn't be overheard.

"Isabelle has been out front talking to the usherettes," Alison said, careful to keep her voice low. "It seems none of them saw Maggie in the auditorium at any time during the performance last night."

"There were two usherettes on duty last night," Isabelle added. "Neither noticed her come through the pass door or go back through it during the UV scene."

"Barbara Denis said she saw her in the wings at the beginning of the routine," Banham said.

"The usherettes did say she could have come in and out without either of them noticing," Isabelle added.

The chorus dancers rolled off the stage into the wings stage left, and immediately jumped up and started peeling their sailor clothes off. They tugged on the new all-in-one black outfits and pulled the balaclavas over their heads.

At the same time Stephen Coombs appeared on stage, having done a very quick change into a green costume resembling a large piece of seaweed. He crossed the stage pulling faces at the audience and picking bits of the material from his legs, arms and bottom. "Someone's weed on me," he announced, making the audience hoot with laughter.

"So if Maggie wasn't out front, that would also shed doubt on Michael's alibi," Alison went on. "He said Maggie came into the kids' dressing room for her binoculars."

"It is possible the usherettes just missed seeing her," Isabelle pointed out. "They didn't seem that bright; if they were chatting a herd of elephants could have passed through and they might not have noticed."

"Unlikely though." Alison shook her head. "I think you'd notice someone walking down the aisle in the middle of a show."

Stephen came off the stage still picking at bits of dark green seaweed. Then the stage dimmed and went into darkness.

Crowther had been standing with his arms folded, watching the dancers changing. Banham managed to catch his eye, and he walked over to join the team.

"He managed to get spare costumes at short notice," Crowther said.

"I'm surprised Know-all Col didn't help out and make a few bob on the side," Alison said sarcastically.

"Just keep your mind on the job," Banham said looking the young DC in the eye.

"Go thunder and waves." Alan's voice sounded around

the backstage area, then he put on the head-cans to hear the sound engineer confirming his instructions.

The roar of thunder echoed across the audience, followed by the crash of waves and lighting effects to signify lightning. Slowly the light dimmed and the thunder became fainter, as echoes of the storm slowly died away. The stage went completely dark, and silence fell for a few seconds as the audience and the actors waited for the UV scene to start. Then there was the sound of bubbles, as if someone was sinking beneath the water.

Banham watched the actors in the wings, all dressed from head to toe in black, each holding a large ultra-violet fish. He tried to work out who was who, but it was impossible to tell. "You and Isabelle go round the other to the other side," he whispered to Alison.

The pianist hit the opening note of the music and a large octopus crossed the stage in mid-air. The black-clad figure holding it was small, so Sophie Flint, or possibly Fay. She gyrated the strange creature in time with the music, stepping sideways across the stage toward him. The audience clapped their appreciation.

Next came the four dancers, entering from Banham's side. Above their heads they wriggled a long bright yellow eel with psychedelic pink feet. The audience squealed with delight.

The music speeded up and everything began to happen more quickly. Banham couldn't tell who was who. He thought he recognised Vincent Mann with a lethargic blue fish; he bumped into someone crossing from the opposite direction. Banham guessed it was Barbara, but she and Maggie were a similar height and build.

Alan McCormak was waiting for the dancers. He took the yellow eel from them and handed each of them single fish, and they set off back across the stage, passing Barbara or Maggie. On the opposite side Michael was handing out the fish. Banham had completely lost track now; everything was moving at such a pace.

The audience oohed and aahed, and clapped in time with the familiar seaside song that the pianist was playing. Some of them even sang along. Then the music moved even faster, and the actors speeded up to keep pace. Two people collided, and their sea creatures tangled together as if they were fighting. Banham realised it was impossible for the actors to know who was in front or behind them. And yesterday would have been even more chaotic, with six extra children in the routine and no one at the side.

How easily an accident – or a murder – could take place.

He tried to keep his eyes on Fay as the line crossed and recrossed the stage; Lucinda should have been in the same position the night before. But on one occasion Sophie's eyes appeared in the beam of Alan's torch as she tugged at the balaclava. It was simply impossible to tell the actors apart.

Banham rubbed his mouth thoughtfully. So it wouldn't be out of the question for someone to join in the routine – easier still if they knew neither Michael nor Alan was at the side of the stage. The murderer could cross the stage, do the deed, then leave.

The music slowed, and the cast walked into the dark, holding the last fish in the air. As they pushed and shouldered each other, Banham wondered how many of them were in the right positions. This time he identified Fay, squeezed in at the end of the line at the opposite side of the stage, in the very place where Lucinda had fallen. But as the audience clapped and cheered the finale, he failed to spot anyone else in the line-up.

As the scene ended the girl dancers ran off the stage and discarded their black costumes, revealing their tiny white G-strings. Crowther's eyes were more prominent than a cartoon bug as the girls wriggled into coloured, chiffon belly-dancing costumes.

Sonia, the tallest of the girls, looked straight at Banham, smiling broadly. She wore no bra, and he turned away in embarrassment. Then curiosity got the better of him; he turned back to find her smiling at Crowther.

What's the matter with you, he asked himself. You're surrounded with half-naked women and you feel absolutely nothing!

Now even more self-conscious, he moved away and stood in the entrance to the wings, keeping his back to the girls. Within seconds Alison had come round the back of the stage. She wore that bad-tempered squirrel look again, and the dark specks in her sludge-coloured eyes shone out. He had a sudden urge to reach out and stroke her face.

He was distracted by the clatter of high heels rushing down the corridor. It was Stephen Coombs, dressed in a red and white old-fashioned bathing costume and matching bonnet. In his hand he carried a pair of flippers.

"Mind out," he said, pushing past them. "I'm going to be off." He disappeared speedily toward the stage, shouting, "I'm the only man on the Island."

Banham looked quizzically at Alison.

"'Going to be off' means going to miss your cue," she informed him.

Michael Hogan walked from the stage and joined them in the doorway. "Thank God that scene's over," he said rubbing the back of his neck.

"What happens now?" Banham asked him.

"Oh, a quick scene between the principals: that's the

dame, Alderman FitzWarren and the principal boy and girl, and the comic. Then the dancers do a spot, and then it's into the last scene, The Palace of the Sultan of Morocco." He emphasised the title of the scene as if it were a pop group. Banham hoped the palace was better than the plywood ship

"That's what the work experience boys are doing now, at the back," Michael told him. "Moving the palace scenery into place. We're going to miss the children in that scene. They play the mice, and the cat's supposed to chase them, and eat them. I'm having to use toy mice." He produced an ugly fluffy toy from under his arm and showed it to Banham and Alison. "Actually I couldn't get mice, so I'm using fluffy hedgehogs. I have to hope you can't tell from the front."

Banham tried not to smile.

"I wish I could cut the scene," Michael said sadly, "but it's vital to the legend of Dick Whittington. Dick's cat is famous for ridding the island of mice. Then King Rat appears, he and Dick have a big sword fight and Dick defeats him. He wins his freedom, marries Alice, and becomes Lord Mayor of London and they all live happily ever after. That's the story."

"Real life's very different," Banham said.

"You're so right," Michael replied. "Well, I'd best help the lads to get the palace into place; we're already running late."

"Twenty minutes to the end of the show," Banham said to Alison. "Everyone's busy – let's have a swift nosy around that company office."

Sophie Flint was furious. She was standing in the stage right wings waiting to go on, and watching the actors on stage. The scene was going very badly; Fay had messed up

123

all her lines, and Barbara was becoming impatient with her and fluffing her own lines. Maggie should have been following at Barbara's heels, but was obviously having trouble seeing out of the eye-holes in the cat's skin, so was following Fay by mistake. And Vincent was cracking jokes about it, which made Stephen lose concentration and mistime his own jokes – which Vincent used to get more laughs at Stephen's expense. The audience squealed with laughter.

Then Alan McCormak, who was also in the scene, forgot his line altogether, so Vincent said it and told the audience it was Alan's – so Alan stormed off the stage and went to the pub.

Stephen decided enough was enough and marched off the stage towards Sophie. "I want words with you," he raged.

"Not now," she snapped.

The scene on stage finished, and Vincent left the stage to clapping and cheering from the audience. The pianist began to play tinkling, fairy-like music, the lights dropped and a pink spotlight shone in the corner. Sophie walked into the light and delivered her pretty fairy speech, assuring the audience that she was there to make sure there was nothing to fear, all would end well and Dick Whittington and his cat would be safe.

When she came off stage Stephen was nowhere to be seen. She carefully laid her glittering wand down in the corner so it would be there for her final entrance in the Palace scene. Then she dropped her head and body forward so her long hair brushed the floor, bent her knees and took a couple of deep breaths. Calmer now, she straightened up and walked to the back of the set.

The dancers were performing the harem belly dance the

audience always loved. Backstage, the two boys were still pushing the palace scenery around. It was a big scene change, and Sophie decided, as she often did, to stay out of their way and cross under the stage via the two spiral staircases.

In the company office, Banham was looking down at a large box full of what looked like bric-a-brac collected for a white elephant stall. There were bits of crockery, glittery wands and crowns, several swords and knives and a whole jumble of kitchen equipment.

"What on earth is all this rubbish?" he asked helplessly.

Alison looked across from the mirrored wall, where she was examining the contents of Sophie's strawberry pink towel. "Props, Guv. He probably keeps a roomful of stuff at home – saves buying new for every show."

Banham shrugged, and moved to the filing cabinet, where he began opening drawers and speedily going through their contents. Alison gazed at the shelf in front of the mirror; bottles of glitter sprays, silver false eyelashes and three open pink lipsticks lay next to a lip brush smothered in cerise colour. Long blonde hairs hung from a plastic hairbrush, and a stand-up shaving mirror stood beside it. A mauve and pink shoulder bag hung on the back of chair; Alison quickly unbuckled it and pulled out a thick filofax with a zebra-print plastic cover.

"She keeps a diary," she said, flicking through the pages.

There was a faint rap at the door. Alison's eyes locked with Banham's, but neither spoke.

Sophie walked quickly down the winding staircase. The bottom was in almost total darkness now the juveniles' dressing room wasn't being used; the basement light switch was the other side of the passageway, and the small worker light was a few feet in, on the right wall, above the costume skips. But she was familiar enough with the area; if she took care, she wouldn't collide with anything.

Her foot hit the concrete floor with a small shock; she hadn't realised she was on the last step. She lifted her foot and rubbed her sole through the flimsy white ballet pump. No harm done.

The darkness was creepy, and she thought about going back into the light. Don't be silly, she told herself crossly; you've worked in this theatre every year since you were a child, you know the layout down here with your eyes closed.

She had never known the basement so silent and dark; it felt eerie. A few steps in she froze; was that a noise?

"Is someone there?" she asked the darkness.

No one answered.

She began to hurry, desperately feeling in the darkness for the wooden skips; the worker light switch was just above them, and she'd feel much happier with its blue glow around her.

She jumped with fright as she bumped into one of the skips – then another sound turned her blood to ice. Someone had got to the worker light switch before her.

Sophie slowly turned to face the shaft of light now stretching blue and thin across the basement, and came face to face with a tall figure. It was another second before she saw the large knife in the leather-clad hand. Her heart thudded against her chest as she turned to hurry back the way she had come, her arms outstretched, grappling desperately for the iron banister.

In her panic she missed her footing, and in that same second the leather-covered hand clamped itself firmly over her mouth and dragged her backwards into the dimly lit passageway. She pulled and clawed at the hand, fighting for breath. Another strong hand gripped both of hers together and pulled them away, then the grip on her face tightened and an agonising pain shot around the inside of her head. A ghastly crack and crunch told her her nose was broken and had disintegrated into her face.

The pain overwhelmed her and she nearly lost consciousness. But she had to fight to stay alive; she tried to kick out, but to no avail since she only wore a satin ballet shoe on her foot.

She felt herself being shaken like a rat caught by a dog. She could taste her own blood now, and almost choked as it slid down her throat and then up into her mouth. Her eyes were closing against the pain; then the hand moved from her face. And she heard that laugh. She tried to stand up, but fell back against her assailant.

She felt the razor-sharp edge of the knife, and heard the grisly sound like a zip fastener. The knife sliced the soft white skin of her throat, and the last thing she felt before she dropped to the ground was a jet of blood shoot high into the air like a cork from a bottle of champagne.

Then there was darkness.

10

The knock on the door took them by surprise. Alison swiftly replaced Sophie's filofax in the handbag, and Banham moved the pile of unpaid bills back into the drawer and sat back in the chair. The door opened and Vincent Mann's head appeared. He became noticeably flustered when he saw the two detectives.

"Oh... Is... er... is Michael not around?"

"He should be on the side of the stage with Alan," Alison said.

"Right... Sorry... I... er... I didn't see anyone on the side of the stage, but then it's very dark down there." He looked uncomfortably from Banham to Alison. She noticed his voice sounded unsteady.

"Anything else?" she asked curtly.

"No, no, nothing." He withdrew from the room, closing the door behind him.

Banham opened another of the desk drawers and found a laptop. He opened the lid and fired it up. Nothing happened; he let out an impatient sigh. "Damn. It needs a password," he muttered.

Alison was reading the December pages of Sophie's diary. "Try *pantomime*," she suggested.

Banham did, and the computer whirred into life. "What would I do without you?" he said.

She looked at him, confused. His eyes met hers for a couple of seconds, then he turned back to the computer. He clicked on Documents, then on Actors Wages, and scrolled down the list and figures.

Why these little comments, she asked herself. Perhaps he

enjoyed leading her on then shutting the hatches; perhaps he felt that was part of the chase. Well, he'd chosen the wrong woman. Whatever she felt, she had no intention of exposing it again. There was a new year approaching and she'd made resolutions: she was giving up her occasional cigarettes, and getting involved with a man was a no no. She was going to be like Crowther – keep them casual and focus on work.

For now, Sophie's diary was the priority.

After a few moments she looked up, straight into Banham's eyes. "This is interesting," he said.

"So is this."

"Didn't he say he wasn't paying Vincent Mann a wage?"

She nodded.

"According to the salary records, he pays him three thousand pounds a week. And Barbara gets the same as Maggie, the wardrobe woman – one thousand a week."

"Now, that is interesting. Why does he pay Maggie so much?"

"You tell me." He looked back at the computer. "Stephen Coombs, five hundred pounds."

There was another knock and Stephen Coombs appeared in the doorway. Large yellow papier-mache flowers decorated the fuchsia pink hat that bobbed on his large head. His shoes and the stripes on his gaudy dress matched exactly. Perspiration ran down his heavily pan-caked face on to his neck.

His eyes travelled from Alison to Banham. "I'm looking for the boss," he said, frowning.

"As you can see, he's not here," Alison said dismissively.

"What are you doing then?" he asked, suspiciously eyeing the laptop lying open in front of Banham.

"The same as you – waiting for Michael."

"Right." Stephen hesitated for another second before backing out and closing the door.

"Sophie is keeping a diary," Alison said to Banham. "Listen to this." She turned back a page and read, "Stephen's temper is the worst I've ever seen it this year." She turned another page. "It's been a really difficult day. Stephen and Vincent Mann have been fighting, and Vincent and Lucinda were rowing. Lucinda was crying again in the lunch-break." She turned more pages. "Stephen was very angry after the rehearsal. He threatened me again. Michael had to threaten to sack him. He apologised, but I could tell he didn't mean it. Then he accused Lucinda of standing in his light. Barbara stuck up for Lucinda and Stephen gave Barbara a load of verbal abuse. He seems even more unstable this year." She turned more pages. "Lucinda was crying a lot today." She looked up. "And I've only got as far as the rehearsals. I'll sneak back up here when they are doing the finale and…"

She didn't have time to finish the sentence. The door flew open and Michael Hogan stood in the doorway.

"Isn't Sophie up here?" he asked urgently.

"No."

He noticed that his laptop was wide open but made no comment. "Where would she be?" he said turning to Alison. "She follows this dance number. Did you hear a call on the tannoy?"

"Yes, I did." Alison flicked a worried glance at Banham. "But she hasn't been up here. She must still be downstairs."

Michael hurried away, leaving the door open; Banham closed the computer and they followed. Fay and Maggie were standing at the bottom of the stairs.

"Where is she? Barbara's going berserk," Fay said. "She should be in the wings, waiting to go on."

Maggie was still wearing the cat costume, complete with

the large furry head. Her own green eyes were just visible through the thick black mesh under the large plastic ones protruding from the top of the head. Her voice sounded strangled as she spoke through the half-moon-shaped, bright red mouth. "Has someone checked the toilets?" she suggested.

Banham headed for the ground floor toilet. As Alison ran back up the stairs she heard Michael calling to Alan, "Get Sonia to say the fairy's lines over the mike."

Both cubicles in the upstairs loo were empty. Alison hurried along the corridor to the Green Room. The two work experience boys, one short with red hair and freckles, the other tall and dark with enormous feet, stood by the vending machine sipping canned drinks.

"Shouldn't you be downstairs?" she said.

"We've finished," the red-haired one told her, a mottled blush creeping over his pimply face. "After we push the scenery on for the Sultan of Morocco scene, there's nothing else for us to do."

"Have you seen the fairy anywhere?"

Both shook their heads. The red-haired one added, "She went under the stage after her last entrance. I don't remember seeing her come up the other side."

Banham walked swiftly down the corridor opening each door in turn. Trevor was in the chorus room, in front of the mirror getting ready to play King Rat. He wore the full costume except the rat's head, which faced him from the dresser.

Sonia's voice sounded through the tannoy: "Our hero has been captured, but never fear, Dick's beloved cat will save the day."

Trevor looked up at the tannoy in bewilderment. "What's

happened?" he asked. "Where's Sophie?"

"When did you last see her?"

"Not since the Island scene." He frowned and his frog-like eyes moved from side to side. "Jesus! That's so unlike Sophie. She never misses a cue."

Alison, Banham and Isabelle Walsh arrived at the foot of the stairs at the same moment.

"Isabelle, you come with me to check the basement," Banham said. "Alison, you stay up here and keep looking."

Alison unclipped the torch from her belt and handed it to Isabelle, then went back into the wings. Banham and Isabelle walked to the bottom of the haunted staircase and found the light switch. Something wasn't right. The children's dressing room should have been in total darkness, but there was a light at the far end of the room. He quickly crossed the room and opened the door. The sight that greeted him made him stagger back.

"When did you last see her?" Alison asked Crowther.

Crowther drummed his fingers against his thighs. "I don't even remember her coming off after her last bit. The girls were next on stage, and to be honest, Sarge, I was talking to them and didn't take much notice of Sophie. I'm pretty sure she went off on the other side, though."

Trevor appeared at the side of the stage, dressed as a large rat.

"She would have gone off on the opposite side," he said. "It's pantomime tradition: the good character goes on and off stage right, and the bad guy goes on and off stage left. So I'm here, stage left."

Crowther looked puzzled.

"King Rat," Trevor added. "The bad guy."

"Well, you live and learn," Crowther said.

"Did the dancers do a quick change in the wings before they went on?" Alison asked Crowther.

He nodded, grinning broadly.

Alison narrowed her eyes. The whole of the British army could creep unnoticed past Crowther while three sexy girls were changing their clothes; duty had no chance against his testosterone.

On stage nothing was going well. Barbara Denis was trying to stay calm. There were no little rats running around, and Michael's toy furry hedgehogs hadn't materialised. Barbara bent towards down to Maggie and whispered, "Eat some invisible rats, for God's sake. Let's keep the show going."

Maggie didn't respond. She crouched in a cat position, unmoving. Barbara was anything but pleased. She walked downstage to address the audience. "Don't be afraid. My faithful cat and I will rid the island of these rats for you."

"What rats?" shouted someone in the audience. Barbara looked furious. She raised her voice and tried to speak over the laughter. "The rats don't scare us," she told them. "My faithful cat will rid the island of them." She gave Maggie a little shove. Maggie ignored her. Barbara addressed Sonia, now dressed in a long white robe and playing the High Priestess of Morocco. "And in return, you will give us our freedom." Barbara held her hand out and took Fay's. "Then I can wed my Alice."

Trevor stepped on the stage in the full King Rat's costume. Barbara looked out front and gave a theatrical gasp, then drew the prop sword from her waistband. "I'll fight this one," she told the audience. "I am not afraid."

The audience started cheering in true pantomime tradition.

Trevor pulled out his own prop sword.

"Prepare to fight to the death," Barbara shouted to Trevor. He lifted his sword and swung it toward Barbara. The two swords crashed together and the fight leapt into action. It was very well choreographed, Alison thought – probably the best bit of the show. Barbara and Trevor were completely in sync; blow followed blow, one ducked as the other jumped, the swords met and the pace and excitement started to build. The audience were loving it. Barbara ducked again as the sword flew past her head, then jumped back up and rushed at Trevor, aiming her sword at his chest. Trevor shielded himself and stretched his sword arm toward Barbara. The audience screamed and cheered on Dick Whittington.

"Jesus," Banham said.

Michael Hogàn was kneeling at the bottom of the spiral staircase on the opposite side of the basement, holding Sophie in his arms. Her head was hanging back over his arm. Blood dripped from a gash in her neck and rolled down her face into her long blonde hair. Her arms hung limply by her side and the blood slid down on to the sparkling fairy tiara lying beside her on the floor.

Within one hour the whole of the theatre was cordoned off with blue tape.

The murder squad, a full forensic team, uniformed police and a couple of sniffer-dogs now swarmed through the building. The show had been brought to a close and the curtain dropped in just as Dick had defeated the King Rat in the famous sword fight. The actors sat in stunned silence on the stage waiting for forensic officers to take their costumes. The three girl dancers, shivering in their harem outfits, huddled against Trevor's warm, furry rat costume, and DC Crowther sat on a chair near them.

Vincent Mann stood on the opposite side of the stage facing the wall. Every few seconds he lifted his hand and hit the wall. Stephen Coombs was a few yards away, perching uncomfortably on a canvas upright garden chair barely wide enough for his bulk. The cheery yellow and cerise hat lay on the floor by his large pink stiletto shoes. One dirty foot rested on his lap, and he whiled away the time picking at it.

Maggie and Barbara sat on the chaise-longue used as the high priestess's throne, with Fay by her mother's feet on the floor. Alan had brought the stool from the prompt corner, and sat next to them, his hand covering his mouth. The only sound came from Stephen, rubbing his corns and picking his toe-nails.

Forensic officers, dressed from head to toe in plastic overalls and gloves the colour of bluebells, scoured the basement and the surrounding area. Penny Starr was scraping spots of fresh blood from the dirty floor, while another officer rubbed at the steps which had led Sophie to her death. Flashbulbs were popping more frequently than at a star-studded film premiere; the exhibits officer was photographing the dead girl and the pattern of blood stains from every conceivable angle.

Another female forensic officer knelt on the ground and used a pair of tweezers to lift scrapings of a substance around a shoe print a few feet away from the body. She dropped them into a small transparent evidence tube, and quickly closed the rubber cap.

Banham was now at the far end of the basement, looking at the mirror outside the children's dressing room. The brown Good Luck bunny still hung from the mirror.

Alison and Isabelle both wore protective forensic suits to search the skips and overflowing crates in the basement. The three skips blocking the fire exit were only a few feet away from Banham; when Alison reached them she lowered her mask and whispered, "Are you OK, Guv?"

"We let this happen," he said in a low, dull voice. "Four of us in the building and this happened under our noses."

She moved closer to him. "Get a grip," she said firmly. "We're not clairvoyant. We were doing our job and investigating another murder." She took a deep breath. "And frankly, Guv, if you think your personal history will get in the way of this enquiry you should stand down and hand it over to someone else."

For a few seconds anger almost overwhelmed him. Then a small part of his mind realised she was right. It took guts to say that to her superior officer; she had guts in abundance, and he admired her for it.

It did the trick. He turned to face the crime scene and shouted to Isabelle Walsh, "When forensics have finished with Mr Hogan and bagged his clothes, can you get him a dressing gown and bring him through to the children's dressing room? Sergeant Grainger and I will take his statement."

Alison was still eyeing him apprehensively. "Thank you," he said quietly. "Let's get on with our job."

Max Pettifer the scene of crime manager walked over to Banham. He pulled off his rimless glasses and rubbed his eyes.

"It would have been a lot easier if that clown hadn't picked her up," he said, throwing a black look in Michael's direction.

"Wouldn't it just?" Banham replied. The skin under Max's chin was getting flabby, he thought – probably something to do all the malt whisky he consumed. "And the quicker you can get his clothes bagged up the better. I want to talk to him first."

Banham studied Michael Hogan in the mirror. The producer was still sobbing as Penny Starr and other forensic officers scraped at the dirt on the sole of his shoes Isabelle stood by with a dressing gown as a blue-gloved forensic officer bagged his clothes. Michael's body started to jerk and shake. Banham recognised the symptoms: he was going into shock.

Alison brought Michael into the children's dressing room. She offered him a hard-backed chair and sat opposite him, beside Banham. The laundry basket served as a table between them, and she took Sophie's zebra-print diary from her bag and laid it down. Michael did not react.

"What was your relationship with Sophie?" Banham asked him.

"I was in love with her," Michael said, lowering his head.

"So she was your mistress?"

Michael looked up. "She was the love of my life."

"And your adopted daughter?"

He shrugged. "That too."

"Where were you when Sophie made her last entrance? And when the dancers were on stage?" Banham asked.

"I had to make an important phone call." He spoke in a quiet, flat tone. "I went to the stage door phone."

"There's a phone in your office," Banham said. "Why didn't you use that?"

"People come in all the time. I didn't want to be over-heard."

"Not even by Sophie?"

"Especially by Sophie. I had to phone my bank. I'm very overdrawn and I didn't want her to find out. She would have worried."

"You've got a mobile," Banham said.

"The battery was flat. I forgot to charge it last night – hardly surprising, with everything that happened."

Banham tapped the side of his face.

"Exactly when did you go out to the phone?" he asked.

"As the harem dance started. Alan had just come back from the Feathers; he settled back on the stool to run the show so I took the opportunity to make the call."

"And when did you realise Sophie was missing?"

"As I put the phone down, Alan came up and asked if I knew where she was. He said the dancers had come off stage, and Fay was just going on. Sophie was always in the wings standing by, but she was missing. That's when I went upstairs, and found you in my office."

This could all be checked; Crowther could call the bank to confirm the phone call. Banham decided to go in another direction.

"Why did you lie about the wages you pay your actors?" he asked.

Michael opened his mouth to speak but seemed to think better of it.

"You said you didn't pay Vincent Mann," Alison reminded him coldly. "But according to your accounts you pay him three thousand pounds a week."

"Only on paper. I don't actually give it to him. It was his idea, and it suited me just fine." He ran his hands through his hair. "He said if his wife found out he wasn't getting paid, she would get suspicious. I took it out in cash, pocketed two thousand to pay off some debts, and gave Barbara an extra grand a week in cash, on top of the thousand on paper." He shook his head sadly. "None of it matters without her." He began to shake violently and pulled the dressing gown around him. Banham stood up and moved the fan heater closer to him.

"Why give Barbara an extra thousand pounds?" Alison asked

"I feel responsible for her," Michael said flatly. "She was my wife and I treated her badly. She never remarried and her career is all she's got. The least I can do is give her work, and help her financially."

"It's still a lot of money," Alison said. "For someone who's going bankrupt."

Michael's eyes rested on the diary. He looked at Banham. "I need to ring Valerie, Sophie's mother."

"Our family liaison office will take care of that."

"It'll be better coming from me." Michael spoke quietly but insistently.

Banham shook his head. "No. I'm sorry."

Michael banged his fist on the table. "She's her daughter, for Chrissake."

Banham stood up. "That'll be all for now, Mr Hogan," he said formally. "Sergeant Grainger will escort you upstairs. I have to ask you to wait with the rest of your cast while we finish here. I'll keep you informed, but I will be asking you to accompany us to the station for further questioning."

Banham walked upstairs, round the side of the stage and into the ground floor corridor, where sniffer dogs and their handlers were searching for Sophie's scent, or something else that might lead them to the murder weapon.

After taking Michael to the stage Alison walked into the corridor and joined Banham. "I'm speaking as a friend now," she said gently. "You handled that interview really well…"

He bristled. "I'm the senior officer here…"

She ignored him and continued, "You're a great detective, but you're in danger of letting your personal life take over." She glanced around to make sure no one could hear. "I know why the young female victims get to you – but it's been eleven years, Paul. If you want to survive in this job you've got to move on."

He didn't answer. How did she know how hard it was for him? He thought he was doing a good job of hiding the turbulent feelings this case was stirring up. Some of the time he even hid them from himself.

She added, "You have stop feeling everything's your responsibility. The murder's happened, so let's find the bastard responsible. That's our job – that's what we do."

She really had front talking to her senior officer like that. But though he could hardly bear to admit it, she was right. He took a deep breath. "I know the murders were very different, but I believe it's the same killer," he said. "And it was definitely an inside job." He paused. "It has to be one of five people, and they are all sitting on that stage. It would help enormously if we could find the weapon."

She touched his arm briefly. "We've got the dogs. We'll find it."

Max Pettifer approached Banham. "Ah, there you are. I knew you wouldn't want to hang around down there, under the circumstances."

Alison gave a gasp, and Banham found himself fighting an urge to hit the thoughtless SOCO man. "What have you got?" he asked.

"Haven't found the knife yet, have you?"

His superior tone that was starting to irritate Banham.

"I'd say the blade was between six and eight inches. It wasn't a clean slicing either; there are bits of muscle and the edge of the oesophagus is splintered. That's a very ragged cut. I'd say your killer wasn't experienced with a knife."

"And in a hurry," Banham suggested.

Pettifer left, and Banham looked at Alison, who was flicking through Sophie's diary. "When we solve this murder, will you let me buy you dinner?" he asked her.

She avoided his eyes, focusing on a page of the diary. "No. I want us to work together and be friends. There's no room for anything else."

"And if I agree, can I buy you dinner as a friend? To say thank you for keeping me in line?"

"No."

Her eyes met his for a moment and he saw determination in them. Maybe best not to push it, he thought sadly.

"There's an entry in this diary for the day before the show opened," she said briskly, flicking the pages. "Sophie threatened to tell Vincent Mann's wife about his affair with Lucinda if he hit Lucinda again." She turned another few pages. "And a couple of days ago Stephen hit Sophie when she intervened in an argument between him and Barbara. She didn't tell Michael because he might have sacked Stephen, and they needed to keep the show running. They couldn't have replaced him easily. Apparently pantomime dames don't come cheap – certainly not at the rate they were paying him."

"What does it say, exactly?"

Alison began to read from the diary. "'Stephen's temper is out of control. He is showing signs of violence again.' Those are her exact words."

Banham rubbed a hand across his mouth. "Did she write anything last night or this morning?"

"No, unfortunately."

"Time we did some background work. Get Isabelle to

run a check on Stephen for previous convictions."

"Will do, Guv." She headed in the direction of the basement.

"And Alison…"

She turned her head.

"You're a great detective too."

Vincent was wearing a red, white and blue, striped dressing gown, and no glasses. He paced the dressing room floor, his agitation coming out as aggression.

"I told you Lucinda was murdered," he shouted. "This wouldn't have happened if you'd listened to me."

"Sit down, please, Mr Mann," Banham said sternly.

Vincent stood still, and leaned against one of the mirrored walls. "I'd rather stand."

"Whatever. Talk me through your movements after you left the stage, just before Sophie went missing."

"I left the stage and went to find Michael." There was still an edge of hysteria in his voice. "You were in the office, you saw me yourself. I'd just had another run-in with Stephen Coombs on stage." He blew out a gusty breath. "I came to tell Michael that I'd had enough. That whatever he threatened, I wasn't putting up with any more. I was walking out."

Banham folded his arms and studied the man. Vincent couldn't look him in the eye. For a few moments neither of them spoke, then Banham asked, "Did you go straight up to Michael's office after leaving the stage?"

"Yes, you saw me yourself. You were in the office when I got there."

"You went straight from the stage to the company office?"

"Yes." Vincent narrowed his eyes. "What are you getting

at?"

"You had your glasses on when you came upstairs," Banham told him. "When did you put them on?"

Vincent shrugged. "I've no idea."

"I presume you leave your glasses in your dressing room?"

Vincent opened his mouth to reply, but closed it again as the door opened. It was Alison.

"Was Mr Mann wearing his glasses when he came to the company office earlier?" Banham asked her.

"Yes. Yes, he was," she answered.

"So where did you leave them while you were on stage?" he asked the comic.

Vincent shook his head like a dog flicking away water. "I'm sorry. I'm in a bit of a state. I'm not sure, but I think I left them on Alan's desk and picked them up as I left the stage." He screwed up his eyes and sighed. "I can't think straight. It's the shock…"

"Was Alan at his desk?" Banham asked.

"No. No, I'm sure he wasn't," Vincent said.

"You remember that, then." The tiny smile on Banham's mouth didn't reach his eyes. "So where did you go when you left this office?"

"I'm sorry, I've gone blank. Back down to the dressing room, I think."

"Did you see anyone, or notice anything unusual?"

He lifted a finger. "I saw Michael Hogan on the public phone, the one by the stage door. He was getting quite heated, so I decided against approaching him. I do remember thinking that it was unusual to see him on the public phone."

"Then where did you go?" Banham pursued.

"To the dressing room."

"Was anyone in there?"

"Stephen wasn't. And Alan's never in there during a show. When he's not on stage he should be at the side of the stage running the show. But as you know, he's more often in the pub next door."

"Did you see anyone else in the corridor on your way to the dressing room?" Banham continued.

Vincent laced and unlaced his fingers in a repeating pattern. "Trevor. I saw Trevor, the boy dancer. He comes off halfway through the dancers' spot to change into the King Rat costume." He exhaled and looked at Banham. "To be honest, I think I saw him. But we do this show twice a day, and I normally see him at this time, so…"

"He normally changes in your dressing room," Banham reminded him. "Today he was changing with the girls."

Vincent laced his fingers and held them still. "Yes, he was. I'm sorry, my brain won't work properly."

"How did you know Stephen Coombs was going to complain about you?" Alison asked him. "You said you didn't see him when you came off stage."

"He told me on stage. He swore at me."

On stage, in front of a theatre full of children, Banham thought, exchanging glances with Alison.

Vincent pulled a pair of glasses out of his pocket and started cleaning them with a red handkerchief. "He whispered to me on stage – called me a foul name and said he was going to Michael about me. I'd had enough. If anyone in the audience heard and told the press, that would be my career as a children's television presenter down the swanee." He rubbed the glasses vigorously and held them up to the light, then started rubbing all over again. "He said I was speaking across his laughs. In comedy if someone says a funny line everyone on stage stays still and waits for the audience to laugh before carrying on with the next line. It's called comic timing." He glimpsed his reflection in the mirror opposite and gazed at it for a moment. "You could wait for a herd of donkeys to pass, and Stephen's lines still wouldn't get a laugh."

His shoulders slumped and he stopped fidgeting with his hands. "Without Lucy, everything seems… irrelevant. I wasn't even concentrating." He put his glasses on and stuffed the hanky in his pocket. "But I can't stop myself ad-libbing when there's an audience in front of me. I'm a comic. I do it without thinking. Anyway, I really don't care. I've had enough of this damned show."

"Did you leave the stage at the same time as Stephen?" Alison asked him.

Vincent shook his head. "No, Stephen made his exit stage right today. The same way as Sophie. I took advantage, and scooted up to Michael's office, to tell him I was leaving there and then."

Suddenly there were raised voices outside the dressing room. Banham raised his eyebrows, but Alison was as puzzled as he was.

"I'll have to ask you to wait back on the stage until further notice, Mr Mann," Banham said in his formal tone. "And I will need you to accompany me to the station for further questioning."

Alison opened the door to find DC Crowther in the corridor trying to fend off a hysterical middle-aged woman. Banham had no idea who she was, and as he approached her she tried to push him aside. Her eyes were firmly fixed on the cordoned-off area leading to the basement.

11

Alison would have known the woman was Sophie's mother even if Valerie Flint hadn't been screaming her daughter's name; the likeness was uncanny. Michael Hogan's attempt to comfort the hysterical woman confirmed her identity.

"Mr Hogan, you were asked to wait on the stage," Banham almost shouted. "This is a murder enquiry. Please do as I ask and leave the police to deal with police business."

Alison managed to detach Valerie Flint's clawing hands from Crowther's lapel. Crowther dusted himself down and led Michael back to the stage.

Valerie was still demanding to see her daughter. Alison stepped in; Banham wasn't good at handling these situations. She introduced herself and spoke soothingly, taking the other woman's arm and pulling her away. For a small woman Valerie was certainly strong.

Eventually she allowed herself to be led through the pass door and into the empty auditorium. Alison settled her in one of the red velvet seats in the front row, and Valerie started to compose herself. Banham had followed them, and sat on the other side. He looked thoughtful but not upset by the woman's behaviour; his mind was firmly on the job. Alison was glad. Her pep talk had worked.

The actors were now sitting on stage in their street clothes or their dressing gowns as Penny Starr bagged up their costumes and shoes, labelling the plastic evidence containers with blue-gloved hands. She put the containers side by side and walked into the wings to ask Crowther to have them driven to the lab.

Maggie McCormak had settled herself back on the

chaise-longue beside Barbara. Fay was sitting on the floor in front of them. "Go and give Michael a cuddle," Maggie said to her.

"I don't think that's a good idea, under the circumstances," Barbara said.

Stephen looked up from the large canvas chair into which he had squeezed his bulk. "It's none of your business as it fucking happens," he said to Barbara a little more loudly than necessary. "You ain't in charge of everything, see."

The four dancers looked away, obviously hoping there wasn't going to be another scene.

Crowther gave the stage his full attention. Barbara stared coldly at Stephen, taking her time before answering – a little unsteadily, Crowther noticed.

"I'm just suggesting," she said, "that as we've been told to sit here and wait, we should do just that. And I think that considering the circumstances, Michael would prefer to be left alone."

"That isn't 'cos you're considering the fucking circumstances, lady. It's 'cos you can't fucking bear anyone near him except yourself," Stephen snarled.

"Oh, for heaven's sake!" Barbara turned away.

Vincent Mann lifted his glasses and rubbed his eyes. He looked at Crowther, blinking nervously. Crowther gave the brewing row his full attention.

"Leave it, brother." This was Alan McCormak. He winked at Stephen and raised his hands appealingly.

"Leave it? Oh, I'll fucking leave it all right. As soon as she leaves this family alone and stops pushing us about!"

"It wasn't meant personally, against you or your family," Barbara said to Fay.

Vincent Mann covered his ears with his hands as Barbara

continued, "But I'm sure you can see as well as anyone else that Michael is upset, and best left alone."

"We didn't take it personally, Miss Denis," Maggie said sarcastically. "We didn't take it any way, actually, because we weren't taking any notice." She leaned towards Fay and tapped her shoulder. "Go on, give Michael a cuddle."

Michael stood up. Crowther had the sense that everyone was holding their breath.

"Actually, Barbara's right, as it happens," Michael said. "I would rather just be left alone." He turned and walked to the back of the stage.

Stephen glared at Barbara. "Don't fucking look like that!" he growled.

"Oh, for heaven's sake," Barbara said. "Can't you for once in your life show some sensitivity?"

Crowther walked briskly on to the stage. "OK, that's enough. If you're going to start fighting and acting like children, that's how you'll be treated. From now on you'll all sit in silence; anyone who speaks will be arrested for breach of the peace." He looked at everyone to be sure they knew he meant business, then walked back into the wings.

Penny was handing the last of the costumes to a uniformed policeman. Crowther winked at her as she followed, and she smiled at him. It was almost worth having to work his holiday, Crowther thought.

Michael Hogan called to Crowther. "I've some brandy and coffee in my office. I could go and make us all some."

"No can do, mate." Crowther raised his hand. "I have orders that no one is to be left on their own."

"Send one of your officers with me, then I won't be on my own," Michael suggested. "I'm sure a coffee and a nip of brandy will help keep everyone calm."

"I want to see her, and I have a right to know what happened," said Valerie Flint, tears flooding down her face.

Alison took her hand. "I'm afraid that's not possible yet. Is there anything I can do, anyone I can call for you?"

Valerie shook her head. "There's only Michael. He phoned me – I was doing my food shopping."

Valerie pulled free of Alison's grasp and clutched the fingers of her other hand. Her facial resemblance to Sophie was uncanny, and they were the same height; but Valerie was stocky whereas Sophie was slightly built. They had the same natural white-blonde hair, but Valerie's had an old fashioned pink rinse and was slightly bouffant, like the young Dusty Springfield.

The closest similarity was the indigo eyes; there was no mistaking them, as small and sharp as her daughter's. She turned them on Banham. "At least tell me what happened."

Banham couldn't answer. He looked at her helplessly for a moment, then stood up and walked over to the stage. Alison watched him climb the stairs at the side and disappear into the wings.

"We're trying to find out what happened," Alison told Valerie, one ear picking up Banham, shouting at Crowther to call the family liaison unit and get someone down to the theatre immediately. "Will you help us, and answer some questions?" she asked.

"Is there any chance she may still be alive?" Valerie asked tearfully.

"No, I'm afraid not." Alison spoke quietly.

"How did she die?" Valerie asked.

Alison swallowed hard. It was always difficult, breaking this kind of news. "Her throat was cut," she said. "I'm very sorry."

Banham came back into the auditorium and quietly

149

settled three seats away from Valerie.

"We need to find the person that did it," Alison told her. "Will you help us?"

Valerie nodded, sitting up and wiping her face.

"You were married to Michael Hogan, weren't you?" Alison asked.

"Yes."

As if on cue, Michael Hogan walked through the pass door, carrying a tray of freshly brewed coffee, three plastic cups and a miniature bottle of brandy. "This is for Val," he said.

Banham's face darkened. He stood up, banging the seat, and strode towards the stage. Leaning over the tray until his face was less than two inches away from Michael's, he said threateningly, "I told you to stay on the stage. If you disobey my orders once more, I'll lock you up for obstructing a murder enquiry. Do I make myself clear?"

The colour drained from Michael's face as Banham drew back and yelled into the wings, "Crowther, take Mr Hogan back to the others, and don't let him out of your sight."

"Valerie was my wife," Michael argued. "She needs me."

"Go," Banham said pushing the tray. The jug of scalding coffee wobbled dangerously.

Michael went.

"Don't be hard on him," Valerie said as Banham sat down again. "I'm sure he's hurting a lot too. He always acts before he thinks, and he so loved Sophie."

"How long had Sophie been living away from home?" Alison asked her.

"She left home when she was fifteen. She didn't have to, but she wanted her own space. She was always very grown-up."

"What about boyfriends? Was there anyone in particular?"

Valerie shook her head. "She wasn't interested in boys.

Surprising, I know, because she's… she was… so pretty…"
A sad smile spread across her face. "The truth is we didn't
get on too well. She didn't tell me her secrets. When she
was a little girl she used to write them all down in a diary.
We were never close." She closed her eyes and took a deep
breath. "Her life was dancing. And when there was no
dancing, she worked with Michael. He treated her like
a princess. Valerie looked at Banham. "This is going to
crucify him. He loved her so much."

"How long had she been working for Michael?" Banham
asked.

"All her life. She was a dancing babe. I suppose it was in
her blood - I was a dancer too. That's how I met Michael.
Sophie was only two, and I was in his production of
Cinderella. I'd just got back into shape after having her, and
I used to take her to the theatre with me - there was always
someone backstage to keep an eye on her. Michael and I
fell in love, and we married soon after." The smile left her
face. "It didn't last long, but that's Michael. No woman lasts
with him."

There was a brief pause, then Banham asked her, "Did
Sophie have any enemies in this show?"

"Did she have any friends, more like?" Valerie's voice was
steely.

"You mean everyone disliked her?"

"This is a jealousy-ridden profession. She choreographed
the show and she was very good at her job." She lifted her
hands in a resigned gesture. Alison noticed she wore no
jewellery but her nails were well manicured and painted
white. She felt a little ashamed of her own reddened,
neglected hands and short unkempt nails.

"I don't know about that Vincent Mann," Valerie said. "I
only met him on the opening night. He was in a corner,

whispering with that poor girl Lucinda. I went over and introduced myself. He was a bit stand-offish, I thought. I couldn't believe it when I opened the paper this morning." She paused, then continued, "I rang Sophie straight away." She fished in her pocket and brought out a white handkerchief decorated with embroidered flowers. "I'm sorry." She wiped her already tearstained face with the hanky. "I'm glad now I spoke to her. As I said, we don't speak very often." Valerie turned to Alison. "Sophie said it was a mistake. 'Who would want to kill Lucinda?' That's what she said. She said the line-up had gone wrong, and Lucinda was standing where Barbara should have been."

Banham stroked his mouth thoughtfully. "So did anyone hate Barbara enough to want to kill her?"

Valerie looked at him as if he had dropped from another planet. "Every one of them. She's a cow of the first degree." She sighed. "Stephen Coombs nearly did her some damage a few years ago. Irish gypsies, that family, and a law unto themselves."

Banham was puzzled. "What family?" he asked.

"The McCormaks. Stephen's real name is McCormak – he and Alan are brothers. Maggie's married to Alan, and Fay is their daughter." She paused briefly before adding, "And Maggie's a slag. That's common knowledge."

Alison began to make notes.

"She broke my marriage up," Valerie continued. "She seduced Michael, and she was pregnant with Fay at the time. I tried to forgive him, and we stayed together for a while, but…" She gazed into the distance for a few moments, then shook her head and looked at Banham.

As usual Banham's face gave nothing away. Valerie continued, "Michael's weak; he got sucked in. He didn't really want her, but he's like any man: he'll take it if it's there."

"Did Alan know?" Banham asked.

"He found out, but he's Catholic and they don't believe in divorce. He couldn't handle it. So now the poor man's an alcoholic."

"Who's Fay's father?" Banham asked.

"Not Michael, if that's what you're thinking," Valerie said quickly. "You only have to look at Fay to know she's gypo too. Oh, Alan's her father all right. Michael would have told me if he'd fathered a child."

Alison lowered her gaze.

"How did Fay get on with Sophie?" Banham asked.

"Fay's jealous of her, always has been. They were dancing juves together. But unlike my Sophie she wasn't born to dance, and it shows."

Valerie reminded Alison of the ballet school mothers she had known: ambitious for their own children, trying to push them in the front, when half of the children didn't want to be there at all. Alison certainly hadn't.

"Is there still friction between them?" Banham asked.

"It's the mother that's the problem, not Fay."

"Maggie?"

Valerie nodded. "I was a dancer too, but you wouldn't hear me shoot my mouth off like her. She goes on as if she knows it all." Her mouth twisted into a sneer. "She knows nothing – she just resents my Sophie because Michael loves her so much." She looked at Banham. "You're a father, I'm sure, Inspector; you'd understand. Do you have a daughter?"

The silence was like a solid wall. Alison held her breath.

Banham wrapped his arms round his chest.

"No," he said quietly. "I don't."

Alison let out her breath. A tricky moment, but he had

coped. When his mind was on a case, there was no better detective. She swiftly changed the subject. "Barbara must have resented that too?"

"Barbara is a sad woman trying to hang on to her youth. She's childless because there's no room in her world for anyone but herself. She picks on everyone for the tiniest mistake, and everyone hates working with her." She sighed heavily. "But Michael always stands up for her. He's a weak man, and naïve. He says she's a perfectionist and just wants the best for the show; the truth is she's a selfish cow, and wants everything to revolve around her."

"Do you think she's capable of murder?" Alison asked.

"She's evil enough to do anything, that one."

"When was it that Stephen Coombs attacked her?" Banham asked.

"I'm not sure exactly. Many years ago."

"Do you know why?"

"Yes I do, as a matter of fact." Valerie looked from Alison to Banham. "She was blackmailing Michael. He had an affair with an underage dancer, and she found out."

Banham shifted in his seat and waited for her to continue.

"I'm quite sure he didn't know the girl was underage," Valerie said. "He wouldn't do anything to make Sophie think badly of him. He was like a father to her – he legally adopted her less than a year after we married."

She screwed her face up in thought and put a finger to her temple. "It happened after his marriage to me, so a long time after his marriage to Barbara. She blackmailed him into giving her good roles and top billing." Her mouth curved down again. "Well, she was never going to get either on talent. Throwing her weight around didn't get her anywhere, though. She wanted Alan sacked for drinking, but I told you why Michael wouldn't give in on that one. Then Stephen found out, there was a hell of a row and it ended with Stephen attacking Barbara."

"Were the police called?"

"God, no. No one would have wanted that."

"How was Sophie with Stephen?" Banham asked.

Valerie pressed her lips together. "She stayed out of his way, kept him out of dance numbers. He can't dance anyway. But she knew he had a vicious streak – she's a clever girl." She stopped suddenly and shook her head violently like a dog coming out of a pool. "Please tell me I'm dreaming."

"Can I get you some water," Alison asked quietly.

"No." She took several deep breaths then looked across at Banham. "Let's get this over with."

"If you're sure…"

"I'm sure. Carry on."

"OK," Banham said. "Going back to Lucinda Benson: would you know if she was having an affair with Michael?"

Valerie put her hands in the air. "No, of course she wasn't. He wouldn't take advantage of a young girl who wanted to break into showbusiness. He's not like that."

"One last question," Banham said. "Was Sophie short-sighted, Mrs Flint?"

"Yes. We both are. She wears contact lenses, and never takes them out. She doesn't miss anything if the dancers go wrong on stage."

"Mrs Flint, you've been very helpful." Banham stood up. "Thank you very much." Alison made to get up too, but he waved her back into her seat. "My sergeant will stay with you until an officer comes to take you home. We'll be in touch again soon."

"Thank you, but I want to wait until Michael is free."

Banham nodded agreement and headed for the stage. As he walked through the pass door into the corridor DC Crowther approached him. "Guv, can I have a word?"

Banham glanced at the stage to check Michael Hogan was back there.

"Something's just come to my notice Guv," Crowther said, keeping his voice low.

"Go on."

"Penny has taken all the suspects' clothes to the lab for testing. She'll do it in the next couple of hours."

"Is that it?" Banham was irritated with Crowther. The young DC never missed an opportunity to point out that it was his influence that had made Penny Starr give up her holiday. But something more pressing was on his mind at the moment. "What I want to know is, who gave Michael Hogan permission to wander around the backstage area?" he asked crisply.

"I'm sorry, Guv." Crowther still spoke with the confidence of a detective superintendent. "He wasn't alone; I sent one of the uniforms with him. He only went to make coffee, in the upstairs area which is cordon free."

"I said no one was to leave the stage," Banham said, looking the lad in the eye.

"Won't happen again, Guv."

"It better not."

"Um, Stephen Coombs, Guv," Crowther went on, a little chastened. "We've taken a bright pink and yellow outfit from him to send away to forensics for testing, with a matching hat and stockings and gloves…"

Banham recalled it. "He changed into that after Sophie's last scene." He thought for a second. "What about the red and white old-fashioned bathing costume he was wearing in the underwater scene? That'll be in his dressing room.

Send that over too."

"That's what I'm trying to tell you, Guv," Crowther said urgently. "It isn't there, and no one can find it. I've got uniform looking, but it seems to have disappeared."

"You didn't ask Coombs where it was?"

"No. After I realised it was missing, I decided to say nothing till I spoke to you, Guv."

Banham rubbed his mouth, and looked over at the spiral staircase at the side of the stage. "How certain are you that no one went down that staircase while the dancers were on stage?"

Crowther looked like a schoolboy caught in the tuckshop out of hours. He hoisted at the waistband of his droopy jeans. "I was standing in that groove." He nodded towards the edge of the stage. "By that big lump of scenery."

Banham's face hardened. "Watching the girls," he said flatly.

"Guv, I couldn't put my hand on my heart and swear nothing could have gone unnoticed behind me."

Banham stared at him, too angry to speak. The lad had cocked up badly this time; if his attention hadn't wandered the second murder might not have happened. Banham wasn't about to let him off the hook.

"I'm really sorry, Guv." For once Crowther sounded sincerely penitent. "But never in a million years did I think that someone might be underneath the stage committing murder."

Banham looked round the wings, where Crowther was supposed to be positioned for security purposes. "I hope for your sake that no one did creep past you," he said, making no attempt to hide his anger. "There were four of us on duty and a murder still took place. If any of us could have prevented it…"

"I'm pretty sure I would have noticed, Guv. It just wouldn't be true if I said I'm certain."

"Pretty sure isn't good enough." Banham spoke in a low voice; all the suspects were in hearing distance. "If important evidence is lost because you can't keep it in your trousers, you can expect to find yourself in front of the DS on a disciplinary charge."

Colin Crowther looked devastated. "Guv, Alan McCormak was in the corner. He would have seen anyone coming or going."

"He walked off the stage and went to the pub! You didn't notice that either?"

Crowther sounded increasingly desperate. "I did, Guv! He was hardly gone a minute. I saw him come back in too. He was back at his desk by the time the girls had started dancing. I've had a word with the work experience boys too - they were pushing the big palace scenery on at the back. They say they did see Stephen Coombs squeeze around the back of the set, but they couldn't say how long after Sophie's entrance."

"And you didn't see him?"

"No, Guv, I didn't as it happens."

"So they could be mistaken?"

"I'd say that's unlikely. It would have taken about ten minutes to push the scenery on – they'd have it timed down to the last second. I saw them leave the backstage area as Trevor left the stage. So Coombs had time to follow Sophie into the basement, kill her and come back up the same staircase, then squeeze around the back of the set, change his costume…"

"…and go up to Michael's office to give himself an alibi," Banham finished. "Just one thing, though – when did he get the knife?"

"That I don't know, Guv. Perhaps it was premeditated and he had it in his costume. He has got form. Isabelle checked his CRO. He attacked someone called Joseph Blake. With a knife."

Stephen Coombs blew his nose into a tissue, examined the contents and sniffed noisily as he dropped the paper into the bin and pulled a greying handkerchief from his pocket.

Banham said, "I want you to go through your movements from your last appearance on stage, up until we found Sophie's body at 3.23 pm."

Stephen shifted in his seat in front of his dressing room mirror, and tugged the enormous beige cardigan he was wearing around his vast bulk. Banham and Alison stood close to him, leaning against the Formica-covered shelving in front of the mirrors.

Stephen Coombs was a very nervous man.

When Alison picked up her notebook and turned to a clean page, he covered his mouth with a grubby hand and bit into the skin by his thumbnail.

He started to speak very quickly, his eyes darting from Banham to Alison and back. "Lucinda's death had left us all at sixes and sevens, see. The 'Only Man on the Island' scene didn't go well. Barbara was angry and Vincent was being his usual prattish self, no bloody help to anyone. We had two understudies on stage and all he could do was make jokes at everyone's expense. That made me angry, see."

He paused and looked at Alison. When she stopped scribbling and looked up he carried on. "It don't seem important now, but I was doing my best to hold the scene together. Maggie couldn't see out of the cat costume – the head had slipped. Barbara was too self-absorbed to notice, so little Fay was guiding her round the stage. Maggie should have been next to Barbara, but she stayed close to Fay because Fay held her hand, see. Then Vincent started going off the script, and Alan walked off. The scene went from bad to worse."

Banham looked at Alison, unsure what Stephen was talking about.

"So you were very angry when you left the stage?" Alison said, looking up from her notebook.

"I'm a professional, love," Stephen answered. "Vincent needed reporting. Instead of helping, he made fun of Maggie and Fay and scored laughs at their expense." He shifted in his chair and tugged at the beige cardigan, which was trapped under his large bottom. "Any professional would have been angry."

"In what order did you come off the stage?" Banham asked.

Stephen's eyes shifted sideways. "I always come off first, always – I have costume changes..."

"Where did you come off?" Banham interrupted.

"I do that change in my dressing room. I have time to get there and change during the dance. Sometimes when I'm in a hurry I have to change at the side of the stage, see..."

Banham interrupted him again. "Which side of the stage was this?"

Stephen stared into his capacious lap. "I make my exits on the side nearest my dressing room. It gives me more time..."

"And you did that today?" It was Alison's turn to interrupt.

He nodded, chewing more skin off his thumb. "And Sophie always exits on the other side. Fairies come off and on at the opposite-prompt side, see; that's the rule in panto. It's the side of the good."

"Just the relevant facts please," Banham said sharply.

"It is relevant, mate!" Stephen slumped even further back in his chair.

"So you came off on the stage left side? Alison repeated.

"Yes."

There was a brief silence while Alison made a note. Stephen shifted uneasily.

"Did Sophie always cross under the stage after that entrance?" Alison asked him.

"Oh, I couldn't be sure of that, lass. I just rush and do my change, see. But I expect she would have done what she always does; why wouldn't she?"

"I don't know," Banham said, "but I'll find out. So you did your change, and then what?"

"I came looking for Michael. You saw me. You were there when I came up to the office." His voice picked up speed again. "I wanted to report Vincent, see." He suddenly stopped for a second, then said quietly, "Seems petty now. But the truth is Vincent Mann's a prat. He knows nothing, it's his first pantomime, and my twenty-second..."

"Not a quick change then," Banham said dryly. "If you had time to do all that."

"Where did you go then?" Alison asked coldly.

"Back downstairs. I went to the bog before my next entrance, in the Sultan of Morocco's palace. That's when Sophie should have been there, and that's when you two came and joined us."

"Did you see anyone in the toilet downstairs?"

He shook his head. "I saw Barbara walking toward the stage in time for her entrance as I came out."

Banham watched Stephen carefully. "We'll need the costume you changed out of – the red and white bathing costume. We need to send it along to the lab with the others. Where would it be?"

Stephen was silent for a second. "In the laundry basket, outside in the corridor. I was sweating like a pig in that last scene. It needs a wash."

He became very uneasy, flicking his eyes away from Banham to Alison, then down to the floor. After a long moment Banham said, "Sergeant, go and get that costume, and make sure it goes to forensics."

Alison left the room. Beads of sweat had broken out on Stephen Coombs's temple. He pulled out his grubby handkerchief to dab the perspiration, and Banham noticed a small tic at the top of his fat upper lip.

Banham spoke again. "Last night during the ultra-violet scene you didn't do your normal costume change. Why was that?"

"Of course I did. Who told you I didn't?" Before Banham could answer he carried on, "I always change while the scene is going on, see. I change into the red and white bathing costume for the 'Only Man on the Island' scene."

"From your green dress?"

He dabbed at his perspiration again. "That's right."

"Sophie Flint told us she saw you after the ultra-violet scene, and you were still wearing your green outfit. In fact, she was going to make an official statement this afternoon at the station saying just that."

Stephen shook his head and wiped his hands on the grey handkerchief. "How would she know?" For the first time he looked Banham in the eye. "She can't see two inches in front of her without her glasses, and she don't wear them during the show. Did she say she saw me after the UV scene?"

Banham nodded. Perspiration was still breaking out at Stephen's temple and running down his face. "When the ambulance arrived?" he demanded.

Banham nodded again, keeping steely eyes on the nervous man.

"I was cold. It gets bloody cold backstage, see, and that bathing costume is flimsy." His voice had risen in pitch as well as volume. "I put my dressing gown on over it. My green dressing gown. See?" He gestured with his head to the back of the door, where a dark green dressing gown was hanging. "There. Satisfied now, are you?"

Banham said nothing for a few moments, and Stephen's face grew even more sweaty.

"Tell me about the GBH incident in you were arrested for."

The colour drained from the big man's face. "I might have known that would come up." He leaned forward and Banham got a whiff of his body odour. "It was seventeen years ago, and none of your business. I'm not under arrest. You've seen my dressing gown. You've got nothing on me."

The door opened and Alison's head appeared. "Can I have a word, Guv?" she said urgently.

12

Banham followed her into the corridor.

"It's not there, Guv." Alison lifted the fraying lid of a wicker laundry basket standing against the wall next to the toilet door. "A few sweaty socks, half a dozen pairs of tights, one white shirt. No red and white bathing costume."

"Well then, someone's took it." Stephen's voice was loud with fear.

The same fear was written across his face when they returned to his dressing room. "I tell you, I bloody put it there," he shouted. A spot of saliva landed on Banham's cheek. "Some bastard's taken it if it isn't there. That's where I bloody put it, see."

Banham lifted a hand and wiped his cheek on the cuff of his sheepskin jacket.

"Ask Maggie. She's in charge of wardrobe." Stephen's voice was still loud and unsteady.

Banham turned and walked toward the door.

Stephen turned to Alison. "What is this?" he shouted accusingly at her.

Banham swung round. "This," he said angrily, "is a murder enquiry. And you, Mr Coombs, are a suspect. You are not free to leave the building." He opened the door. "Sergeant Grainger will escort you back to the stage. You'll wait there until I decide what to do next."

Stephen turned a grubby finger in the end of his nose. He struggled to get out of the chair, and when he succeeded he walked through the door without looking at Banham.

When Alison returned from escorting Stephen Coombs back to the stage Banham was walking the corridor from the dressing room to the phone at the stage door.

"Maggie McCormak said she hasn't been near the laundry basket," Alison told him. "She was playing the cat, and had no time to cover the wardrobe duties as well. Shall I get DC Walsh to take Stephen to the station for further questioning?"

He rubbed his mouth in a familiar gesture, his mind still on the distance between the stage door telephone and the dressing room. "Not for the moment," he said after a few seconds. "Let's see if we can find the costume."

He continued down the corridor and stopped outside the chorus room, looked to his right towards the door to the haunted passage, then back to the stage door.

"We'll take Maggie McCormak's statement next," he said still absorbed in his train of thought. "Forensics have been over all the dressing rooms, haven't they?"

"Yes, Guv. And uniform have searched every inch of the building. They've brought their best dog in now. If the weapon's here they'll find it."

"Good." He opened the door to the chorus room. "Bring Fay in after we've spoken to Maggie, and Maggie can stay with her if she likes."

"The chorus have asked if they can go home. Crowther's taken their statements. They were all on stage at the time of the murder, so they can't be suspects. Shall I let them go?"

He looked up. "No one goes," he said sharply. "Not until I have read and approved the statements."

"Fine," she said, giving him the squirrel look. "Why don't you get yourself a coffee from the machine upstairs?"

He didn't answer, but when she went to get Maggie, he went to the Green Room and did as she suggested. The coffee was sweet and frothy, and it hit the right spot. He bought Alison a cup too, careful to press the No Sugar button.

In the chorus room he had to move an assortment of make-up and sweet wrappers to find a place to put the plastic cups down. He pushed half-drunk, lipstick-stained bottles of mineral water to one end. He was amazed at the quantity of make-up, brushes and gadgets the young dancers needed. Three gadgets were plugged into a single adapter in the wall socket – a pair of curling tongs, some-thing with *hair-straightener* written across the plastic casing, and a third he couldn't make out. He turned it one way then another, then squinted between the ridges; finally, holding it at an angle towards the light, he made out the word *Crimpers*. He was none the wiser, but they all felt too hot, so he pulled the plugs from the wall.

In the far corner stood a tall can of men's deodorant, and a red plastic container with *Afro-Caribbean Powder* written across the lid. A packet of Marlboro Lights also marked the place, a green plastic throwaway lighter beside them. He didn't need his detective skills to work out that they belonged to Trevor Bruce, the boy dancer, who had obviously moved in with the girls to keep them company since the death of Lucinda.

Maggie and Fay had made themselves a place at the other side of the room, on the floor in front of the floor-to-ceiling mirror. With a shock he caught sight of the back of his head in the mirror; his balding patch was worse than he had thought. He told himself he wouldn't worry about it; at least he had lived long enough to start ageing. Nevertheless he lifted the collar of his sheepskin coat to hide the view.

He sipped the coffee and read the messages on the Good Luck cards that decorated the mirrors in front of the crowded dressing table. There was a card signed by Lucinda, and another from Sophie, both written only days ago. Now both of them were dead. A deep sick feeling filled the pit of his stomach, and he didn't know if it was grief for himself or for the girls' families.

One thing he did know was that four of his team were on duty, and they had failed to prevent a second murder. Sophie's mother would never wake up happy again.

He gave himself a mental shake. Alison was right: if he let his personal feelings get in the way, they would cloud his thinking and give the killer an edge. But Banham wasn't a quitter; he was going to put this murderer behind bars. Sophie's mother wouldn't be let down as he had been over his lovely Diane and little Elizabeth. This was the reason he had moved from uniform to CID and applied to join the murder division: to bring killers to justice.

His mind was working overtime: how long would it take to come off the stage, get the knife from wherever the killer had hidden it, then get down in the basement, cut Sophie's throat, come back up one of the staircases, hide the knife again, and go to wherever they had to be on the stage – all without anyone noticing? Whoever had murdered Sophie would have had to be quick; getting the knife from its hiding place would take time…

Unless… A light seemed to go on inside his head. What if the knife was hidden somewhere on the stage? That was the one area which hadn't had a thorough search.

A maroon sheepskin jacket hung on a rail by the door. He recognised it as Maggie's; she had been wearing it last night, after Lucinda's death. He slipped his hand in the pocket and felt a piece of paper. He pulled out a cheque, made out to her, signed by Michael – for the sum of five thousand pounds. He quickly replaced it as the door opened; Alison came in, followed by Maggie.

Maggie settled herself on the canvas chair in the corner without waiting to be asked. She was dressed in her street clothes, a white, low-cut t-shirt, heavily decorated with silver diamante and tucked into blue, figure-hugging jeans. She crossed her legs so that the frayed slit on the top of the thigh was in full view, allowing tanned skin to peep through. She clutched the edge of her red angora cardigan round her shoulders as if she was cold.

Her eyes were very brown and set quite close together, and her hair heavily streaked with thick blonde highlights. Banham perched on the far end of the dresser, arms folded. He watched her for a few moments; she checked her appearance in the mirror, and lifted a hand, heavily decorated with gold jewellery, to hook a lock of hair behind her ear. He realised she wasn't cold at all, but was holding the cardigan to prevent it obscuring his view of her ample bosom. She hooked her hair behind her ear again, apparently enjoying the attention.

Alison settled in a chair next to Banham and opened her notebook.

"When was the last time you saw Sophie?" he asked Maggie.

Maggie voice had a hard edge and she had obviously trained herself not to drop her hs and ts. But she hadn't trained away her flat estuary accent. "To talk to?" she asked.

"Yes."

"In the interval, when we were rehearsing the moves for the UV scene."

Banham's hand unconsciously strayed to his mouth.

"But I actually saw her last during the 'Only Man on the Island' scene." She crossed one leg over the other, and turned at an angle which revealed more of her large breasts. Banham noticed the dark flecks in Alison's eyes; she didn't like this woman.

"She was standing by the stage waiting to make her

entrance." Maggie's bosom rose as she took a thoughtful breath. "While we were on stage."

"Did you see anyone else in the wings at that time?" Banham asked.

"Alan, my husband, should have been – not where she was, but on the opposite side. But he wasn't. I didn't know that at the time, the bloody cat's head had slipped, it was all lopsided, and the netting I'm supposed to see through was practically under my chin. I could hardly see anything. Fay was leading me around the stage, and then off at the end of the scene. That's when she said Daddy had gone off to the pub again."

"But you saw Sophie on the other side of the stage waiting to go on?"

There was a beat, then she nodded. "Yeah, I saw her there, before my head slipped. She was watching the scene and didn't look pleased."

She flicked at her hair, and Banham studied her. She had a sharp mind and a cunning face. But she was obviously nervous and trying hard to hide it.

"Where did you go when you left the stage?"

"To the loo. To sort out the cat's head." The fingers flicked at her hair again.

"Which loo?"

"The ground floor one, next door to here – it's the nearest. Fay had to lead me. That's when she told me about Alan going walkies." She looked away, clearly uncomfortable now. "He really can't help himself," she added. "He can't handle it when people start getting nasty."

"Was anyone else in the loo?" he asked.

"Yeah, Barbara was in there."

"How long were you there?"

"Just long enough to fix the cat's head. I took it off and

Fay showed me how to tighten the back so it fitted me and wouldn't slip." She shrugged. "Well, then I went after my old man. When I came back everyone was looking for Sophie."

"Did anyone see you go into the pub?"

She looked a little surprised. "A lot of people would have noticed a woman with a large cat's head under her arm," she said.

"You went via the stage door?"

"Yes."

"Was anyone nearby?"

She thought for a moment. "No, I don't think so."

Banham folded his arms. "How well do you know Michael Hogan? he asked her.

Maggie became still. "I work for him," she said, turning her hard eyes on Banham. "We all do, all our family, and have done for many years. He's a…" She paused, and Banham's eyes held hers. She was first to look away, and the finger pushed her hair behind her ears again. "He's a good friend too."

Banham's mouth curved in a tiny questioning smile. "A good friend?"

"Yeah." She pursed her lips. "I do the wardrobe, and I help out with stage management when my husband finds it all a bit much. And I look after the children in the show. General duties really – anything Michael needs."

"How much does he pay you?"

"Gosh! One thousand pounds a week, that's for all of us, including Fay. Hardly a fortune."

"Sounds pretty good to me," Banham said. Then, holding her eyes, he asked, "Who is Fay's father?"

"I beg your pardon?"

He turned to the mirror and adjusted his collar. "Fay's

father," he repeated. "Who is he?"

She looked at Alison. "Do I have to tell him that?" she asked.

"Yes," Alison said bluntly.

"I don't think I do," she said looking back at Banham.

"Answer the question please," Banham said in a tone that brooked no argument.

"It isn't relevant," she said, tilting her chin. "I refuse."

"A young woman has been murdered in cold blood," Banham said coldly, "and someone in this building murdered her. I'll decide what's relevant."

She shrugged. "All right. The truth is I don't know." She began to massage the skin behind her ears. "I really don't."

"But Michael Hogan thinks he's her father – so he keeps your husband in a job, and he gives you money."

Maggie was staring at the ground.

"Doesn't he?" Banham shouted.

"Yes." Her hard front was starting to crumble.

"And I bet you didn't like it that he thought more of Sophie than your daughter…"

Her head shot up. "No, he didn't."

Alison opened her mouth to speak, but Banham got in first. "Michael's heavily in debt, but he still keeps you and your family."

"We work for him."

"And you get very well paid for it. Did Sophie know that? Did you argue with her over it?"

"Is that an accusation?" Maggie's voice was full of panic. "Are you accusing me of…"

"Guv!"

Banham ignored Alison's plea. "Where is the red and white bathing costume that Stephen changed out of after his last scene?" he asked Maggie.

"I don't know. Ask Stephen." She was one frightened lady now.

"He told me to ask you."

She opened her mouth and closed it, shook her head, fidgeted with her hair again. "I don't know," she said, clearly more agitated than she sounded.

Banham took a deep breath to calm himself. "You are responsible for the wardrobe?"

"Well, yes, but…" The fingers raked her hair again.

"But what?" He raised his voice again. "If it's your responsibility, why don't you know?"

She lowered her eyes. "I was playing the cat today. I wasn't doing wardrobe duties."

"So who was?"

She shrugged. "No one."

Banham took a deep breath. "OK. So where should it be?"

"In Stephen's dressing room. Or if he wanted it washed he'd have put it in the laundry basket in the corridor." She raised her eyes and looked him in the face. "That's common knowledge," she said quietly. "Costumes are either in the dressing room, ready for the next performance, or in the laundry basket waiting to be washed."

Banham rubbed his mouth. "Do you know anything about the spare black leotard and tights that are kept in the company office? In one of the filing cabinet drawers?"

"Yeah." She hesitated, then said, "It was originally made for Stephen, but Sophie wouldn't have him in the ultra-violet routine." She paused again. "She said some of the mothers had complained that he smelled."

Alison caught Banham's eye. "That must have created bad feeling," he said.

"No more than there was already," Maggie said

dismissively. "He and Sophie hated each other. We all knew that." The corners of her mouth turned down. "She gave him a costume change during the UV scene, so he couldn't be in it." She hesitated again, looking from Banham to Alison.

"Go on," Alison said.

"Go on where?" she said contemptuously. "There's no more to tell. The leotard and tights were made specially for Stephen 'cause the others wouldn't go anywhere near him, but after he was kicked out of the routine it got kept as a spare. That's all."

"And everyone knew where it was?" Banham asked.

She shrugged again. "I suppose."

Banham closed his eyes. Why did it have to be so hard? It was a constant struggle to keep his mind on the job when unwelcome images kept invading his thoughts.

He stood up and walked to the door. "I'll be back in five," he said to Alison, aware of the concern on her face. "I think we've finished with Mrs McCormak; can you ask one of the uniforms to fetch her daughter?"

As he closed the door behind him he registered that Maggie was looking pretty worried too.

Banham walked down the corridor a little way, then stopped and put both hands flat against the wall. He breathed deeply, fighting to clear his mind of the image of his eleven-month-old Elizabeth, her tiny chubby fingers bludgeoned and one blue eye staring up in terror.

DC Crowther appeared at his side. "Are you all right, Guv?"

He looked at the young detective. "Four officers in the building and another mother's lost her daughter – and you ask if I'm all right?"

"It's happened," Crowther said. "You're not responsible."

Banham looked at Crowther, his eyes burning with anger. "We were on surveillance and a young woman has been murdered right under our noses. How am I not responsible?"

"I'm very sorry, Guv," Crowther said, with more sincerity than Banham had ever seen in the lad.

"You will be if I find you were more interested in three half-naked girls than in being a good detective. Do I make myself clear?"

"Crystal." Crowther hung his head like a scolded school boy. "Um, Guv… Penny has just phoned through some lab results from the buccal swabs."

"And?"

"She tested Vincent Mann and Michael Hogan against the semen found inside Lucinda. At first neither matched, then she tested again, and realised the first came up negative because there were two matches. Lucinda had sex with both of them within three hours of her death. She said chances are high Michael Hogan was the last."

Banham made an effort to calm himself. "So Hogan's telling the truth. Anything yet on the large black costume that I sent separately?"

"It's in hand, Guv," Crowther said, his confidence returning.

Angry though Banham was, he couldn't dislike this lad who dressed as if he bought his clothes at the local market and didn't know what size to buy. Crowther made a lot of mistakes, but he was consistently enthusiastic, hardworking and honest.

"Get Isabelle to check the CCTV in the pub next door," Banham told him. "We need the exact time that Alan went in there, and the exact time his wife went to fetch him."

"Will do, Guv. Anything else?"

"Yes." Banham began to walk away. "Find that red and white bathing costume. It has to be here somewhere."

Beside the cordon by the spiral staircase, Banham slipped a forensic overall over his clothes and pulled on the matching shoe covers before going down to the basement.

The forensic team, all covered from head to toe in identical bluebell-coloured overalls, were still busy. He focused on a pair of hands covered in colourless gloves so fine that they could have been made of skin. They scraped at the fresh bloodstains beginning to coagulate on the rail just behind the dead girl. Sophie's lifeless blue eyes were wide and terrified. He wondered what she was thinking as the blood pumped from her neck. Just a few hours earlier he had promised her and the rest of the cast that his team would protect them during the show. Was she still alive, he wondered, as the knife carved into the thin white skin, nudging through the carotid artery and up into her jawbone?

Another forensic officer, careful not to touch the blood, delicately lifted particles and the odd hair from the floor with a pair of tweezers, and skilfully enclosed each minute piece of evidence in a see-through bag.

Max Pettifer, the elastic of the blue forensic cap clinging tightly to his receding hairline, was brushing at the blood pattern around the body. He looked up at Banham.

"I'm not surprised you're not a happy bunny," he said. "The building swarming with cops, and another murder right under your noses." His mouth widened into a sarcastic smirk. "Best not let the press in on this one."

Banham ached to take a swing at him. "Anything helpful you can tell me?" he asked flatly.

"Apart from watch where you're walking, in case there's another footprint?"

"You've got a print?"

"A faint one, and it isn't hers." Another condescending smirk. "Don't worry, we're on the ball. We've collected all the suspects' shoes, so it's just a matter of time. Another bit of luck for you: there's particles of food in the print. Find out who had what for lunch and you're home and dry."

"Unless someone walked in someone else's lunch." Banham couldn't resist a touch of one-upmanship. He nodded towards the children's dressing room at the other side of the basement. "Have you been in the passageway beyond that dressing room yet?"

"We're working our way across."

"There's a door in the wall – it leads to a passageway to the ground floor dressing rooms. It isn't used much, though it has been recently, and not just by my team." He paused. "It's rumoured to be haunted."

Max chuckled. "Oh, no worries there then, pal. We've no fear of ghosts – they pay our wages."

Banham gritted his teeth. Why did this man have to be so irritating? He walked back across the basement and up the stairway on the stage left side. Behind the scenery flap he peeled off his overall and shoe covers. The actors were all sitting in silence, immersed in their own worlds. Sonia, the tallest dancer, was in the wings on the far side, giving her statement to Crowther. The other two girls and Trevor sat on the stage huddled together for comfort. They were hardly more than kids themselves, he thought; hardly the stuff murderers were made of. Once he'd read their statements he would let them go.

The four actors were a different matter.

Barbara Denis's face was strong and hard, but sad as well. It was becoming plain that this was a dog-eat-dog profession; she probably had to be tough to survive in it.

Stephen Coombs still looked nervous and uncomfortable. He was sitting on a cheap, canvas chair that wasn't big enough for his bulk, picking at the skin around his fingernails.

Michael Hogan's face looked vacant, and Vincent Mann's was worried. He was having trouble keeping still; he sat on the floor tapping his fingers on his buttercup-yellow jeans.

Which one of them had just committed murder? He needed evidence. Why did forensics always take so long? Too much of the budget was given to other less important police work.

Michael Hogan could have had time, but he loved Sophie, so what motive did he have? Maggie wouldn't have had time if she went to the pub to get Alan – and there was CCTV to prove where Alan was. Barbara was still in the loo when Maggie went to the pub, and changed her costume as well. Vincent and Stephen both had time to commit the murder, and Stephen was sweating badly when he came to the office.

If Penny Starr could identify that footprint in the next few hours, he had the bastard. And if he did, he owed Crowther a thank-you, not a dressing down. If the young DC hadn't charmed Penny, she wouldn't have offered to give up her leave, and he would have been waiting two weeks for the evidence he needed.

Fay was crying when he went back to the chorus room. Alison was sitting patiently beside her, and Maggie was sitting on the floor cleaning the make-up from her own tearstained face.

Banham sat down beside Fay.

"Daddy left the stage in the middle of the scene," Fay said, then started crying again.

Maggie pulled a handful of tissues and brought them to her. "And when the scene finished we went to the loo to fix my head," she prompted, kneeling beside her and dabbing at her face.

"I'd like Fay to tell us in her own words," Alison said firmly.

Fay wiped her face with the back of her hands and blew her nose.

"Take your time," Banham said gently.

"Which loo did you go to, to fix the cat's head? Alison asked Fay.

"The one next door to here," Fay answered. "Barbara was in there, in the cubicle. Mummy took the cat's head off, and I tightened the elastic at the back."

"And then what did you do?"

"I ran to the pub to get Daddy. Everyone was looking at me, because I was in my stage costume and carrying a cat's head."

13

Crowther was sitting on the floor by the stage, taking statements from the chorus dancers. The barking of one of the sniffer dogs distracted him, and he stood up and followed the agitated sound into the corridor.

The dog had picked up a scent and stood barking frantically on the step leading to the haunted passage, its back arched and paw scraping. The animal had been given another of Stephen's costumes to pick up the scent, and clearly he had done his job.

A second dog was now barking too, but neither of the two handlers could find what had caught their attention. They opened the door to the passage, but the dogs pulled back and scraped insistently at the wooden step again. A couple more uniformed police crouched on the floor, prodding at the area around the step.

A tall probationary officer, his uniform jacket too short for his arms, reached over and stroked the side of the step. The dog became even more agitated.

Michael Hogan was standing behind DC Crowther. "There's a lip at the side of the step," he told them. "Put your hand under that and the step will lift up like a trinket box. Shall I show you?"

Crowther hadn't realised Michael had followed him. "No," he said quickly. "We'll sort it. Go back to the stage. Please."

The young constable's hand moved down the side of the step and located the lip. It opened, as Michael had said, like the lid of a box.

Inside was Stephen Coombs's red and white bathing costume.

The first thing Banham saw when he and Alison came out to find out what was going on was Michael Hogan disappearing through the door to the stage. Crowther and a small crowd of uniformed and blue-clad forensic officers now surrounded the entrance to the passage. Max Pettifer had been in the secret passage; he was standing by the step with a see-through evidence bag. He carefully lifted the bloodstained costume in his gloved hands, and was about to drop it into the evidence bag when something slipped from inside it. Max managed to catch it before it hit the floor: a large, sharp knife, smeared with blood. He looked round for another evidence bag, which another forensic officer handed him.

"Looks like the ghosts have been busy," Pettifer said. "You're in luck; that should save you a bit of face with the national newspapers."

Crowther held out his hand for the bag. "I'll take that," he said cockily. "I'll drive over to the lab so Penny can work on it straight away."

Banham opened his mouth to remind Crowther that it wasn't his call, but Max Pettifer hadn't finished. The SOCO officer twisted his mouth into an insincere smile and said, "DCI Cartwright is still on that cruise until the day after tomorrow. With all that overtime from Penny Starr, you'll have the case sewn up by the time he gets back. It'll do young Crowther's promotion prospects the world of good. You should ask him to put in a good word for you."

Banham's eyes flared but he didn't answer. Instead he spoke to Crowther, "Isabelle can drive the evidence to the lab," he said. "I want you to arrest Stephen Coombs, and take him to the station."

"Aw, Guv…" Crowther protested.

Banham's eyes hardened, but he kept his voice low. "Don't push it, Crowther; you're already in trouble. I want Penny's mind kept on the job. Go and arrest that bastard."

Alison was frowning at him; another dissenter. "Arrange for uniform to drive the rest of the cast to the station," he told her crisply. "But keep Maggie and Fay apart until we've checked the pub's CCTV." Alison didn't move. "What now?" he asked irritably.

"Far be it for me to contest my DI's orders," she said quietly. "But remember the only reason that Penny is working over her Christmas holiday is because she's madly in love with Crowther."

"Work is what I want her to do! This is a murder investigation in case you'd forgotten!"

Crowther and Alison exchanged chastened glances.

Banham was in his stride now. "I want to talk to Barbara Denis before you take her to the station. She was in the ground floor toilet at the same time as Maggie and Fay McCormak."

The stage door banged closed and DC Isabelle Walsh appeared. "I've just heard you've found the weapon," she said. "That's great. I've got the CCTV footage from the Feathers. And I've spoken to the barman. He said the young girl ran in, and shouted, 'Daddy, you've got to come back now.' And there was a blonde woman behind her."

Everyone began to talk at once, and Banham had to shout to make himself heard.

"OK," he said when he was sure they were all listening. "Here's what we're going to do. Isabelle, you can organise getting the cast to the station for official statements. Then you can go through the pub's CCTV. Crowther, bring me the dancers' statements. As soon as I've had a look through them, they're free to go. Make sure you've got their contact details, though – we may need to speak to them again."

"How will they get home? Shall I drop them off?" Crowther said.

"For goodness' sake," Banham snapped, "it's five o'clock in the afternoon and public transport is running."

"They've had a terrible shock, Guv, I just thought…"

"That's family liaison's job. Fancy a transfer to them, do you, Crowther?"

"No, no, no." Crowther backed off.

"Then go and arrest Stephen Coombs."

"Guv." Crowther set off towards Stephen's dressing room. "Trevor Bruce, the black boy, wasn't on stage for most of that dance," he said over his shoulder. "You know that, don't you, Guv?"

Banham nodded. "He was changing his costume when I was looking for Sophie. I saw him in his dressing room. And you've taken his statement?"

"Yes, Guv. He only did the first half-minute of that dance routine. He walked on stage on his hands and turned a couple of somersaults, then he lifted the girls on to the stage one by one. That was it – he went off to change then. That left about eleven minutes unaccounted for."

"I'll bear that in mind," Banham said, fixing Crowther with his hardest stare. The young DC beat a hasty retreat towards Stephen Coombs's dressing room.

"Have we got anything to link Stephen to Lucinda's murder?" Isabelle asked Banham. He looked at Alison, who shook her head.

"Not unless there's something on the costume from Michael Hogan's office. We haven't had the forensics back yet. That was the only one big enough to fit Stephen – if we can link that to Lucinda, we've got enough."

Banham watched thoughtfully as Crowther marched

182

Stephen out of the door. "The murders were so different," he said. "But I still believe it was the same killer. What I'm not certain of is why he killed Lucinda."

"Lucinda's killer was very strong, Guv." This was Isabelle again. "That stage weight is so heavy, I couldn't lift it. Stephen Coombs is a very big bloke – he would have had no difficulty."

"Trevor would have no trouble either," Alison said. "He's fitter and stronger than Stephen. But he was in the front line for the UV routine, so he's out of the frame."

"Alison lifted that stage weight," Isabelle joked to Banham. "She's got some muscle on her. Cop a feel of that!" She squeezed the top of Alison's arm and Alison snatched it away.

"Everyone in the cast could lift that stage weight," she said, putting some distance between herself and Isabelle. "Dance training builds your muscles and gives you strength."

"Even Fay?" Banham asked.

"No, possibly not Fay," Alison conceded.

"We're relying on the forensics tests for something on that black costume then," Banham said.

"Good old Crowther," Isabelle answered dryly. "He's going to be the office hero, and all for screwing Penny Starr."

Alison felt Banham's eyes on her as she dug in her bag for her notebook. "What?" she asked, checking her reflection in the mirror on the dressing room wall. "Have I got coffee froth on my mouth again?" She flicked her ponytail behind her ears and wiped her mouth with the back of her hand.

"No."

"What, then?"

"I'm looking at your muscles."

She flushed. "Can we keep personal remarks out of this?"

He lowered his eyes. "Of course," he said. "I apologise."

"Good."

"But you have got great muscles, and you should be proud of them," he added, realising how lame it sounded.

The black flecks in her eyes started to shine. "I'm more proud of my karate training. It means I can deal with any bloke who makes sexist remarks."

Before Banham could respond the door opened to admit Barbara Denis. She settled herself in the chair in front of her mirror as if she had every right to be there. Which of course under normal circumstances she had, Banham thought.

She had removed her thick stage make-up and her face was taut, pinched and heavily lined. Her skin was pale and her lips colourless. Her speckled grey-blonde hair was pulled into the nape of her neck and secured with a thick black scrunchy. She wore a thick, well worn grey wool jumper, over black leggings tucked into black snow boots. She was thinner than any of the chorus girls; from the back she could have been an eighteen-year-old, but from the front, without the help of make-up, she now looked her age.

Alison ran a finger down Barbara's statement. "You said earlier that you went straight to the loo when you came off stage."

"That's right."

"Were you in there when Maggie and Fay came in?"

"Yes. I was dying to go, so I headed straight there. Maggie and Fay were struggling with the cat's head in the wings. They followed a minute or so later."

"How long were they in there?" Banham asked.

"I heard them fiddling with the cat's head. Fay was telling Maggie how to stop it from slipping. Then they went out."

"Did you hear them say where they were going?"

"No. Fay showed Maggie how to fix the clips on the head, in case it slipped again, but I didn't hear them mention anything else." She shook her head slowly. "To be honest I wasn't paying much attention. It didn't seem important at the time."

"Did you notice anything unusual at the end of that last scene before Sophie made her last appearance?" Banham asked her.

Barbara nodded. "Yes, Stephen exited stage right, that I can say for sure. He never does that. All his exits are stage left, nearest his dressing room, because of his quick changes." She pulled the black velveteen scrunchy out and shook her hair free, then gathered it in her hands and slipped the band back. "Stephen and Vincent had been arguing on stage again. Maggie and Fay were all over the place because of the cat's head. Alan walked off in the middle of the scene, but that's not unusual as you know. It's unprofessional of course, but that's what I have to put up with." She lifted her hands in the air. "Oh, that's not important now."

"Did Maggie and Fay leave the toilet together?" Alison asked.

"I'm afraid I couldn't be sure of that. I wasn't taking a lot of notice. I was in the cubicle doing my own thing."

"How long were you in there?" Banham asked a little self-consciously.

She looked as embarrassed as he felt. "As long as it took me to go."

Alison was trying to hide her amusement; he deliberately

avoided her eyes. "And then what did you do?" he asked Barbara.

"I came in here; I have to change my costume at that point in the show, to get ready for the Palace of the Sultan of Morocco scene."

"Did anyone see you?" Alison asked.

"Yes – as it happens, Trevor did. Normally I don't see anyone, because of course the star of the show doesn't have to share a dressing room." She caught sight of herself in the mirror and raked long thin fingers through the front of her hair. "But today Trevor knocked on the door. He was doing his own change, into the King Rat costume, and his cigarette lighter wouldn't work. He asked to borrow mine."

"That would have been towards the end of the dancers' scene?"

"Probably. He only does the lifts at the beginning, then he has to come off and change into that big King Rat skin." She looked at the ceiling. "Budgets again, I'm afraid."

Suddenly she pressed her lips together and the lines on her forehead deepened. She opened her mouth to speak, then seemed to think better of it. Banham lifted his eyebrows.

"I know it's a million times worse for Valerie, and for Lucinda's family," she said, "but I really needed this show to work. Not only because I have to try to resurrect my career and pay my bills, but for Michael. He needs the money desperately, he's in so much debt." She looked sadly at Banham. "So that's why I'm so tough about standards, and everyone hates me…" Her voice trailed off and she gazed at the wall.

Banham leaned forward. "Go on, Barbara."

She looked squarely at Banham and Alison. "I think we

could have been in the wrong order in the UV routine last night," she said. "Lucinda was where I should have been."

"Ah." Banham exchanged glances with Alison. "Are you saying you think someone tried to kill you?" he asked.

Fear crossed Barbara's face. "Possibly."

"Who?" Alison said quickly. "Who hates you enough to want you dead?"

Banham watched her closely.

"Stephen," she said quietly. "Maggie is blackmailing Michael, and that whole family knows that I know."

"When you say that whole family, you mean Fay, Alan, Maggie and Stephen?"

She nodded. "But Alan isn't capable of murder, and Fay was in the line in front of us in the UV scene."

"Which leaves Stephen and Maggie," Alison said, looking at Banham.

There was another pause. Barbara looked away, then said, "Lucinda told me Stephen had a large knife in the boot of his car. She said when she asked him about it, he told her he goes fishing, and he uses it for gutting his catch."

"Does he go fishing?" Alison asked her.

"He never has to my knowledge."

Trevor looked frightened to death. He stood in the doorway of the chorus room and waited for Banham and Alison to tell him to take a seat before choosing his own chair at the corner of the dresser.

"Feel free to smoke, if you like," Banham said. "I'd offer you a cigarette only I don't."

"Oh, I've got some here, man." Trevor opened a packet of Marlboro Lights and put one in his mouth.

"How long a break do you have between the dancing and the Sultan of Morocco scene?" Alison asked him.

"About ten minutes, and I have a change."

"And a cigarette?" Banham asked casually.

"'Fraid so." The way he put his hand to his mouth reminded Banham of a naughty schoolboy.

"Today too?"

"Yes." He lifted his lighter. "I got a light from Barbara; she's the only one in the company that smokes. She'll vouch for me. My lighter wouldn't work."

"It's working now," Banham remarked.

"It was wet. Someone knocked water over it, I suppose," he said with a shrug. "It's a bit overcrowded in here. There's four of us dancers and now we've got Maggie and Fay too." He looked at Banham and then over to Alison who was writing. "I dried it on the radiator."

The boy's brown eyes bulged fearfully. Banham thought he looked like a frog. "I noticed you were very shaky earlier," he said.

"I always am, man. Have you seen what I have to do at the beginning of the dance? I walk on on my hands, then I do a triple somersault, then one by one I have to lift the dancers and carry them on. That's enough to make anyone shake, man."

"Is it?" Banham said flatly.

"Yes, it is," he said nearly spelling out the words.

"Did you know about the hidden staircase behind the door at the end of this corridor? Alison asked him.

"I didn't until a few minutes ago. The girls told me."

His grey towelling dressing gown had heavy perspiration stains under the arms and another large patch down the middle of his back. He was tall, broad, and very muscular. He looked Afro-Caribbean but his accent was pure London. Banham put him at no more than twenty-one or -two.

"Have you ever worked in this theatre before?" Alison

asked.

"No, never."

He took a nervous drag on his cigarette and tapped the ash several times over the small, rusting metal bin by his chair. "I've been here before though," he said. "I came to see a mate of mine in a show in the summer. He was on tour and they were playing here for a week. I came backstage after the performance."

He inhaled and flicked his cigarette again, several times.

"Did you see anyone in the corridor when you came off stage to change?" Banham asked him.

Trevor's bulbous brown eyes moved from side to side, making the whites even more prominent. After a second he said, "Yeah, I saw Stephen, the dame."

Banham's chin lifted a fraction. "Where was this?"

"In the corridor. He was going in his dressing room as I was going into Barbara's for a light."

"Coming from where?" Banham asked quickly.

"I presumed the loo. There is only the loo, this room, the boys' room, and Barbara's room along here. It wouldn't have been Barbara's room, they hate each other, and I had just come out of this room, so it…"

"Which direction?"

Trevor shook his head, as if trying to remember. "From the upstage end?"

"Near the haunted staircase," Banham said.

"I suppose. As I said I didn't know about the passageway then, and I wasn't taking much notice at the time. People come and go all through the show and you don't wonder about it."

"Isn't the loo down here a ladies'?" Banham said.

The tension seemed to slide from Trevor's face. He looked at Alison and his face broke into a wide smile.

"Gents or ladies, no one cares. They're all unisex around here," he said with an amused shrug.

Banham glanced at Alison. She was amused too. He looked at the floor to hide his embarrassment.

"When did you first realise that Sophie was missing?" Alison asked Trevor.

"When Mr… er…?" He looked at Banham questioningly.

"Banham, D I Banham."

"When Mr D I Banham came in here. I was changing into my King Rat costume and you were looking for her."

Banham nodded. "Thank you, Trevor, that's been very helpful. I'll need you to come to the station and make an official statement."

He opened the door and left the room.

"Is that it?" Trevor asked.

"For now." Alison got up and followed Banham. As she reached the door she looked over her shoulder. Trevor was tapping his cigarette on the dustbin again, and the fear had returned to his face.

14

Before setting off for the station, Banham gave his sister a call on his mobile. Lottie worried about him, and her little family was almost like his own.

"Madeleine lost her first tooth this afternoon," she told him. "Scared her half to death – she was in floods of tears."

He smiled; if a lost tooth was the most frightening thing that ever happened to Maddie, she'd have a great life.

"Let me talk to her," he said to Lottie.

Maddie still sounded tearful. He comforted her and told her to wrap the tooth in a tissue and put it under her pillow.

"Why?" she asked him.

"Because Miranda the tooth fairy is looking for teeth to build a grand stairway in the palace for the wedding of Cinderella and Prince Charming. I'll give her a call, shall I?"

"What will she do?" Maddie stopped crying as Banham explained that Fairy Miranda would take the tooth and leave a pound coin for her moneybox. "But you have to go to sleep first – fairies don't come while you're awake."

"Like Father Christmas."

"Yes – just like Father Christmas."

His sister's house was almost on the way to the station. When he arrived, Lottie put a finger to her lips to shush him. "I think she's asleep. You're brilliant, you are!"

"Have you got a bit of silver foil?"

"What for?"

"To wrap this in." He held up a pound coin.

Lottie gave him a strip of kitchen foil, and he wrapped it round the coin. Then he quietly crept into Maddie's room and carefully placed it under the sleeping child's pillow.

It turned into another late night at the station, taking statements from all the actors and production staff. Maggie McCormak changed her original statement; she now said she followed Fay into the pub to haul Alan out, and Fay had been carrying the cat's head. Alan's statement confirmed that Maggie was following Fay.

When the statements were completed Banham conferred with Alison about the next day's allocation of tasks.

"I want Isabelle to go through that CCTV footage and report back to me," he said. "If it confirms Maggie McCormak's statement, she and her daughter can be released."

"That will take her most of the morning, Guv."

"Should be done by the time we get Sophie's post mortem results, then."

"Are you going to interview Stephen Coombs?"

"No, you and Crowther can do that. It'll keep him out of Penny's hair – if Coombs is still refusing to confess, we'll need the forensic evidence before we can charge him."

"That could be another twenty-four hours, Guv."

"Yes, but it's just a formality. A full confession would make our job a lot easier, but he'll fold when he realises there's no way out."

"What about you? Where will you be?"

"There's something I have to do. I'll be at the station by midday."

The something was Banham's first appointment with Joan Deamer, the sex therapist. He had thought long and hard, and decided to keep it. Alison was more than capable of overseeing things at the station, and though he was tired and more than a little apprehensive, it was time he began to face his demons.

He hadn't yet met Mrs Deamer, and was dreading it. The thought of talking about his non existent sex life face to face with an attractive young woman made him want the floor to open up and swallow him.

Luck was on his side. She was old enough to be his mother, and made it easy for him to open up. All the same, for the first twenty minutes he was tense and monosyllabic, answering her gentle, carefully phrased questions with yes or no. Then she asked if he wanted to talk about the case he was working on - and a floodgate opened. Tears overcame him as he described walking through the children's dressing room into the basement, and seeing Sophie lying in Michael's arms, her head hanging back and her white neck open from ear to ear, blood covering her face and arms and soaking into the shiny white fairy dress.

Then the memory he had been pushing back, of finding his wife and baby Elizabeth lying in their own blood, flew into his mind and shook him like a hound with a rat. He heard himself tell Mrs Deamer what a failure he felt, as a detective as well as a husband and a father.

"I let them down. I wasn't there to protect them, and I couldn't even track down the bastards who did that to them."

"Were they never caught?"

"We didn't come close. They're still out there somewhere – and not a day passes when I don't imagine how long it took Diane and Elizabeth to die, and how much pain they had to endure first. And it was all my fault."

Sobs overcame him again, and he huddled in the chair,

shoulders shaking and tears pouring down his face.

"Tell me why you blame yourself. When you're ready. Take your time."

The therapist's soft voice had a calming effect. He took the handful of tissues she held out and mopped his face.

"I stayed late at work that evening. I was always staying late – I was desperate to make a good impression, I wanted promotion so badly. There was a fight outside the football ground after a match, and I had to write up the statements…"

Ten years of grief seemed intent on pouring out of him. He told her how he would give anything to change places with them, to have taken the fatal beating himself, to save them from all the pain and fear they endured before they died.

Mrs Deamer barely blinked as she listened, only moving once to offer more tissues when his tears began to flow again.

"Let me ask you something else now," she said when the wave of grief began to subside, leaving slight embarrassment in its wake. "What are you hoping to get out of these sessions? What would you like to achieve?"

"What do you mean?"

"Clearly you want to come to terms with your grief and move on. But where do you want to move to? Another relationship, perhaps? It's been eleven years, after all. Have you had any relationships in that time?"

"I… I can't."

"Can't what?"

"Have a relationship."

"You mean you can't commit yourself to another woman?"

"Yes, and…"

She waited, and he looked at her helplessly.

"I'm guessing that since I'm a sex therapist, you're telling me you can't have sex."

He nodded, relieved not to have to spell it out to this kind-faced woman.

"And is there someone you'd like to have sex with? Is that why you decided to seek my help?"

Banham nodded again. "Someone at work. My sergeant, actually. We've been good friends for a while, and I asked her out, but then when we… got close… I… I couldn't. I let her down."

"You were impotent?"

There, it was out in the open. He nodded, feeling as if something inside him had been released.

Mrs Deamer led him gently through his futile attempts to get close to any woman over the past eleven years, and eventually to his feelings for Alison. He had no idea how she did it, but by the end of the hour he was feeling lighter, less trapped and more optimistic than he could remember. Mrs Deamer thanked him for talking to her and suggested he make an appointment for the same time next week. "We've made some progress," she said, "but there's still a long way to go."

As he stood up to leave she asked if he had any questions for her.

"Do you think you can cure me?" he asked with a rueful smile.

She looked at him from behind her large glasses. "I doubt it, but I might be able to help you cure yourself."

He opened the door and turned to thank her again.

"We have something in common, you and I," she said. "I do manage to save some of my patients. Not all, but some."

As he walked down the street outside her office, he felt as if he had finally started to crack the heavy carapace that had shielded him from life for so many years. It was a crisp, cold morning and the sun was shining; the mortuary was only a few streets away, and he decided to walk there and pick up the post mortem report on Sophie Flint before making his way back to the station. On the way he rang Lottie's house, and Madeleine picked up the phone.

"Did Fairy Miranda tell you she came to my house, Uncle Paul?" the little girl asked him excitedly. "I put my tooth under the pillow like you said, and when I woke up there was a silver coin."

"That's great, Maddie. What are you going to do with it?"

"It's in my money box. I'm saving up to buy *Mary Poppins* on a CD." She sang the first line of *A Spoonful of Sugar Helps the Medicine Go Down* in a clear, sweet voice, and he heard himself hum along. He and Lottie had taken the children to see the film a couple of weeks before Christmas, and Maddie had been entranced. He ended the call with a promise to visit them later in the week, and made a mental note to buy her the CD himself.

At the mortuary his positive energy started to evaporate, and he regretted the decision to go there. The smell of death, disinfectant, and stale flesh was too evocative; his hands began to tremble as he breathed it in.

Heather Draper, the pathologist, looked surprised to see him, but if she noticed him shaking she made no comment. She handed him the report and said, "This one should be quite straightforward. I gather you've already got the murder weapon."

"Anything I should know?"

"There's no sign of recent intercourse this time." She

thought for a moment, then continued, "Forensics picked up some crumbs on the floor in the basement, didn't they? Well, her stomach contents contain pizza. She ate it within a couple of hours of death."

When he arrived at the station the smell of freshly baked fruitcake lingered down the corridor as far as the lift. He followed the aroma to the staff canteen, where an array of metallic helium balloons bobbed from the ceiling. One bore the greeting Happy Birthday; another had a large 30 across one side.

Peggy the motherly canteen manageress explained. "It's a party for Wendy Roberts. It's her first day back on the beat." She poured coffee for Banham from a large metal pot, and he recalled the incident which had put the young WPC in hospital for two months. She had been stabbed in the stomach breaking up a street fight and almost lost her life; the two months had been followed by five more at home recuperating. "She was unconscious on her birthday," Peggy told him, "and uniform are giving her a belated party. It's a welcome back as well."

She indicated the collection bowl on the counter for contributions and Banham took a five pound note out of his wallet. He hardly knew Wendy Roberts, but he was glad she had survived her ordeal. Her attacker was behind bars. His own wife and child hadn't been so lucky.

He found he could think about it calmly now, without the horrifying flashback images flooding his mind. Perhaps this therapy thing had its uses.

The pink heart-shaped balloon bobbed in front of him as he sat down with his coffee and the pathologist's reports. Diane had never reached thirty; she and Elizabeth had been dead for over a year when his own thirtieth birthday came around, and on that day he had made them a promise that he would find their killer. He had failed them.

He wasn't going to fail the two dead actresses. All he needed was confirmation from forensics, then he would charge Stephen Coombs with Sophie's murder. He had nothing yet to help him pin Lucinda's murder on the man, but there was a nagging feeling in his stomach that he had missed something. He decided to interview Coombs himself, and push hard for a confession.

He opened the report and heaped sugar into his coffee. Alison had hinted that he should give up sugar for his New Year's resolution, suggesting that his waistline was expanding, but there were still two days of the old year to go. He actually had no intention of giving it up; he had other resolutions, much more important than the odd spoonful of sugar. This was the year when he would face his dragons and overcome them. He was over the first hurdle; he'd met the therapist and had managed to open up and admit his fears and feelings during the first session. He had left feeling positive, even if it was shortlived. Next time might be better still, and if the improvement continued his sexual problems might even disappear, and he could try to pluck up the courage to ask Alison to give him another chance.

He sipped the coffee and reread Lucinda's report. There was brain movement prior to the haemorrhage which killed her, proving the blow to the side of her head was delivered before she fell. Without a doubt, then, the fall was no accident - someone had hit her.

Bruise marks a few days old were found on Lucinda's cheeks and upper arms. They tied in with the notes in Sophie's diary about Stephen Coombs's attack on Lucinda a few days earlier. Stephen's only response to a question about the bullying was a terse "No comment."

Sophie's diary had also recorded that Vincent Mann had hit Lucinda on the day before her death. There were small abrasions above the bruising on her arm, and the skin had been broken. So whoever had gripped her and shaken her wore something sharp – jewellery, perhaps. Michael Hogan, Barbara Denis, Alan McCormak and his wife Maggie all wore watches, but Banham had noticed they took them off before going on stage. Even the dancers wore strange bracelets in the Sultan of Morocco scene, curled around their bare arms up to their shoulders; they looked distinctly scratchy. Vincent Mann wore a thick gold identity bracelet.

The marks probably came from Vincent; he had already admitted he had a temper. But would he have wanted to kill her? A man who had given up his own salary to get his lover a job was an unlikely murderer.

It all pointed to Stephen Coombs. And Sophie found out so he had to kill her too.

He took a sip of his sweet coffee and picked up the other post mortem report. Sophie's murder was quite different. Her throat was cut by a knife, six to eight inches long and razor sharp, a kind used by butchers, but on sale in shops as well. That murder was cold and calculated. Penny Starr's tests of both the knife and the bathing costume had revealed Stephen's DNA, and shown that the blood on them was Sophie's. Of course his costume would be covered in his DNA, Banham reasoned; and since the knife was wrapped in the costume, the DNA would transfer to it.

Some bodily fluid found on Sophie's face also matched Stephen's DNA. He could have put a sweaty hand around her face before he cut her throat. Stephen's explanation was that he had a cold, and sprayed saliva on everyone when he said his lines. But Stephen never stood close to Sophie on stage; in her fairy scenes she stood at the side of the stage talking to the audience.

Banham took out a pen and began to list the evidence he would need to bring Stephen Coombs to trial.

The crumbs on the floor by the footprint in the basement could have fallen from Stephen's clothes; he had admitted eating pizza earlier in the day. But so had everyone in the show; they had sent out to Pizza Hut for lunch as they had been rehearsing until five minutes before curtain up.

If forensics proved that the footprint was Stephen's he had the bastard; Stephen had said he didn't go down to the basement.

If the tests on the black costume in the office came up positive with fragments from the stage weight, that was Lucinda accounted for. Sophie was about to make a written statement saying that Stephen hadn't changed his costume during the UV scene on the night of Lucinda's murder and that he always changed during that scene – but Sophie was murdered before she could make that statement. This supported the theory that Stephen killed Sophie to silence her because she found out about Lucinda's murder.

Stephen claimed he had changed as he always did, but he was cold and had wrapped his green dressing gown over the bathing costume. He had also argued that without her glasses Sophie couldn't see her hand in front of her face – but her mother said she wore contact lenses.

So many ifs, so many contradictions. He felt as if his head would explode. He gave himself a shake and swallowed the last of his coffee.

At the same moment Alison walked into the canteen. She looked quite different from the previous day. She wore a clingy cream t-shirt over khaki jeans, with ankle length brown kicker boots, and a thick rust-coloured sweater tied around her waist. Her hair was pulled into a pony-tail, and she had obviously spent some time twisting it into an elaborate braid; it hung over her shoulder, and the end was decorated with a pretty brown ribbon. She was wearing eye make-up, and shiny red colour on her lips. She looked stunning, and she smelled gorgeous.

"Why are you so dressed up?" he demanded.

"Do I have to have a reason? I felt like it."

The black specks in her green eyes were shining. He decided not to pursue the subject; the look that she was giving him said very plainly that it wasn't his business. In a way it was; he realised that he cared for her, very much. But now wasn't the time to tell her.

"I've got the PM reports," he said briskly.

"And we've got some forensic results." She handed him the papers and sat down opposite him.

Banham read the report, rubbing his mouth in concentration. "Lucinda's blood and hair were on the side of the stage weight that rested against the floor and her balaclava was torn. That backs up the evidence of brain movement from the post mortem. The concrete weight was definitely lifted; she didn't fall. Without a doubt Lucinda was murdered. Trouble is, it doesn't prove Stephen Coombs murdered her." He looked at Alison, mesmerised by her reddened mouth. He wanted to kiss it. "Check that Penny has got DNA from every person that worked in the show," he said quietly. "We might have enough to frighten him into a confession."

"That isn't looking likely," Alison said warily. "Crowther's getting very wound up with him. Stephen's refused a solicitor and is answering 'No comment' to everything."

"If forensics tell us the footprint in the basement is his, we've got him," Banham said confidently. "The likelihood

201

is that Sophie knew who killed Lucinda, and that was the reason she was killed. We know Lucinda's death wasn't an accident; we just have to wait for forensics to give us a bit more."

Banham stood up. "Come on, I'll have a go at Stephen, see if I can get a confession. Sit in with me."

"I'm going to go for a bluff," he told her as they walked back along the corridor to the interview room. "I'm going to tell him that we've got the proof that the shoeprint was his."

"Good idea," Alison nodded. "Oh, I meant to say, Isabelle's finished scanning the pub's CCTV footage."

"And?"

"It shows Fay going into the pub carrying the cat's head and Maggie McCormak following a little behind. She also has written statements from a barman and a customer, and they tally: a blonde woman dressed all in black followed a young girl into the pub and yelled at Alan. The young girl was carrying a cat's head. So we've released her and Fay."

"So Fay wasn't lying."

"No. Maggie was probably trying to protect her. And listen to this: Michael Hogan came to pick up Maggie and Fay and Alan about an hour ago – and he asked for permission to carry on with the show!"

"What? I don't believe that man!"

"Nor do I. He said it's what Sophie would have wanted. The real reason is money, of course. According to his bank statements he's up to his ears in debt."

Banham shrugged. "I suppose he can go ahead; forensics have already got all they're going to. I want the cordons left up, though, and he has to respect them: no access to the understage area, or the haunted passage."

"I'll tell him." They turned the corner into the corridor

that led to the incident room, and Alison stopped at the vending machine. "By the way, did you have sugar in your tea?"

"Coffee. Yes, I did. It's not New Year yet." He dug in his pocket for coins. "What do you want?"

"Black coffee, but I'll get it," she said fishing around in her purse.

He fed money into the machine for her. "Black coffee?"

"Yes please. I don't want an expanding waistline."

He handed her the plastic cup and she sipped the hot liquid.

"I'm surprised any of them want to go back to the theatre after what's happened," she said. "And how can you have a pantomime without a dame? Stephen Coombs was one of leading players."

"Michael will probably do it himself."

"Seems wrong somehow. He was so close to Sophie."

"I want you to be at the theatre, at least for the first few performances," Banham said. "Tell them it's for protection. Keep digging about, see if you can find anything more to nail Stephen. I'll sort out some uniform back-up. Are you OK with that?"

"Fine," she said, her painted mouth breaking into a smile. "As long as I don't have to go on stage and play the dame."

Isabelle Walsh was behind her desk in the incident room as Banham and Alison passed through on their way to interview Stephen Coombs. A pile of papers lay beside her computer, and the printer began to chatter out more. "Bank statements for Michael Hogan," she told Banham. "He had overdrafts and loans all over the place. Hardly surprising - he was paying the bills on Sophie Flint's flat, as well as his own and Maggie McCormak's."

"Why doesn't that surprise me?" Banham said, picking up a pile of mobile phone bills and flicking through them.

"Lucinda Benson made a call to Stephen Coombs on the morning she died," Isabelle told him. "And Sophie Flint called him twice, but he said he doesn't remember."

"Interesting." Banham turned to Alison. "We couldn't find Stephen's mobile. Perhaps he'd hidden it." He ran his eyes down the two lists in his hand. "Lucinda made four calls to Michael Hogan that day, before she had sex with him," he said lifting the next page. "And she received calls from Vincent Mann, and her mother." He moved his eyes to the next list of numbers. "Sophie rang Michael twice on the day she died. Popular man." He screwed an eye up thoughtfully. "Sophie received calls from all the cast, and rang Maggie, Barbara and Vincent Mann as well as Stephen – twice. Right, I'm going to interview the fat bastard."

Alison set off and he let her go on ahead. "Have you noticed Grainger is dressed up today?" he said to Isabelle.

The young DC put a hand over her mouth. "Is she?" she said.

"Any idea why?"

Isabelle sucked in her cheeks. "Dunno," she said. "Perhaps she's in love."

Stephen Coombs looked exhausted, and it was hardly surprising; they had been holding him for nearly twenty four hours. His body smelt rancid, there were bags under his eyes, he had refused a solicitor and had spent all night arguing his innocence. It was time to get heavy.

Banham settled in the chair beside Crowther, and Alison sat in the corner behind them. Crowther turned on the tape and gave the identifying information.

Banham leaned back in his chair and stared at Stephen.

"You know, it would be very much in your interests to co-operate with us," he said firmly.

Stephen lowered his eyes and said nothing.

"You're going to be charged with the murder of Sophie Flint," Banham continued.

"I didn't do it."

"Do you go fishing?" Banham asked him.

"What? Yes, I do, as a matter of fact."

"I hear you gut your own fish."

Stephen stared back at Banham then lowered his eyes again.

"What happened to the knife that you had in the boot of your car?" Banham asked.

Stephen shook his head. "I've been set up."

"Really?" Crowther drawled. "So who else has a key to your car?"

"I don't know!" He wiped sweat from his temple with his hand. "The keys are always in my coat pocket."

"That's handy," Banham said dismissively. "Go through your movements for me again, after you came off stage, from the 'Only Man On the Island' scene."

Stephen kept his eyes focused on the table and said nothing. His big hands were curled into tight fists, making the dimples in the fat more prominent.

"You were wearing your red and white bathing costume," Banham prompted. "The one we later found wrapped around the knife that killed Sophie."

Stephen slowly looked up. "I didn't kill her," he said again. "How many more fucking times?"

Banham moved forward and put his elbow on the table. He ignored the strong body odour and rested his chin in his hand. The other man's bulk seemed to spill over the sides of the chair. He wasn't comfortable, Banham thought, and that could only help in his effort to push for a confession.

Banham put his other elbow on the table and linked his fingers. He held Stephen's gaze for a few seconds. "Do you want legal representation?" he asked.

"What for?"

"You're looking at being put away for a very long time, Stephen."

"You've got nothing on me. Anyone could have wrapped that knife in my costume."

"And stolen it from your car first?" Crowther said.

Stephen looked from Banham to Crowther and then back to Banham but said nothing.

"Did you kill Sophie because she knew you'd killed Lucinda? Is that what happened?" Banham pushed him.

"No!"

"Oh, so you didn't kill her because she found out?" He left a beat before adding, "So why did you kill her?"

Stephen just shook his head.

"We know you did kill her. And we can prove it. But tell us why you killed Lucinda. Was it a mistake? Did you kill her by mistake? Did you mean to kill someone else?" Banham kept firing the questions.

Stephen sniffed and wiped his hand across his nose, then rubbed his forehead and temples with the arm of his grubby polyester shirt. Droplets of perspiration formed on the top of his head. Banham knew he was getting to him.

"It must have been hard," he goaded. "To get the right person in the pitch black. Let me tell you how I think it happened. You changed quickly into your black costume, the one that's kept in the company office, then you snuck down to the stage. No one was looking, so you crossed the stage, picked up the stage weight and waited for your opportunity. Is that how it was?"

Stephen didn't answer.

"How did you cross the stage, Stephen? Did you squeeze around the back, or did you cross behind the others? Dressed in that black costume, no one would have seen you. Is that what you did, Stephen?"

Stephen let out a large sigh.

"It should have been so easy, shouldn't it?" Banham carried on. "But it wasn't, was it? You got the wrong person." He edged his face in nearer to Stephen's.

Stephen lowered his gaze.

Banham's voice grew louder. "That's what happened, isn't it, Stephen? You got the wrong person, didn't you? And Sophie found out, and you had to kill her too."

"No!" Stephen shouted, flinging his head up and facing Banham. "No, I didn't! I didn't kill anyone!"

"We can prove that you did," Crowther butted in. "We've got your DNA on the knife that killed Sophie, and it was hidden with your bloodstained costume."

"I told you, anyone could have hidden it." Stephen's voice rose half an octave. "I put the fucker in the laundry basket."

"We found your footprint by Sophie's body," Banham said softly.

For the first time, Stephen looked very afraid.

"No one but you could have put that there," Banham continued. "Yet you say you weren't in the basement. Now, that's a lie, isn't it, Stephen?"

Stephen opened his mouth to speak, then changed his mouth and looked down at the table.

"And your saliva is on her face. Did you spit at her when you cut her throat?" Crowther asked with quiet disgust.

"No, I bloody didn't," Stephen said through gritted teeth. "But I'd like to spit at you lot."

Banham leaned towards him. "We think you did, Stephen."

"All right, all right," he shouted. Then he lowered his voice to a whisper, and Banham heard the crack in his voice. "I'll tell you the truth."

Both detectives became very quiet.

Stephen spoke slowly. "I've got a cold, see, and I sneezed on stage." He raised his voice again. "I bloody well sneezed during one of Vincent Mann's unfunny jokes. The only thing I killed was one of the comic's laughs. Comic indeed. That's a joke in itself. That's what started the row with that bastard."

"Go on," Banham said.

"Go on what?" The man's voice was cracking with emotion as it increased in volume. He squeezed his fat white hand into a fist on the table. "That's how my spit got on her face, see. I went to her in the wings, to complain about Vincent's attitude, and get her to sort it." His shoulders began to shake, and Banham realised he was near breaking point. "I was angry, see. I must have spat then." He turned back to face Banham and repeated softly, "I must have spat then."

"So you admit that you left the stage on the opposite side to the one you claimed in your statement?" Banham said.

"Yes," he whispered.

"Louder, please, for the tape," Banham almost shouted. "You left the stage by the stage right exit. You admit that?"

"Yes." Stephen snarled.

"So if you didn't kill her and you're innocent as you protest, then why did you lie?" Crowther butted in.

Stephen wiped his face with his sleeve again. "Because I was afraid," he said without emotion.

"Of what?" Crowther asked impatiently.

Stephen looked up. "Of this. Afraid you'd blame me. And I was right because you bloody have."

"Because you are to blame, Stephen," Banham told him coldly. "And what about the basement. Was that another lie? That is your footprint down there, isn't it? So you were there, weren't you?"

Stephen covered the top of his head with his hands.

Banham raised his voice. "You were in the basement, weren't you, Stephen?" Stephen looked up. "Yes," he shouted.

"Yes." Banham leaned back in his chair. The truth was finally on the tape.

"Yes, I was there." Stephen was still shouting. "I told Sophie she had to do something about Vincent Mann, and she ignored me – just walked away, down the stairs and into the basement to cross the stage. She told me to grow up." His voice began to crack. "I decided to complain to the boss, but I had to change first, so I squeezed around the back of the set." He looked at Crowther. "You never saw me. You were watching those dancing girls."

Crowther folded his arms and leaned back in his chair. Banham recognised bravado when he saw it.

"I did my change, mega quick like, and headed for Michael's room. You were in there, with that young woman of yours."

"Go on," Banham said wearily.

"I didn't kill her," Stephen pleaded. "I wanted to find Michael before Vincent did, see. Get my side in first. When he wasn't in his room I thought he'd be in the basement. I took the quick route down the haunted passage and through the kiddies' room. I expected to meet her, Sophie, coming up, but I didn't." His voice developed a quaver. "I walked into the basement, turned on the light, and I saw her dead body. Well, I panicked, didn't I, and ran back upstairs."

Banham stared at him. How much longer was this – this

209

pantomime going on?

"I've been set up," Stephen pleaded.

"How could you have been set up?"

"My costume was in the wardrobe basket, in the corridor. Someone must have took it, wiped the knife on it, then hid it in the step in the passageway." His eyes flicked from Banham to Crowther like a frightened rabbit caught in a headlight. Beads of sweat had broken out again, and again he wiped them with his forearm of his shirt. "I'm telling you, I didn't do it. Someone has set me up."

Banham put his elbows back on the table. "OK, let's think about this. Who knows you put your costume in the laundry basket?"

"I don't know. I don't always put it out to be washed." Desperation was clear in his voice. "Sometimes I make it last two or three performances, if Maggie is busy. You don't notice from out front if it's a bit grubby, see."

"Who knows about the haunted passage?"

"Everyone says there is a ghost backstage. The theatre's famous for it, see. I don't really believe in that sort of stuff. But everyone knows there's a haunted passage."

"Vincent Mann doesn't. You just said yourself that you used the passage to get to Michael before he did."

Stephen pushed his dirty bitten thumbnail against his mouth and chewed on the dry skin. "I suppose."

Banham banged his hand on the table. "Two young women have been murdered," he shouted. "And you are facing two life imprisonment charges. If you want to help yourself *I suppose* isn't good enough. My patience is wearing very thin. You've just admitted to being in the basement, something you lied about in your statement…"

There was a knock on the door. Banham went to answer it and Crowther informed the tape they were taking a break. Outside stood Isabelle Walsh. Banham closed the door behind him and she handed him some papers. "Just in from forensics," she said, a broad smile lighting up her face. "We've got a match, Guv. Residue from the stage weight that killed Lucinda has been found on the black gloves. The ones from the company office."

A smile spread across his face. "That's great news," he said.

"That's not the best part," Isabelle went on. "The footprint in the basement matches Stephen's, and the crumbs with it are from a salami pizza. Guv, we've got him. For both murders!"

15

It took Michael Hogan less than twenty-four hours to get a replacement actor to take over as dame. Alison Grainger arrived at the theatre accompanied by two uniformed constables to find the cast gathered on stage and waiting for the producer to arrive. She told them she would be backstage during the show for their added protection, then settled herself on the high stool in the wings to observe the rehearsal.

Hardly a word passed between the actors as they waited. Only the chorus dancers, huddled together in the corner as usual, were talking to each other.

A few minutes later the stage door banged. Michael came into the wings followed by a tall middle-aged man who reminded Alison of a tree; he was tall and willowy, and wore a sage green poncho over a brown shirt. His arms waved as he fired questions at Michael Hogan, but the producer wasn't giving much back.

"Sorry to keep you all waiting," Michael said to the cast. "This is Rory Harrison. He has kindly agreed to take over as dame. We've less than two hours to curtain up, so I'll save the introductions until later; let's just all give him a welcome, then Alan will top and tail the show, cutting to cue, and rehearsing the important scenes and the dialogue Rory is involved in. He's learned the lines."

There was a spatter of half-hearted applause, then Barbara stepped forward offering Rory her outstretched hand.

"I'm Barbara Denis," she said. "You're welcome to call me Barbara."

"I've just said introductions later," Michael snapped. "Places, please, for Rory's opening scene And if there's anything Alan is unsure of, Fay is the one to ask." He pulled his mouth into a plastic smile for Rory's benefit, and glared angrily at Vincent Mann, who glowered back.

"Actually, it's mainly the changes." Rory's voice was light and breathy, and his head bobbed like a nodding dog. "I could do with a bit of help with the really quick changes. And if someone could help me decide which outfit to wear for which scene?"

Maggie had been keeping very quiet. She was dressed in a different cat costume, one with even less fur than the previous one. Her own suntanned face and gold-streaked hair jutted from the neck, reminding Alison of a spring daffodil that had just emerged from the earth. She held a large, ugly and extremely dusty cat's head under her arm, its large green and black flecked eyes staring out, and the red plastic half-moon mouth grinning.

"Normally I'd be there to help you," she said, "but as you see I'm having to play the cat." She looked across at Alan. "So perhaps…"

"Yes, yes, I'll be there to help," Alan answered, catching on for once in his life. "I'll be in the wings most of the time."

"And when he's on stage playing Alderman Fitz, I'll be in the wings," Michael said with another of his plastic smiles. "In fact, I'm in the wings at all times, for the rest of the run."

Rory nodded politely. "If we've time, I'd like to go through the changes after the rehearsal…"

Michael was hardly listening. His eyes moved from one cast member to the next. "I'd like to take this opportunity to thank you all for sticking with it," he said. "Sophie…"

His voice stuck in his throat. "Sophie would want the show to go on…" None of the cast looked him in the eye; they were all clearly uncomfortable.

Michael's eyes now rested on Sonia. Instead of the villager's costume the other two girl dancers wore, she was wearing a sugar pink tutu, with layers of different coloured netting. A tiara glittered in her blonde hair, and she held a sparkling fairy wand.

"I… I'm grateful for the costumes you've all managed to get together," Michael said, unable to take his eyes off Sonia. "As you all know, Stephen has been charged with Sophie's murder…" He paused to collect himself. "The police have said the original costumes will be released in the next few days."

Sonia grew uncomfortable as Michael's eyes lasered into her; she let out a long breath when he turned away and started to walk off the stage.

"I'll be upstairs in my office if anyone needs me," he said.

"He's being very brave," said Trevor. "I mean, it was bad enough that Lucinda was killed. But Sophie! She was his daughter! And he's picking the pieces up and carrying on the show." He inhaled on a Marlboro Light and he shook his head. "I tell you, man, I could not do it."

"He has to," Barbara said quickly. "He's about to be made bankrupt; he doesn't have a choice. Her eyes burned into Maggie. "Someone is bleeding him dry."

Fay clapped her hands. "OK, let's get going," she said with the authority of a forty-year-old. As an impersonation of Sophie it was spot on.

She instructed them all to spread out and take their positions while she talked Rory through his first entrance. Barbara glared at her, and Maggie smiled like the doting mother she was. Vincent walked about like an over-wound clockwork toy, his face saying nothing. The dancers just got on with it.

"Daddy has the script in the wings, if you forget anything," Fay said to the nervous Rory.

"If I forget something," Rory said with a nervous laugh, "I'll just make it up. It is panto, after all."

"We'd like you to keep…" Barbara began. Her voice was drowned by Vincent's.

"We'll keep to the script as much as we can," he said. "If you forget anything, I'll cover for you. I'm a comic, and I'm used it."

"I'm a comic too," Rory said. "I'm sure I'll manage to cover for myself."

"Right, let's move on." Fay clapped her hands again. "That scene will be fine. Places for the next one, please."

They rehearsed more scenes, then Fay said, "We'll skip the ultra-violet scene; you're not in that. We'll do the Palace of the Sultan of Morocco."

"We should walk through the whole of this scene," Barbara said. "It leads into the big sword fight between me and the King Rat, and we should all be absolutely certain that Rory knows where he is standing. We don't want to risk an accident."

Everyone agreed and Fay clapped her hands again. "OK, everyone to your places for the fight between Dick Whittington and the King Rat. Quickly, please."

"Can you stop doing that?" Barbara through clenched teeth.

"Stop doing what?" Fay asked.

"Clapping your hands together like a penguin at dinner time. You're giving me a headache."

Maggie shook her head at Fay, behind Barbara's back.

Fay made no reply.

The girl dancers stood either side of the entrance at the back of the stage, arms bent at the elbow and hands above their heads, palms together in a prayer pose. They had quickly changed into their harem costumes, chiffon blue bodices with bare midriffs and baggy, hipster trousers, ankles and arms decked with jangling imitation jewellery. The tension was almost visible.

Barbara drew the stage sword and held it in a threatening pose toward Trevor.

"Fight till the death," she said.

Alan touched Rory's shoulder. "When Barbara picks up the sword and holds it at that angle you'll need to stand well back, boy. That's Maggie's cue to run around and eat up all the little rats."

Maggie looked bemused.

"Mummy, all you do is sort of paw into the air." Fay demonstrated. "They'll just run off the stage." She tittered nervously. "Well, they used to, anyway."

Alan spoke again. "And that's the moment when Barbara and Trevor start the big sword fight."

"We haven't got any baby rats to chase off," Vincent said to Alan. "There aren't any juveniles, remember?"

"The swords are blunt, aren't they?" Rory asked Trevor.

"'Course they're blunt, mate," Trevor assured him. "They've been used in Michael's pantomimes for years. They're one hundred per cent safe, and the fight has been very tightly choreographed. Nothing can go wrong. It's best to stay back though, if you don't want to be hit by a swinging arm."

"Doesn't sound too bad then," Rory said with a nervous giggle and a wink. Trevor's face broke into a lively smile, displaying his perfect pearl-like teeth.

Alan stared at Fay. "So we've no rats at all?"

"Well, yes," Fay said. "Michael got those big furry hedgehogs. He was going to throw them on stage last time, but he forgot." She turned to Barbara. "I don't know if I should remind him, or whether he's got too much on his mind?"

"It's not your job," Barbara told her. "I'll speak to him."

"I'd rather you didn't," Maggie said. "Have you seen those hedgehogs? They're embarrassing. Couldn't we just cut that bit?"

"No, Maggie, you can't cut that bit," Barbara snapped. "The show wouldn't make sense. It's part of the legend of Dick Whittington and his famous cat. The cat rids the island of rats, and Dick helps him by taking on King Rat. Dick wins the fight and they all get a pardon from the Sultan of Morocco and their freedom. Dick is made Lord Mayor of London and gets very rich, so he asks for Alice's hand in marriage. That's the story; you should know it."

"I do," Maggie said indignantly.

"So no matter how bad the hedgehogs look, we have to leave them in." Barbara's patience was fraying. "And the cat has to pretend to chase them off."

Maggie gave a resigned shrug of her furry shoulders. "Fine."

"OK, that's done," Fay said to everyone. "Now all we have to do is the walk-down. Rory, you go down after Dad. We'll run through it quickly, and then we'll do a sound check."

"I go down last in the walk-down," Barbara said to Rory.

"That's because she's the star," Maggie added. "But she doesn't get the biggest cheer from the audience."

Alison slipped from her stool and decided to have a quick check around the backstage area while they were still rehearsing and bickering. She walked into the corridor, past the toilet and down to the end. The area around the haunted passage was still cordoned off with police tape. Barbara's dressing room with the tarnished star and the number one on the door was next to it. She turned the handle; it wasn't locked, so she looked inside. Everything seemed as it should: make-up set out ready for the performance, costumes hanging on the rail by the far wall next to her sofa and fridge.

She closed the door and checked the toilets. Again everything was fine. But when she opened the door to the chorus room she nearly jumped out of her skin. Michael Hogan was standing in the far corner by the clothes rail. He was as startled as she was.

Alison spoke first. "I'm just doing a quick check," she said.

"I'm making sure there are enough costumes," he said flatly. "Would you like some coffee?"

"You've got enough on your plate," she said. "But can I help myself when I do? I know where it is."

"Of course."

She left the room, closing the door behind her. Next door Rory had already made his space at the end of the shelving. Stephen's few remaining possessions had been pushed into the far corner. There were three unopened bottles of lager, an empty pizza carton with the large letter S written across the front, and a half-used box of tissues. She lifted the lid on the pizza carton; just a few crumbs were left, and a shrivelled slice of something that looked like ham or salami. She checked that the windows were locked and then left the room.

The Green Room obviously hadn't been cleaned in weeks. The plastic Christmas tree with the lopsided fairy was full of dust, the shelf it stood on was grubby and the waste paper bin overflowed with used polystyrene cups, sweet wrappers and fast food containers. Alison pulled a face, checked that the windows were shut and left.

After checking the toilet on that floor, she knocked on Michael's office door. No one answered, so she went in. The desk was as untidy as ever, with piles of papers weighed down by an assortment of props. Alison shifted a dull block of what looked like stone; it was heavier than it looked, and the documents underneath were only the bank statements they already knew about.

The stone had left traces of oil on her fingers; she wiped them on a tissue and leaned over the metal filing cabinet to plug in the kettle for coffee. The plug was beside another overflowing waste paper bin; two large, flat pizza boxes stuck out of the top; the initials M and S were written across the top. So Michael and Sophie even ate their pizzas together, she thought. Another thought leapt into her head. She pulled a carton from the bin and opened it, then took out her mobile phone and punched a number in.

Stephen Coombs was a large man, but he looked hunched and sunken in the chair opposite Banham and Crowther. His arms rested on the desk with his fat dimpled hands clenched into fists. Beside him sat the police duty solicitor, an undistinguished, well-presented middle-aged man with hair toppling over his forehead and eyebrows a little too heavy for his small face.

Banham sat with an elbow on the desk, watching Stephen. Crowther glowered.

"I've got enough evidence to put you away for Sophie's murder," Banham said to him.

"I didn't kill her," Stephen said. "I've told you what happened."

"You've told it different each time," Crowther snapped at him.

"I just went down there, and panicked and ran away," Stephen said. "I only said I didn't go down there because I was afraid this would happen, see." Stephen's voice was cracking and fear filled his eyes. "I didn't kill her. I swear I didn't."

Banham stared at Stephen. His mind was working overtime. He had enough evidence to charge him with Sophie's murder, but not Lucinda's. There was residue from the concrete weight on the black costume belonging to Stephen, but to get a murder charge to stick he needed Stephen's DNA on it, and that test hadn't proved positive. He needed a confession.

"If you admit the charge it will go in your favour." He glanced at the dull-looking solicitor, who offered nothing in the way of advice to his client. "In the long run," he added.

"Why should I?" Stephen's aggression was returning. "I didn't do it, see. I couldn't kill anyone."

"Oh, I think we all know that's not true," Banham snapped. "You stabbed a man called Joseph Blake and received a suspended sentence. You must know that we'd find that out."

Stephen looked at the duty solicitor. He wiped his nose with his sleeve. "That was a one-off," he said, dropping his gaze.

"Don't insult my intelligence," said Banham. "We've got Sophie's diary; it's written in black and white that you physically threatened Lucinda Benson, and Sophie, and Barbara Denis."

Stephen's eyes shifted from side to side. "That's not true; Sophie was a liar and a troublemaker." When no one disputed this, he added, "OK, I'll tell you what happened with Joseph Blake."

Banham's eyes fixed on Stephen and he became very still.

Stephen seemed to be picking his words very carefully. After a few seconds he said, "My brother Alan McCormak is married to Maggie. She's a bit of a girl see – has a colourful past. I warned my brother against her, but…" He stretched his fat lips. "He was besotted, wouldn't listen, see."

Banham held the eye contact. Stephen looked away. "Go on," Banham said.

"Maggie was having an affair with that Joe Blake," Stephen continued. "She was having it off with Michael too. Alan didn't know about either, see, but I did. I confronted her, but she begged me not to tell Alan, said it was over with both of them and she was pregnant." He sniffed hard. "I asked her who the baby's father was, see. She said it was Alan's, so I agreed to keep shtum. Then Maggie must have told Joe Blake that he was the father. He was rich, see, a property developer. And they needed money. He must have given it to her; she didn't tell me, and I never asked. Then the baby was born. Fay Mary McCormak." He glanced at his solicitor and sniffed again, wiping the back of his hand across his nose before continuing. "Then Joe Blake bloody turned up, asking to see his baby. A fight broke out and he attacked my brother." He paused and uncurled his fingers. "Maggie rang me. She was hysterical, so I rushed round." The hands hit the table. "Joe had a kitchen knife in his hand. I went for him and in the struggle he got stabbed in the stomach. The police were called in, and Joseph said he wouldn't press charges if he was allowed to visit his daughter. Maggie told him it wasn't his daughter. DNA samples were taken from them, proving without doubt that he wasn't the father. My brother Alan was." He looked down at the table. "So the bastard pressed charges against me, and Alan too, for aggravated assault. Alan got a complete discharge, and I got a three month suspended jail sentence. He made Maggie and Alan pay his money back too – said he'd get them done for deception." He looked from Crowther to Banham and shook his head sadly. "Alan's drinking got worse than ever then, see, and they got heavier in debt. So Maggie went to Michael for help. Michael had been married to Valerie for a couple of years by then, and had already adopted Sophie – it was common knowledge how Sophie was the apple of his eye. But Maggie told him he was Fay's father." Again he looked from Crowther to Banham. "She was desperate, see, she felt responsible for Alan's drinking. She asked Michael for money. And said she wouldn't tell Valerie Fay was his daughter if he agreed to keep Alan and me in work every Christmas and pay towards Fay's upkeep. He didn't want to break his marriage up, or lose Sophie, so what choice did he have?" He looked again at Crowther and then back to Banham. "That's been going on for years. Now he is about to be declared bankrupt. And now you know the truth."

"And he isn't even the father," Crowther added. "Poor bastard."

Banham watched Stephen carefully but said nothing. He told the tape they were taking a break, and beckoned Crowther to follow him out of the room.

"We'll leave him to consult with his brief for a few minutes," he said dryly, setting off for the staircase.

In the incident room Isabelle Walsh was still at her computer. "Can you get me all the details on the suspended sentence that Stephen Coombs got for GBH?" he asked her.

222

"Guv."

Crowther was ending a call on his mobile outside the interview room when Banham arrived back.

"Alison's just phoned, Guv," he said. "She found a whole lot of pizza containers in the bins at the theatre. I rang the lab and checked with Penny; the crumbs on the shoe print in the basement are from salami pizza. The container in Stephen's room was salami. Alison is sending her the remains of another one to check against the shoe print – from Sophie and Michael's room."

"Stephen came up to Michael's office when I was in there," Banham said. "That was before he went down into the basement. If the salami one came from Michael's room, he could have walked on some crumbs."

"He only stood in the doorway though."

"Yes, but he still could have walked in the crumbs. Did Alison ask Michael what kind of pizza he had?"

"She said he's walking around in a daze. He didn't even remember eating one. So she's checking out the orders with the Pizza Hut, see if they've kept a record of who ordered what."

Banham blew out a breath. "You know, out of all of them Stephen's the one with least motive. Or am I missing something?"

"Sophie told us he hadn't changed his costume during the UV. She knew he killed Lucinda. There's your motive, Guv, for Sophie at least."

"But what if she got it wrong? His dressing gown is green, I saw that myself. And Sophie's mother's the only person who mentioned that she wore contact lenses, and she said herself that she and Sophie weren't close."

"I think that's all irrelevant, Guv. I think he meant to kill Sophie in the first place and got the wrong person."

"But why?"

"Now that I don't know, Guv."

The pantomime was in full swing. Alison watched from the wings, near Alan McCormak's desk. The atmosphere throughout the first half of the show had been extremely tense, but the actors had got through, and the new dame seemed to manage with little problem.

From time to time Michael Hogan had walked into the wings, watched for a minute or so, then walked away again. Alan had made all his entrances, and hadn't missed any of his lines.

At the interval the cast gathered on the stage again to walk through the second half of the show. Alison was surprised at how friendly Barbara Denis and Vincent Mann seemed to be. They stood side by side at the back of the stage talking quietly, while Fay and Maggie talked Rory Harrison through the routines.

The four dancers were going through the steps in the UV scene, and Alan and Michael were checking the fish. Alison assured the nervous cast that she would not leave the wings, and that the two uniformed police would be on the other side. The lighting technician had rigged up extra worker lights in the wings to make the cast feel more secure.

They finished their rehearsal with five minutes of the interval left, and all went off to change.

The uniformed PCs went to the Green Room to get coffees from the vending machine and to re-check the windows and the fire exit. Alison made another call to Penny. The lab had received the pizza cartons, but the tests would take another hour. Alison rang the Pizza Hut again, but they hadn't so far found anything which would tell her who ordered which toppings.

The door to the chorus room stood ajar, and as she passed she glimpsed her side view in the floor-to-ceiling mirrors reflected her image. The sight depressed her; the twig-like figures of the two chorus girls changing into their sailor outfits made her even more self-conscious.

Sonia put a cigarette to her mouth and lit it with a thick gold lighter.

"I didn't have you down for a smoker," Alison said to her from the doorway.

"I've just started again," Sonia told her. "It's partly nerves. It stops me getting fat too."

Alison only smoked five cigarettes a day, and her new year's resolution was to give up completely; but she decided there and then to scrap that idea. If she put on even one extra pound now, she'd look enormous.

"Could I borrow a cigarette from you?" she asked Trevor. "I'll pay you back later. I can't leave the building at present to buy some."

"No problem," he said passing her the Marlboro Lights with a packet of matches. "My lighter's packed up again," he told her.

"Here, use mine," Sonia said, passing her the gold lighter.

The nicotine had a calming effect, and made Alison feel thinner and happier. Her new resolution was to be more independent, she promised herself. She would stand up to her father when he tried to bully her mother, and ignore him when he tried to wear her down. And as for Paul Banham - he had made it very clear those few days before Christmas that he didn't find her attractive. Crowther had the right idea; she would treat men like he treated women, and use them for a good time and good sex.

Suddenly she felt better.

By the time she had smoked the cigarette right down to the filter the show was well into the second act. She ground the butt in the red sand bucket outside the stage entrance and went to stand beside Michael Hogan.

The UV scene was just ending, and the release of the tension was almost tangible. Michael congratulated the actors and told them they'd done well. She left the two uniformed PCs in the wings, and went upstairs to the Green Room. She bought herself a can of diet Coke from the vending machine, popped the can and enjoyed the sharp bubbles as the drink ran down her throat, then checked her mobile for messages. There were none, so she made her way back to the side of the stage.

When she reached the bottom of the stairs, a faint tapping noise made her stop in her tracks.

At first it sounded like someone playing ball against the outside wall of the building. She stood still and listened; no, it was coming from inside and on this floor.

The music playing over the tannoy was the opening of the Sultan of Morocco scene – the last scene of the show. Everyone was in it, so who could be making that noise? She closed her eyes and listened carefully.

It was coming from the chorus room.

She remembered that one person wasn't on stage at this point. Trevor had to change into his rat's costume.

She hurried along the corridor to the chorus room. The tapping was coming from inside the room, and the door was locked. "Trevor," she called, rattling the handle again. "Trevor, are you in there?"

The tapping became more urgent.

All the dressing room keys hung on a rack behind Alan's chair; she ran to the stage and beckoned to the uniformed PCs as she skimmed the rack for the chorus's key. It was the only one missing.

"Get that door open," she told the PCs. "Break it down if you have to."

She left them to it and ran back to the stage to find Michael Hogan. There was no sign of him in the wings. The Sultan on Morocco scene was in full swing; Dick Whittington was promising to rid the island of rats with the help of her amazing cat, in return for freedom for herself and her friends. Alan would be on stage. So where was Michael?

Sorting out the hedgehogs, she realised. There was no time to find him.

She ran back to the chorus room. The door was open and Trevor was on the floor wearing only his underwear and a red and white spotted handkerchief tied tightly around his mouth. His wrists were strapped together and bound to the pipe under the sink with the strong grey sticky tape – gaffer tape, she remembered – which was used in abundance backstage. He was sobbing and trying to free himself, helped by the uniformed PCs.

"What happened?" Alison asked.

"I don't remember anything," he sobbed. "But I've got a terrible pain in the back of my head. I suppose someone hit me."

"OK," Alison said gently. The two constables wrapped his towelling robe around him. "Call an ambulance and get him comfortable."

"I've got to be on stage," Trevor cried desperately. "I've got to be King Rat."

The large furry costume was nowhere to be seen – and through the tannoy Barbara Denis was telling King Rat to draw his sword and fight for his life.

Alison snatched her mobile from her pocket and

furiously stabbed the keys. As she raced from the room, the phone pressed to her ear, she heard the swords clash. The fight that should have started slowly was already moving at a galloping pace. It grew faster and louder as she reached the wings.

"Guv, I need urgent back-up," she hissed when Banham picked up. "There's an impostor King Rat on stage and I think he's about to kill Barbara Denis."

16

"Mushroom, got it." Crowther clicked his phone shut and ran after Banham, who was striding away down the corridor pocketing his own mobile. "That was the lab, Guv. The pizza in Sophie Flint's stomach contents was mushroom. The salami fragments came from the shoeprint."

"Never mind that for now. We've got to get to the theatre – that was Alison on the phone."

They clicked their seat-belts and moment later were following two patrol cars at top speed, lights flashing and sirens screaming.

Alison's brain was racing. The sword fight was more frantic than usual, but whoever was in the rat costume knew the moves. None of the actors seemed aware anything was different from usual.

Alison tried desperately to think what to do for the best. She had to do something; there was no time to wait for back-up. Not only was Barbara's life potentially at risk, there were also five hundred people sitting in the auditorium, at least half of them children; and if she stopped the show, the unknown person could jump into the audience.

Barbara seemed oblivious to the fact that she could be in danger. Alison's eyes darted around the stage; all the actors and dancers should be there at this point in the show, and she started to count them off. Rory the new dame was there, standing well out of the way of the clashing swords. Fay was beside one of the chorus dancers, also well clear of the sword fight, leaning against the back entrance to the set. But which dancer was it? Lindsay or Tanya? They looked so similar.

She spotted Tanya crouching on the ground, fighting a few grey fluffy toys; Alison realised they were the dreadful hedgehogs Michael had substituted for rats. That meant that Michael himself was probably at the opposite side throwing the ghastly furry creatures on to the stage. But Alison couldn't see the other side of the stage. She couldn't see Sonia either, then remembered she was on the stage, playing the Fairy of the Bells.

Again Alison tried to work out who wasn't there. Maggie and Vincent should both have been on stage, but they were both missing.

Barbara was struggling to keep up. She ducked as the large sword swung around her head and jumped as it dropped towards her legs, panic and puzzlement written across her face.

Alison made an instant decision to bring the curtain down. She turned to grab the lever behind Alan's high chair, but it wouldn't budge. She ran to the back of the set to look for the work experience boys, but realised they would have left; their job was done once they had moved the scenery for this scene.

Every second counted if she was to prevent another murder. Where was Alan? He wasn't on stage and he wasn't in the wings. He had promised he wouldn't disappear off to the pub any more – so where had he gone?

There was no more time to waste. If she couldn't bring the curtain down, she would have to walk on stage with the two uniformed officers and stop the show. She decided to give the curtain one last try.

But she was stopped short. Her jumper had hooked itself against the trestle table. The table was overflowing with stuffed hedgehogs, and stood at its usual dangerous and obstructive angle beside the police tapes that cordoned off the basement. The only light was a small worker bulb intended to help the actors find their props in the dark. She felt around to find out what she was hooked on, and her finger jabbed something sharp. She carefully freed the jumper and turned around to see what it was. Her heart started racing like a formula one car. It was one of the rusting prop swords.

So what was the person in the rat's costume using to fight Barbara?

She gesticulated to the uniformed PCs and rushed back to try the curtain lever again. One of the constables followed her and they both pulled and tugged, but the lever still wouldn't budge.

Out front the audience was going wild as the sword fight headed towards a climax. They were out of time; she had to stop the show.

The screams from the audience could have been heard in the next town as Barbara ducked and dived. Today King Rat was winning the fight, and panic was written across Barbara's face. She clearly knew she was fighting a very different fight from the one they had rehearsed; this one was to save her own life.

The audience were on their feet, yelling themselves hoarse. King Rat waved the sword above his head like a madman. Suddenly a voice came through the head-cans draped across Alan's stool. "Can anyone hear me?" pleaded the sound technician, who could see everything from his seat at the back of the stalls. "Bring the curtain in now. Something's very wrong up there."

Alison snatched up the head-cans and pressed the Speak button. "It's Sergeant Grainger," she said desperately. "I am trying, but the lever won't budge."

"Pull it upwards and tug it sharply to your left," he told her. "I'm on my way."

Barbara let out a yell. Alison turned to see her clutching at her shoulder. The sword had landed at the top of her arm, which was shielded only by the thin white cotton shirt under her mini tunic dress. A rush of dark red blood stained the sleeve and she dropped her own sword. The rat's sword landed again, cutting into her shoulder.

The audience fell suddenly into horror-struck silence, and the actors stared in terror. Barbara fell face-down and hit the floor.

A child in the audience cried, "Don't die, Dick. Get up and slay the monster."

Then everything seemed to happen at once. Alison rushed on stage shouting, "Stop! Hold it right there." Trevor and the sound man arrived at the side of the stage and grabbed the curtain lever. The two uniformed PCs walked purposefully towards the unknown person in the rat's costume, but backed away as the intruder pointed the long, sharp sword at them. Panic spread through the cast as the intruder lifted the sword and swung it around.

Alison kept her eyes firmly on the creature standing before her pointing the sword. "Everyone stand back," she ordered. "And someone help Barbara."

The girl dancers rushed to Barbara's aid, kneeling beside her as her face contorted in pain and she clutched her bleeding shoulder.

As slow handclapping from the impatient audience started to mount, police sirens wailed towards the theatre. The anonymous creature took another swipe, cutting the air a few times around the uniformed PCs.

Alison kept her distance but faced the furry impostor.

"You must know you can't get away," she said. "The theatre will be surrounded by police in a moment. Drop the sword and we'll sort this out."

The sirens grew louder then stopped.

Alison stretched her hand out to the rat. "Just give me the sword," she said calmly, taking a step forward.

The stage door opened and banged. Alison used the momentary distraction to take another step. "Give me the sword." She was now standing less than a foot away.

A moment later Banham rushed on the stage, followed by Crowther and half a dozen uniformed officers.

King Rat lifted his sword.

"Drop it," Banham commanded.

The rat seemed to flounder, and Crowther seized the moment. He crept up behind and grabbed the creature by the wrist which held the sword. The rat tried to resist, but a uniformed officer grabbed his other arm, and after a very brief struggle the sword hit the floor.

Alison grabbed it, and ran her fingers across the blade. "Wow," she said. "That could take someone's head off." She looked at it more closely. "It's been sharpened recently." A thought flashed into her head: the oily stone on the desk in the company office. It was a carborundum stone; her father had one in his shed, for sharpening his garden shears.

"Who is it?" Banham demanded.

Two officers took hold of either side of the rat while a third struggled unsuccessfully to pull the head off.

"It's Vincent Mann," Alison said.

Banham pushed the creature against the wall and struggled with the zip at the back of the costume.

"No, I'm here," Vincent said sheepishly. He peered out from behind the set. "That fight was a bit scary. I thought I was better off back here."

Alison looked quickly round the stage. The dancers were all there, comforting Barbara; Sonia had ripped the sleeve off the bloodstained white shirt and was using it to staunch the blood.

The rat continued to struggle, and Banham still couldn't get the head undone.

"It opens at the back. You need to undo the clips as well as the zip," Trevor explained.

"Mummy knows how to do it," Fay said. But Maggie was nowhere to be seen.

Alison moved in to help Banham. She felt for the clips and relieved the creature of its head.

"You?" she said.

"I think I'm going to faint," Barbara Denis. Her head lolled to one side and she lost consciousness. Blood trickled down her thin arm to her fingers.

Alison knelt beside Barbara and lifted her so she rested against her shoulder. "I'll get her to the couch in her dressing room. Chase the ambulance up," she told the one of the PCs. "She's bleeding and it might need stitches." Alison and the dancers lifted Barbara and began to carry her into the wings. "You'll be all right," Alison said to her. "Help is on its way."

Behind her Banham's voice rang out. "Michael Hogan, I'm arresting you for the murder of Sophie Flint and Lucinda Benson, and the attempted murder of Barbara Denis. You do not have to say anything, but it may harm your defence…"

Alison eased Barbara on to the sofa. The actress gulped in air and cupped her hand over the wound in her shoulder.

"Could you go and fetch the first aid box?" Alison said to the dancers.

Barbara clenched her teeth against the pain. "You're going to be OK," Alison told her. "The cut doesn't look deep and the paramedics are on their way." The wound was bleeding and might need a few stitches, but it didn't look too bad.

She felt totally responsible. She should have simply stopped the show when she first realised something was wrong, instead of trying to find out how the curtain worked, and spare the five hundred odd people in the audience. If Barbara had been the third victim she'd never have forgiven herself.

Barbara's eyes started closing. "Water?" she whispered.

She licked her dry lips and Alison opened the fridge door to look for a bottle of mineral water. She found one and was about to close the door when her eyes fell on the pizza carton on the middle shelf. The letters C and T were written across it. But no one in the show had those initials.

The penny dropped. M and S on the ones upstairs in Michael's office didn't stand for Michael and Sophie, but mushroom and salami. And this one was obviously cheese and tomato.

A current of pain shot through her brain as something hard hit the back of her head. Her hair was grabbed and her head yanked backwards. Then something cold slithered around her neck. It was Barbara Denis's arm, and she held a small, sharp knife. She froze at the sudden prickle as the point touched her throat.

"Don't think I won't kill you too," Barbara said, her tone very different from her usual voice. "The only thing stopping me is that you're my ticket out of here."

"Can we come in? We've got the first aid stuff." It was Tanya's voice outside the door.

"Say no," Barbara whispered, turning the knife in her

hand so the handle jabbed into Alison's throat. "And don't try any fucking heroics, or I guarantee you're dead meat."

"We're OK for the moment," Alison shouted to the dancers, trying to sound as normal as possible. "Go back to your dressing room and I'll come and get them."

She watched Barbara in the mirror. A sadistic smile spread across the dark red mouth, and the lips moved back revealing the teeth. Barbara threw her head back and laughed. "Good," she said. "Do as you're told and I won't kill you. But cross me and I will. Do you understand?"

Alison couldn't risk nodding her head. If she moved a millimetre there was a good chance that the knife's sharp edge would break the thin skin on her neck. She swallowed and gasped, to let Barbara think she needed to catch her breath, and to buy herself a few seconds to think. Barbara loosened her grip slightly.

Alison had been trained to deal with situations like this, but nothing in the training had prepared her for the reality. She fought desperately to quell the panic and keep control of herself, but the sharp blade against her throat and the thought of her own blood spilling like the dead Sophie Flint's made logic waver.

Banham signalled to Crowther to take Michael Hogan out of his sight.

"I haven't murdered anyone," Michael protested as Crowther took his arm. "Dear God, don't make another mistake."

"What mistake? What are you talking about?"

"I wanted real justice for Sophie. Surely you can understand that. The law would only give her a few years in prison..."

Banham looked at Crowther.

"Without Sophie, nothing matters," Michael said. He lifted his furry arms in the air. "Lock me up, throw away the key, I don't care. But don't let her get away. "

"What are you saying?"

"An eye for an eye, a tooth for a tooth, that's what it says in the bible."

At the same moment Alan McCormak arrived at the side of the stage with Maggie. "He was in the pub," Maggie said. "I didn't think he could do sword fighting but I had to be sure."

Alan brushed her aside. "You'd better come," he said to Banham. "The dancers went to get bandages for Barbara's shoulder, but she's shut herself in the dressing room with your sergeant…"

17

Alison felt anything but calm; the composed voice sounded as if it belonged to someone else. "You won't get away with this. There's a dozen police just a few yards away."

"Shut the fuck up," Barbara hissed at her. "I'll do the talking."

Alison closed both her eyes to stop herself blinking. Her ponytail was tugged backwards, pulling her head back so the skin on her neck became taut. "Do I make myself clear?" Barbara asked, moving the knife just a fraction so Alison could nod her agreement.

The small movement was a chance; Alison lifted her hand to go for the knife. But Barbara was quicker. The long bony leg was up in a second; she kneed Alison hard in the kidney, then pressed the knife against her throat again. "Do I make myself clear?" she repeated.

Alison was struggling to breathe. She opened her mouth and cold air rushed into her lungs; the sudden shock, the pain in her kidney and the enveloping fear made her lose control of her bladder, and hot liquid seeped down the inside of her trousers. Barbara watched her in the mirror, amused.

"I'll do whatever you ask," Alison she said carefully as their eyes met in the mirror. "I don't want to end up like Sophie and Lucinda. Why did you kill them?"

The hard brown eyes seemed to pierce into hers like the knife. A small part of Alison's mind still worked logically; it weighed up the chances of taking on both the woman and the knife. Strange laughter rang from Barbara's painted mouth, and Alison felt the grip tighten on her shoulder and the knife press harder against her throat. She had never been so terrified in her life.

"Sophie Flint had it coming," Barbara said casually, turning the knife against Alison's throat. "Thieving little slut. He's mine. She stole his money too, and talent from every performer she stupidly choreographed." Her voice sounded deep and distorted. "These pantomimes used to be works of art. When Michael and I directed them they were wonderful."

She turned to check her reflection in the mirror. Alison nearly seized the moment, but then it was lost.

"Then she came along, and all her stupid life she made it her business to take everything. And he was too blind to see it." Her eyes narrowed. "Who'll mourn her? No one but him. No one liked her. I did us all a favour." She narrowed her eyes again. "She had it coming and she got it. She caused everybody nothing but pain."

"What about Lucinda?" Alison asked. The knee in her kidney took her by surprise again; her head jerked up as the pain hit her brain, and her neck nudged the edge of the knife. At first it felt like a wasp sting. Her eyes watered and she gasped for breath. She looked in the mirror to see if there was any blood but Barbara's arm was in the way.

Barbara tightened her grip. "Keep still!" she said angrily. "You wanted to know about Sophie Flint. Well, I'm telling you. She was only three days past her sixteenth birthday when she opened her legs for him."

The key to the room lay on the dresser in front of them. Barbara picked it up with her left hand. Alison watched carefully.

"The mother used to be in the chorus," Barbara said, still speaking in the strange voice. "No talent, so she threw herself at every producer and director that she worked for, hoping to get a leg up on the career ladder. All she got was that bastard child, who turned out the same as her, a grade one slag. I did the world a good turn." The hard, mad eyes turned back to Alison. "Oh, but you're a copper. I don't expect you to agree."

She started to drag Alison toward the door.

"Where are we going?"

"Out of here. You're my ticket. Your boss likes you."

Alison willed herself to stay calm. Her neck stung and her head throbbed, but worst of all was the humiliation at having urinated in her trousers.

"He won't take any chances with you. But I'll kill you too if I have to." Barbara laughed. "So the choice is yours. If you try anything I'll happily cut your throat."

"Fine," Alison answered with more confidence that she felt.

Barbara locked the door from the inside. She was still wearing her costume: short beige suede tunic, bloodstained shirt and thigh-length boots. There was no pocket so she threw the key across the room on to the dresser. She stared at Alison in the mirror. Alison stared back, desperately trying to keep her brain working. Their eyes locked.

"What did Lucinda Benson do wrong?" Alison asked, fighting to sound calm.

"It was her own fault," Barbara said with a casual shrug. "She was in the wrong place."

"You thought she was Sophie?"

Barbara burst out laughing. "You've wet yourself. A nice, clean-living police-woman, and you couldn't wait. I hope he still fancies you, or I'll have to kill you."

"You hit her with the stage weight thinking it was Sophie?" Alison persisted, willing her voice not to shake.

Barbara shrugged again and lowered her eyes. "I got her

eventually, didn't I? I finished what I started." Her forehead creased and she suddenly calmed down. "I didn't mean to hurt Lucinda," she said, her tone now a child caught raiding the biscuit tin. "She had a lot to learn but she wasn't a bad girl. And she was welcome to Vincent Mann. He's a ghastly man, but that's none of my business. She didn't interfere with my Michael, and she didn't deserve to die." She shook her head and pressed her lips together. "I'm truly sorry about that."

So Barbara didn't know everything that had gone on.

The rapping on the door made them both start. Alison winced as the knife delivered another wasp sting to her neck.

"Open up," Banham shouted. Alison recognised the nervous edge in his voice as he banged and rattled the locked door. "Alison, are you in there." Then a second later, "Alison? Alison, answer me."

Neither did. The two women stared at each other.

After a second Barbara whispered, "I told you he liked you." She pulled Alison's ponytail with her left arm and dug the knife hard against her already smarting neck. Alison closed her eyes, willing the pain away.

The banging was suddenly much louder. "Open the door now!"

"Don't answer," Barbara whispered.

Alison knew what was going through Banham's mind. It took all her willpower to stop herself crying out to him that she was alive.

"Get this door open," she heard him command. Bodies banged hard against it.

Barbara twisted Alison's body so they were facing the door. The sharp edge of the knife pressed hard against her throat.

The door was starting to give way. There was desperation in Banham's voice as he urged the officers to hurry. She said a silent prayer that she would stay alive long enough to thank him. If she ever needed proof that he cared for her, she had it now.

Then the lock on the door gave way and the door flew open. Banham stood in the doorway. Alison's head was pulled to one side but they could see each other. His face was a mask.

He held his hand out and took a step forward. "Give me the knife, Barbara," he said.

"One foot closer from any of your dummies, and I'll carve her throat open and you can watch her life drip away." Barbara's voice was cold as ice.

All the police froze.

Alison felt another sting as the knife moved slowly across her neck. It took all her all her willpower not to cry out and her body started to shudder uncontrollably. Banham stood still as a statue.

"What do you want, Barbara?" he asked calmly.

There was no reply.

"Let her go," Banham said, as if he was suggesting she shouldn't have another drink before driving.

Barbara moved the knife a millimetre from Alison's eye. "I'm not messing. If you come any closer, I'll take her fucking eye out."

Then without warning the knife flashed down to her chest and struck through the jumper and into the skin above Alison's breast. Alison cried out as her knees started to give way, but Barbara held her ponytail firmly so she stayed upright. Blood leaked from the wound staining her jumper dark crimson. Then the knife was back against her throat, and Barbara's mouth pulled into an ugly smile. "Just to let you know, I give the orders," she said to Banham.

Warm blood ran down Alison's chest. She didn't know how badly she was cut, only that the pain was excruciating. She forced her eyes to stay open and look at Banham. It gave her strength. His were fixed on her, but showed no emotion. "What do you want, Barbara?" he repeated, showing no sign of fear.

Barbara relaxed and Alison seized the moment. She closed her mind to her own pain and lifted her leg, booting Barbara hard in the groin.

Barbara hunched, gulping for air.

Alison's training kicked in. She grabbed Barbara skilfully by the wrist that held the knife. Banham moved quickly to help, but Barbara was quicker, and a wave of dizziness engulfed Alison. Barbara held on to the knife and pointed it against Alison's face. Banham backed off, putting his hand out to halt the other officers. He was taking no chances, but his eyes were pinned on Barbara, waiting for another opportunity.

Barbara slipped her wrist from Alison's grip and brought the knife back to her throat. She dragged her long nails along the already burning graze on Alison's neck. The pain was nearly unbearable. Alison's shoulders slumped, but Barbara held her upright. Then she moved the knife back to the side of Alison's eye.

"It's up to you," Barbara said, watching Banham. "Not my fault if she falls unconscious on to the knife." She burst out laughing. "Ever heard of King Harold?"

Then her voice changed again, becoming low and distorted. "Get out of my way. We are leaving. And if any of your penguins get in my way, she'll be a one-eyed wonder."

"Do as she says," Banham said, his eyes on Alison. All the police stood back to let Barbara walk out. Alison managed to keep her eyes open and look back at Banham. They had been through a lot together in the ten years she had worked under him, but nothing compared to this. He gave her strength.

The police all backed away from the door. Barbara started to drag Alison. As they reached the door Banham said, "You can go, Barbara. I give you my word we won't try to stop you. But please leave Sergeant Grainger."

"Then give me your car keys," Barbara said.

"Let her go first," Banham answered.

Her voice dropped in tone. "I decide the terms. Give me the keys, or I'll take her eye out."

She opened her left hand, palm up, and he dug in his pocket for the keys.

"OK, that's fine." He spoke in a quiet authoritative tone, and his eyes met Barbara's. "Let her go, then I'll give you the keys."

Barbara took another step towards the door. She was a foot from Banham, and Alison was still within his reach.

"She's coming with me," Barbara said. "She's my passage out of here. Give me your car keys or it's King Harold the second."

His voice was perfectly steady. "You're too clever to believe you can walk out of here with a knife against the face of a police sergeant and get away with it. I'll give you my car keys, and I'll let you drive off, but you're not taking Sergeant Grainger with you."

"The keys to your car," Barbara spat at him.

Alison could see no way out of this. Banham couldn't back down, and Barbara wouldn't. At best she was going to lose an eye; at worst, her life. The odds weren't good. It was now or never.

Adrenalin drove her forward. She swiftly ducked her

head and kicked out hard, making contact with Barbara's thigh.

As Barbara took the kick she raised the knife, but Banham saw it coming and lunged, closely followed by Crowther who was standing right behind him. This time Banham grabbed the hand that held the knife, but before he could shake it free, Barbara dug it into his hand. He hardly felt the pain; he bent her wrist back sharply, and she released both the knife and Alison with a little cry. He held both Barbara's arms above her head. "Handcuffs," he shouted to the uniformed officer next to him. Crowther picked up the knife as the PC happily clicked the handcuffs on Barbara. But she wasn't finished; she managed a final kick, and the heel of her boot landed in Alison's face. Blood spurted from her nose and she fell forward in a heap on the floor.

Banham was on his knees beside her in a second. "Where's that ambulance?" he shouted. Then, unable to resist, he stood up and punched Barbara hard in the face.

The other police all looked away.

Barbara sat in the interview room, her swollen eye nearly ninety percent closed. The other stared at the cold grey walls that surrounded her.

Banham sat opposite, with DC Crowther beside him.

"I don't deserve this," she said.

"That's for a jury to decide," Banham said coldly.

"He should be here. It's his fault."

"Who's he?" Crowther asked, bored.

"My husband. No, sorry – everybody's husband." She laughed harshly, then burst into angry tears.

Banham and Crowther made eye contact. She was clearly mentally disturbed, but Banham hoped the court wouldn't be lenient because of it. She had killed two beautiful young women with their lives ahead of them, and nearly murdered his sergeant and best friend as well.

He was angry that someone so unstable could get a job in a Christmas pantomime show alongside a dozen innocent children who all thought themselves lucky to be doing it, while twice a day five hundred adults and children cheered her on as a hero. He shuddered at the thought.

He stared at the swollen and bruised eye. Crowther's report said she had walked into a wall resisting arrest.

Barbara smiled coyly at Banham. "It really is Michael's fault, you know. He killed us all. He lured me into his nest, got me a hit record, promised to love me for ever." Her voice took on the distorted note. "Then he dropped me when the next little tart came along." Her own voice returned. "He took my life, you see."

"Tell us how you killed Sophie," Banham said flatly.

"I'm only sorry I didn't kill Fay as well."

"Fay? What does she have to do with it?" This woman was unbelievable.

Again the tone of her voice changed. "She was Michael's bastard. He wouldn't give me a child, but he gave Maggie one."

Banham swallowed his anger. "Tell us how you killed Sophie," he repeated.

"You know how I killed her," she sighed. "I cut her throat."

"Talk us through your movements up to and just after the murder."

She looked away. "I married him first. He was mine."

Both men waited for her to continue. She started to cry again. Banham hoped her swollen eye hurt.

"She wound me up," Barbara said through her tears. "She kept saying she loved him, and he was her father." She closed her good eye and shook her head, then stopped crying and smiled again. "He wasn't her father. She seduced him, like all the other tarts. And he gave her my job. I was always his assistant director, right up to last year."

"Tell us how it happened," Banham asked again.

"I took the knife from Stephen's car and hid it in the step with my gloves." She looked at Crowther. "There were plenty of the overall things your little blue people wore – I found one yesterday, in one of the costume skips down in the basement, and thought, what a good idea. Didn't want to get blood all over my costume, did I? So I hid it with the knife." She seemed pleased with herself. "I set my boots out in the toilet to look as if I was in there, then locked the door and climbed out over the wall. Oh, and I fixed the cat's costume so the head wouldn't stay on. The loo was nearer than their dressing room – I knew she'd head straight there after we left the stage." A smile spread across her face. "And I knew she and that halfwit daughter of hers would be stupid enough to see my boots and believe I was in there." She smiled again. "They were my alibi."

"You had it all worked out," Banham said, his eyes burning into her.

"Oh, it was perfect," she assured him. "Even Stephen. He walked into the trap like a stupid rabbit."

Crowther took in a noisy breath, but Banham's eyes remained on Barbara. Her excitement mounted. "I had to be quick. I ran to the step and got the knife and gloves, and the blue suit, then I ran down the haunted staircase and met her in the basement. It was perfect." She looked innocently at Banham. "You didn't know her. She had it coming, believe me."

Banham managed to keep his temper. "I wonder if the judge will agree with you."

"And you took Stephen's costume from the laundry basket?" Crowther butted in. "And wrapped it around the knife then hid it in the step, so if it was found, Stephen would take the rap."

She looked at Crowther and burst out laughing. "I'd already cooked his goose, with the gloves."

"Gloves?" Banham frowned.

"I wore his black gloves when I went to kill Sophie. Except it wasn't Sophie that time – it was the other girl."

Her eyes were glazed. Banham began to wonder if she was losing it, or if he was. Then it fell into place: the gloves from the oversized black costume in the company office, which had incriminated Stephen Coombs when Penny Starr found concrete dust on them. Barbara must have taken them, then returned them to the office after killing Lucinda. What a devious mind she had.

She was still talking. "It was so easy. You didn't even notice me. Your eyes were out on stalks, watching those twits of girls gyrating. You were a walkover."

She looked superciliously at Crowther. He stared at the floor to avoid Banham's eyes.

Barbara smiled again. "I enjoyed it. I heard her coming down the stairs, on the opposite side of the basement. It was pitch black down there until I turned the worker light on. She walked into me, like a rabbit to a fox. And I enjoyed ripping her neck open. I only wish the light had been better – I really wanted to watch her face. But I enjoyed every sound she made. I had to stop myself laughing out loud as her head fell back and the blood shot out." Her eye stared coldly. "I had to be very careful, you see; very careful to stand behind her, so that the blood shot away from me; I couldn't risk getting any on my boots." She smiled and sighed as she said, "She was moaning and writhing on the floor and her body was jerking. But I was careful not to tread in the blood. Mind you, when your little blue person asked for my boots, I gave her the other pair, the spares I left in the toilet, just in case I'd been careless." She laughed, this time like a small child. "Then I came up the haunted passage and hid the knife in the step by the door of the passage. I saw Stephen drop his costume in the laundry basket, so when he went upstairs I took it and wrapped it around the knife and dropped them back in the step."

"What did you do with the gloves and the forensic suit?"

She frowned.

"The blue overall," Banham said wearily.

"I'm coming to that! Maggie and Fay had gone, so I went back into the loo, climbed over the toilet wall again and changed my boots…"

"The overall. Where did you hide it?"

"I stuffed it in the lavatory cistern. The gloves too. Didn't anyone look?" She threw him a triumphant look. "Your penguins really aren't very thorough, are they? They didn't even ask if I had a second pair of boots! The star of the show always has spare costumes. No one else though."

Her look of satisfaction made Banham feel like blacking her other eye. That toilet must have been flushing with pink water for the past twenty-four hours, and none of the forensic team had noticed. And Coombs's bathing costume – why had nobody realised that there simply wasn't enough blood on it? Why had *he* not realised? The basement had been like a horror movie – the killer must have been liberally splashed. The costume was only smeared, from the knife wrapped up in it.

Barbara burst out laughing again. "I fooled you, didn't I, inspector?"

Banham looked away. Yes, he had been well and truly fooled. And Alison had almost died as a result.

"When did you discover that the step opened? Crowther asked her.

"An electrician who worked at the theatre many years ago used to leave me love letters there. He was besotted with me. I could have had an affair with him, but I didn't because I loved Michael." She paused. "He showed me the step. He told me it was a very special place, like my…" She mouthed the ugly little word and smiled again. "It just looks like a step, but it opens like the lid of a box, provided you know which corner to lift it from." She looked at Banham, a hand covering her eye. "Easy really. All your uniformed little penguins searching high and low, and it was there all the time, in front of their noses. In my secret place. And you were sure to find out that Stephen has a record for GBH. Police are very predictable. So it was perfect." She twisted her mouth downward and shuddered. "Anyway, he's a horrible man. He's fat and talentless, and the other way sexually. He should be locked away."

Banham kept himself under control with an effort. She looked at him as if waiting for a reaction; when none came she spoke again.

"Trevor's a queer too, you know." The mouth twisted again. "I threw water over his lighter earlier, so he'd have to come in for a light in his dance break. That gave me another alibi."

"But Michael worked it out, didn't he, Barbara?" Banham said. "And decided to take his own revenge."

The smile left Barbara's face and her forehead crinkled. "He should never have left me," she said starting to cry. "We were a great team – my talent and his brain. If I'd been his business partner, we'd be millionaires by now, not on the breadline." She shook her head resignedly. "I had to stop her. She would have ruined him." She sighed again. "They all used him, bled him dry to get a foot up the ladder, then moved on. But I loved him and I proved it too." She leaned forward towards Banham, her voice was almost a plea. "I did it out of love."

"But he would have killed you for it," Crowther said coldly.

She put her hand to the wound in her shoulder and suddenly looked thoughtful. "Will he be locked up too? It's worked out then. We'll be together at last."

"That's up to a judge," Banham told her abruptly.

"I think it's unlikely that you'll be out in time to enjoy any more precious moments with him," Crowther added. "You're hardly a spring chicken now."

There was a knock on the interview room door and Isabelle Walsh put her head round the door. "Guv," she said, "can I have a word?"

Out in the corridor Isabelle told him, "The hospital's just rung. Alison's discharged herself. But they won't let her go home alone – one of us needs to pick her up."

Banham headed for the stairs. "I'm on my way," he said.

18

Alison felt as if she had been run over by a burning bus. She had eight stitches in the top of her chest and was having trouble catching her breath, but had to spend too much time in hospitals in the line of duty, and couldn't bear the thought of being admitted to one. She just wanted to go home. The doctor told her she could only leave if someone drove her home and stayed there with her. She assured him that she had arranged it.

A nurse tried to help her to put her street clothes back on; in her usual independent way she insisted that she could manage. The nurse suspected that she might not wait to be picked up, so while Alison went to the loo, she phoned the police station and let the CID department know that Detective Sergeant Grainger had discharged herself.

Alison took out her phone to call a taxi, but the receptionist explained that the use of mobiles was banned inside the building and asked her to make the call outside. Alison closed her phone, and slowly and shakily she made her way through the rotating exit doors.

"Car for Ms Grainger," a familiar voice called out as she walked into the cold. She looked round. Banham was leaning against the wall, his hand wrapped in a large bandage and jingling his car keys.

There was a teasing note in his voice. "I thought you might like a lift."

She did, but not from him. He was the last person she wanted to see at this moment. She was suddenly afraid she might start crying.

But he was here, and she would have to deal with it. She took a deep breath and walked towards him, concentrating on every step to make sure she didn't wobble.

"Honestly, Guv, there was no need. I don't know what the fuss is about. It's only a few stitches. I'll be back at work in a couple of days."

"Yes, I know," he said. The muscle in his cheekbone tensed, and she knew he felt responsible for her injuries. "But that's in a couple of days. Meanwhile…" He pointed the key at his car. "I reckoned, seeing that it's down to you we got the right result, that the least I could do was to drive you home, heat up some soup and tuck you up in bed."

"You're not in such good shape yourself," she said, looking at his bandaged hand.

"I'm taking the rest of the day off too."

"You could play Captain Hook next pantomime season," she joked weakly.

All she could think of during the drive home was the state of her flat. She had made a feeble attempt at Christmas decorations: a three-inch paper Father Christmas over the fireplace, and a tree the size of a small pot-plant on top of the television. All her festive spirit had evaporated when the relationship she thought she was starting with Banham ground to a sharp halt before Christmas had properly begun. She had spent the holiday waiting for the phone to ring, and when that didn't happen, neither did the decorations.

Banham pulled up at a red light and glanced across at her. "Are you all right, Alison? You're very pale."

The tenderness in his voice nearly made her weep. But she fought down the hope it raised; she had moved on, and wasn't going to lay herself on the line again. The week before Christmas all she could think of was getting him inside her flat and into her bed. Now it was the last thing she wanted.

"If it's all the same to you, Guv, I'd rather you just dropped me off at me front door. I'd like to go in and get some sleep."

"I'm going to make sure you're OK first," he said firmly.

"I am OK," she argued feebly. "And I really appreciate the lift. But I'd rather you didn't come in."

The lights turned to green and he pulled away, keeping his eyes on the road. He turned off the main high street into the long road that led to her village, and said nothing for the rest of the journey.

When they arrived at the large house her flat was part of, he made no attempt to get out of the car. They sat in silence staring through the windscreen. Eventually he cleared his throat and spoke. "This is difficult for me, and I apologise if it comes out all wrong, I'm no good at apologies…"

That made her smile. "You've just apologised," she said.

Suddenly exhaustion overwhelmed her. The day felt as if it had gone on forever. The painkillers were only just starting to kick in, and the pain that had been with her for the last three hours had worn her down. The last thing she wanted at the moment was a contretemps about what happened the previous week.

She didn't even have the energy for hurt pride. They had both acted hastily, and nearly made a mistake: it was as simple as that. And they both now knew he wasn't ready for a relationship. She wondered if he would ever be capable of that kind of commitment. She was his sergeant, and they were a good team: end of story. The moment for any other relationship with him had passed, and she had moved on. Right now she all she wanted was to get into bed and sleep – on her own.

"I'm going to pull rank," he told her. "I am coming in. I am going to get you some hot soup, and I am going to put you to bed."

Her eyes were drooping and she didn't have the strength to argue. She let him open the car door for her, and use his good hand to help her slowly and carefully to get out. He put his arm around her shoulders and she found herself leaning against him as they walked up the path, into the house and up the stairs to her flat.

"Where are your keys?" he asked when they reached her front door.

"In my pocket… Ow!" A bolt of pain shot across her chest.

"I'll get them. Which pocket?"

"I don't know…"

Her khaki anorak had a dozen pockets, and her attempts to feel for the keys undid all the work of the painkillers. Banham took hold of the fabric and jiggled it to make the keys rattle. Alison's arms had stiffened up, and she struggled to hold them up so that he could search each pocket in turn.

Suddenly they were both giggling like teenagers.

"What a pair of crocks we are," he said, holding up his bandaged hand. "We only add up to one whole person between us."

Finally they got into the flat, and she sank into an armchair while he went to investigate the kitchen.

"There's no soup," he called.

"There isn't much of anything. I haven't shopped since before Christmas."

"Not to worry. I'll phone the Chinese takeaway."

"I need the bathroom," she said, suddenly remembering the line of underwear strung across the bath to dry.

Her arms were stiff and the stitches in her chest pulled, but she started to haul them down. A flicker of movement caught her eye, and she looked up to find his reflection in the mirror. She had left the door open, and he was standing in the doorway. "I'll do that," he said. With his good hand he lifted down the patterned G-strings and small-cupped padded bras and laid them across his bandaged arm. "They're dry. Where do you want them?"

Her cheeks burned. "In the bedroom. Thank you."

"Let's have you in the bedroom too; you can eat your supper tucked up in bed. The Chinese is on its way. I ordered mushroom noodles for me and chicken broth for you."

He walked into her bedroom, opened the top drawer and carefully placed the underwear in it, then pulled the bed cover back and held out his arms. He put his arm around her waist and slowly lowered her on to the bed, pulled the duvet around her, and puffed her pillow behind her. "Close your eyes and have a rest," he said tenderly. "I'll wake you when supper arrives."

He pulled out the dresser stool and sat on it beside her bed. Much as she wanted to, she couldn't close her eyes; she was too aware of his blue ones watching her. She smiled at him. "Thanks for this," she said in a whisper.

"I was worried I might lose you today," he said. His forehead crinkled and straighten out again. "I don't know what I'd have done if I'd lost that bad-tempered squirrel and those sludgy eyes."

She turned away and closed them. She wanted it not to matter.

After a few silent moments he stood up. "I'm going to let you get some rest," he whispered. "I'll bring your supper in on a tray when it arrives."

The takeaway took ages to open, and even longer to eat.

He couldn't do it with just one hand, and she couldn't move her arms enough to help. The giggling started again, and eventually using one hand each, they removed one silver-foiled top. Banham tried to be masterful and said he'd manage the rest, but then he dipped his bandage in the scalding noodle sauce and had to run it under the cold tap to stop it burning through to his already stinging hand.

He fed her hot soup with his good hand, resting the bandaged one on the radiator to dry out. She was skilled with chopsticks, and fed him one-handed with noodles.

After they'd eaten he disposed of the containers and washed the plates. He even managed to make tea in her best china pot, a treat after polystyrene vending-machine cups and canteen mugs. He placed the tray on the dressing table stool by her bed and knelt on the floor beside it. "I'll let it brew first," he said.

Banham wasn't feeling the pain in his hand. For the first time since Diane had been murdered he was aware of sensation in his groin. Perhaps his problem wasn't a permanent one after all. But he wanted to laugh at the timing.

"Thanks for all this," Alison said, visibly wilting.

"Milk?"

"Mm, but only a touch."

"A touch?"

She started to laugh.

"Oh, Paul," Alison said. "You should go home and get some rest. You need it as much as I do."

"Can I stay here and sleep on your sofa?"

"If you want to. But the sofa it is."

They looked each other in the eye.

"I will. I'll sleep on the sofa. And in the morning I'll go and get you some groceries."

She watched him walk to the door.

"We're a good team, Paul," she said softly.

He didn't look round. "Goodnight, Alison."

"Goodnight. Guv."

ALSO FROM CRÈME DE LA CRIME

BY PENNY DEACON
TWO GENRE-BUSTING FUTURECRIME CHILLERS

A Kind of Puritan   ISBN: 0-9547634-1-6

Bodies are bad for business, but Humility, a low-tech woman in a hi-tech mid 21st century world, isn't going to let go until she knows who killed the guy everyone said was harmless.

Help from the local crime boss exacts a high price. But her best friend's job is on the line, the battered barge she calls home is under threat and 'accidents' happen to her friends. She's not going to give up – even when one death leads to another, and the next could be hers!

A subtle and clever thriller…
- The Daily Mail
A bracing new entry in the genre … a fascinating new author with a hip, noir voice.
- Mystery Lovers

A Thankless Child   ISBN: 0-9547634-8-3

Ruthless patriarch Morgan Vinci wants Humility to find out why a man hanged himself – before the fanfare opening of his new marina.

Her mother wants her to track down a runaway niece – but how do you find one child in streets full of terrified homeless kids?

In Humility's world good wine is laced with poison, girl gangs guard their territory with knives and nightmares are terrifyingly real.

… moves at a fast slick pace … a lot of interesting, colourful, if oddball, characters… a good page-turner… very readable.
- Ann Bell, **new**booksMag

BY ADRIAN MAGSON
THREE FAST-MOVING ACTION ADVENTURES

No Peace for the Wicked   ISBN: 0-9547634-2-4

Hard-nosed female investigative reporter Riley Gavin follows a bloody trail from a windswept south coast to the balmy intrigues of Spain's Costa Del Crime, accompanied by the laconic Frank Palmer, ex-military cop turned private eye. They uncover a deadly web of vendettas and double-crosses in an underworld that's at war for control of a faltering criminal empire.

And suddenly facing a *deadline* takes on a whole new chilling meaning...

A real page turner... a slick, accomplished writer who can plot neatly and keep a story moving...
- Sharon Wheeler, Reviewing the Evidence website
... the excitement carries right through to the last page...
- Ron Ellis, Sherlock magazine

No Help for the Dying   ISBN: 0-9547634-7-5

Riley Gavin has always been haunted by Katie Pyle's baffling disappearance: her first assignment – and her greatest failure. So when Katie turns up dead a decade later Riley has to find out where the girl had been all those years, and what drove her to walk away from a loving family. Her probing uncovers more dead runaways, and with the help of Frank Palmer, Riley follows a trail down into the subways of London's street life, and up to the highest levels of society.

Gritty and fast-paced detecting of the traditional kind, with a welcome injection of realism.
- Maxim Jakubowski, The Guardian

No Sleep for the Dead   ISBN: 0-9551589-1-5

Investigative journalist Riley has problems. Palmer disappears after a disturbing chance encounter, her love affair seems set to stay long-distance and she's being followed by a mysterious dreadlocked man.

Frank's determination to pursue justice for an old friend puts him and Riley in deadly danger from art thieves, gangstas, British Intelligence – and a bitter old woman out for revenge.

BY MAUREEN CARTER
THREE GRITTY POLICE PROCEDURALS

Working Girls   ISBN: 0-9547634-0-8

Detective Sergeant Bev Morriss of West Midlands Police thought she was hardened, but schoolgirl prostitute Michelle Lucas's broken body fills her with cold fury.

This case will push her to the edge, and when a second victim dies, Bev has to take the most dangerous gamble of her life – out on the streets.

A hard-hitting debut … fast moving with a well realised character in Detective Sergeant Bev Morriss. I'll look forward to her next appearance.
- Mystery Lovers
Fans of TV from the Bill to Prime Suspect will love Maureen Carter's work. Imagine Bridget Jones meets Cracker... gritty, pacy, realistic and… televisual. When's the TV adaptation going to hit our screens?
- Amazon

Dead Old   ISBN: 0-9547634-6-7

West Midlands Police think Sophia Carrington's bizarre murder is the latest attack by teen yobs. Only Bev Morriss won't accept it.

But a glamorous new boss buries her in paperwork and insults, and even Oz, her lover, has doubts. Birmingham's feistiest detective rebels – then the killer decides Bev's family is next…

…many writers would sell their first born to create such a distinctive 'voice' in a main character.
- Sharon Wheeler, Reviewing the Evidence
Carter's work has style, something that suggests she isn't just passing through. Complex, chilling and absorbing…
- Julia Wallis Martin, award-winning author of *A Likeness in Stone*

Baby Love   ISBN: 09551589-0-7

Rape, baby-snatching, murder: all in a day's work for Birmingham's finest – but when the removal men have only just left your new house, your lover's attention is elsewhere and your last case left you not too popular in the squad room, it's sure to end in tears. Bev Morriss finds herself in serious trouble when her eye slips momentarily off the ball.

SPARKLING DEBUT NOVELS FROM
CRÈME DE LA CRIME

IF IT BLEEDS   BERNIE CROSTHWAITE

Chilling murder mystery with authentic newspaper background.
Pacy, eventful... an excellent debut.
- Mystery Women
ISBN: 0-9547634-3-2

A CERTAIN MALICE   FELICITY YOUNG

Taut and creepy debut crime novel with Australian setting
*... a beautifully written book... Felicity draws you into the life in
Australia... you may not want to leave.*
- Natasha Boyce, bookseller
ISBN: 0-9547634-4-0

PERSONAL PROTECTION   TRACEY SHELLITO

Dark, gripping lesbian thriller set in the charged atmosphere of a
lapdancing club.
a powerful, edgy story... I didn't want to put down...
- Reviewing the Evidence
ISBN: 0-9547634-5-9

SINS OF THE FATHER   DAVID HARRISON

Tightly-plotted debut novel which reveals the dark side of comedy.
*... replete with a rich cast of characters and edge-of-the-seat situations
where no one is safe...*
- Mike Howard, Brighton Argus
ISBN: 0-9547634-9-1

… it is good to see a publisher investing in fresh work that, although definitely contemporary in mood and content, falls four-square within the genre's traditions…
- Martin Edwards, author of the highly acclaimed *Harry Devlin Mysteries*, writing on the *Tangled Web* website

Creme de la Crime… so far have not put a foot wrong.
- Sharon Wheeler, Reviewing the Evidence